Praise for A WAY OUT OF HELL

"Great book for those open to expanding their understanding of complex issues, and serious about building bridges instead of walls. Well-researched. Highly recommend!"

Carl Medearis, author of *Muslims, Christians, and Jesus;* co-author of *Tea with Hezbollah*

"A WAY OUT OF HELL *is a fast-paced, multi-faceted thriller with a secret plot underwriting some of today's most frightening headlines. The lead characters, former jihadist, Abdullah, and savage attack survivor, Sari, are great examples of how Muslims and Christians can come together in spite of a history of years of divisive suspicion and work together to foil the plans of extremists who want to unleash a reign of terror in Indonesia.*"

Dave Andrews, author of *The Jihad of Jesus*

"I am convinced that the fruit of peacemaking is friendship–real friendship between people with real differences who come together to make a real impact in their communities. Jim Baton makes this happen. I have walked his streets, and I have seen firsthand how Jim has fostered a community of Muslims and Christians who live together and work together to overcome intolerance and extremism with love and respect. Not surprisingly, this is the major story line in A WAY OUT OF HELL, *an emotion-stirring journey that in the end leaves you inspired and challenged to love more and thus live better.*"

Thomas Davis, Global Peacemaking Coach with Peace Catalyst International

A Way Out of
Hell

JIM BATON

Visit the author's website: www.jimbaton.com

Library of Congress Cataloging in Publication Data:
International Standard Book Number: 1532765991
ISBN 13: 9781532765995
Library of Congress Control Number: 2016906507
CreateSpace Independent Publishing Platform
North Charleston, South Carolina

While many of the historical accounts of terrorism in this book are factual, and actual
locations are used to add believability to the story, all characters and events in the
story are fictional. Any resemblance to actual persons, living or dead, or actual events
is purely coincidental.

First edition

Acknowledgments

Thank you to the outstanding peacemakers who added insights to this book—Thomas Davis, Robert Pope and Jared Holton, your lives build bridges that inspire me. Thank you to Rick Wallace for sharing your expertise in aviation. Thank you, Joy Park, for your excellent editing skills and Jessee Fish for your beautiful cover. And a special thank you to Carl Medearis, Dave Andrews and Thomas Davis, not just for your kind endorsements, but for your extraordinary lives that model for us a better way.

I dedicate this book to all the beautiful people of Banjarmasin. May you find eternal peace.

List of Characters

Abdullah – former terrorist turned peacemaker, married to Siti with sons Iqbal ("Bali") and Syukran (deceased)

Sari – Christian minority girl, close friends with Bali

Joko – Intelligence Agent with BIN (Indonesia's CIA)

Ardiansyah – local expert on radical Islamic groups

David – youth pastor at the church Sari used to attend

Nina – Sari's childhood friend

Abdullah's former students at the Islamic School ("pesantren") – Hafiz, Juki, Udin, Fani

Terrorist cell members – Achmad, Khaliq, Rio, Hidayat, Amat, Baqri

Chapter 1

After the Friday noon prayers at the Sabilal Muhtadin Mosque had finished, the two men rolled up their *sejadah* carpets, collected their sandals outside, and wandered into the towering pine trees separating this proud center of Banjarmasin's culture from the Martapura River. They moved unhurriedly, to a prearranged spot far from the exiting crowd of worshippers and adequately shaded from Indonesia's fierce tropical sunlight.

A few minutes passed, then a thin, older man in a white skull cap, blue dress shirt and a checkered *sarong* around his waist shuffled up to them, breathing heavily.

"*Assalamu alaikum,*" the thin man greeted them first.

"*Wa alaikum assalam,*" one of the men replied. The giant next to him said nothing.

The thin man swallowed hard and looked hopefully to the shorter man. "You are the one they told me about? You will pay for my daughter's surgery?"

"Yes. We have the money—more than enough for your daughter, and for your wife." The man spoke softly but clearly. "Are you ready to do what we asked?"

The thin man stiffened, then resignedly nodded, almost whispering, "Yes."

"There must be no such hesitation on that day. You must drive with conviction, with courage. Remember, if you do not do what we have agreed upon, I will not give your wife the money. Instead, I will send *him* to visit your family." He pointed his chin at the glowering giant. "There is no going back. Do you understand?"

The thin man was breathing louder now, "Y-yes. Of course I will."

"Then go in peace, brother, and wait for our signal."

The thin man turned back to the mosque, walking much more quickly than he'd come. When he reached the closest of the mosque's four minarets, the shorter man said, "Have Hidayat follow him for a couple of days."

The giant nodded.

"Are the other brothers prepared for their roles?"

Again the giant nodded.

"All assignments must go like clockwork—no delays, no mistakes." He frowned. "I'm not sure the new kid is ready. Let's plan a test for tonight. Let him make a plan and pick the target, then push him to the edge—see if he's worthy of our family."

Another nod.

The shorter man stretched his arms high and wide, gazing through the heat waves at the post-*sholat* crowds eating at roadside stands, the traffic coming back to life, and the skyline of buildings across the river. Without lowering his eyes he rummaged in his pocket for his cell phone.

"Remember Poso? Remember the fear that blanketed that city once we had done our mission?" He didn't need to look at his partner to know that he remembered it well. "That will be nothing compared to the fear this city will cower under."

A teenage girl with no helmet or even a head covering drove by on her motorcycle, her long hair blown back by the wind, prompting a slew of whistles and catcalls from the young Muslim men eating at the roadside stands, then a roar of laughter. This city boasted one of the highest percentages of Muslims in the largest Muslim nation in the world, but what percentage of them were *true believers*?

But that wasn't really the shorter man's concern. Others would handle intellectually preparing the *ummah* for following the *caliph* as the international leader of all Muslims. In this new organization they'd joined, roles were clearly defined, and his was to destroy man's systems that Allah's might be built on their ruins. It was a role he was uniquely suited for.

He smiled at the terror these pleasure-seeking Muslim fakers around him were about to experience while he dialed his phone.

"Ignorant fools. Let the fires burn."

Chapter 2

The Peace Café was one of Sari's happy places in Banjarmasin. She loved the portraits of various peacemakers on the walls, which included some of her personal heroes such as Mother Theresa, Gandhi and Nelson Mandela. The service wasn't particularly fast, but they knew her name and always asked how she was doing. The round stools at the bar gave the place a modernist feel, but of course there was no alcohol served, as precious few places in her traditionalist Muslim city could get a license to serve alcohol. The Peace Café had a great selection of coffee drinks, however, and Sari particularly enjoyed their Peace Frappe.

Bali had brought her here several times on what he called "dates." She didn't argue the term. She'd made it clear that, as a Christian, she couldn't marry someone of a different religion. But he was still her best friend and she enjoyed every moment with him.

Today she and Bali were here for a different reason. The Peace Generation club was holding a special meeting here at their headquarters because the current student-leader, Nitya, was stepping down to prepare for her upcoming wedding.

Fifteen members, mostly university students like Bali and Sari, were seated on black vinyl couches at wooden tables around the room while Nitya stood facing them from the bar.

"We need to choose someone to replace me, and I've been thinking about it a lot. I'd like to suggest a name and hear what you all think."

Sari leaned forward, wondering who Nitya would endorse.

"I suggest our new student-leader be Sari."

Sari jerked back in surprise. She saw a couple others do the same. Next to her Bali started clapping, but no one joined in.

Nitya took a deep breath and continued, "Sari's been a member of Peace Gen for over two years. She's faithfully at every meeting, every event and every social outreach we do. She's one of our best public speakers, and everyone knows she has more ideas than the rest of us put together." She paused. "So…anyone want to say something?"

The bamboo-checkered wallpaper resounded with silence.

Bali spoke first. "Come on, guys, Nitya's right. Sari came up with the Peaceathon, she got us teaching about peace in the prison, she even lobbied the mayor for a city-wide Peace Day celebration. She's the obvious choice to lead us."

Sari blushed. Bali always made her feel more special than she was.

"But aren't we going to even consider other candidates?" Aisyah asked. "What about Lukman?"

The lean, handsome Lukman shook his head. "Sorry, training for wrestling nationals. I won't be around much the next six months."

Aisyah tugged on her pink satin head covering. "How about you, Fitri?"

The girl next to Bali murmured, "Can't do it—college thesis."

Aisyah scanned the faces around the room. "Not everyone is here…" she sputtered.

Nitya calmly asked, "Would you like to be considered, Aisyah?"

"It's not that…it's just, you know, most of the young people we're reaching are Muslims. I think we need a Muslim face in the front, that's all."

"Ah, come on!" Bali protested. "We're supposed to be teaching others not to be prejudiced, to see people apart from their labels—"

"Aisyah's right," Sari interrupted. "It will be easier for a Muslim leader to recruit new volunteers. I'm happy to work behind the scenes. Aisyah, why don't you be student-leader?"

Now Aisyah's face reddened. "I don't want to be the leader. I just, you know, I didn't mean anything against Sari…" She straightened her head covering again and looked down.

Nitya sighed. "Personally, I'd be honored to have Sari as our leader. Are you sure you won't do it, Sari?"

Sari smiled. "We have plenty of good candidates to stand in the front. What's important is that we all work together, right?"

Bali raised his hand. "Fine, how about if I do it? Is that okay with everyone?"

A couple people nodded, but Aisyah frowned. "You're dating a Christian."

"What's that supposed to mean?" Bali retorted.

"We're not dating," Sari added, placing her hand lightly on Bali's arm.

Nitya seized control. "Let's move on to other business for now. Can we hear the report from the committee planning our visit to the orphanage in two weeks?"

Sari couldn't see Bali's eyes behind his long bangs, but she knew they'd be smoldering. Of all the people on the planet, she knew him the best. She had grown up in the same alley as Bali, watching him play street soccer through the window, or race by when he first learned to drive a motorbike, but he hadn't really noticed her until their senior year, when he was class president and she was elected class secretary. At that time he saw himself as superior to her in every way. Since then, a series of tragedies had bonded them together. Along the way, she'd watched him transform into the kind of man any girl would want to marry. *If only...*

Chapter 3

The sun was setting by the time Bali pulled up in front of Sari's house on the motorbike to drop her off. The final "*Allah Akbar*" of the call to prayer rang through the neighborhood, then there was silence. They were the only ones on the street, everyone else already starting their *sholat* prayers at their homes or in the *musholla* at the front of the alley. Sari reflected on how she'd always hated this time of day as a child, when the Muslim kids whose parents allowed them to play with her had to go home to pray, and she, the only Christian kid in the neighborhood, had no choice but to go home too. Her mom had faced years of being ignored by the Muslim women here because of her faith, but last year everything had changed. Hopefully those days were gone.

Bali removed his helmet as Sari got off the bike. "That Aisyah is a jerk. I still can't believe what she did."

"I really don't mind," Sari smiled at her best friend. "But thanks for sticking up for me."

Bali flashed her a grin. "You know it. Why, one of these days you'll be travelling the world and people will stand in line to hear you speak."

Sari gazed into those playful eyes, no longer hiding behind the floppy bangs. She admired Bali's strong jaw and his smile that could light up a room. She loved the musty smell of the leather jacket he wore when on the motorbike. She loved the way…

In a city of only one percent Christians, where would she ever find a Christian boyfriend that was as good as Bali?

Sari forced herself to turn away. "Better get to my homework."

"Hold on a second. I know what will take the sting out of Peace Gen today. I was going to save it for later, but... Come here, close your eyes and hold out your hands."

Sari giggled and returned to the motorcycle, obediently following Bali's instructions. She could hear him rustling in his backpack, then she felt something heavy and round placed in her hands.

"Okay, open your eyes."

A flurry of snow swirled around the tiny village. Sari had never seen snow before, and now she held it inside a little globe, in her own hands. She shook it again and imagined all the places in the world she would one day visit.

"It's beautiful! Where could you possibly have found this in Banjarmasin?"

"Who said I found it in Banjarmasin?" Bali teased, obviously pleased with her wide-eyed wonder.

"Iqbal!" Sari used her best friend's formal name. "Come on, where did you find this?" She turned it upside down then back upright to watch the snow again.

"A mysterious hobbit named Bilbo Baggins traded it to me for my Liverpool soccer jersey." Sari punched his shoulder. "Ow! Okay, the hobbit was my dad. I told him just to bring it when he comes home next month in time for your nineteenth birthday, but he went ahead and mailed it to me. He's never mailed me anything! I think he has a soft spot for you."

"Where do you think this village is? Switzerland? Russia? The Himalayas?" She turned with her treasure toward her home.

He zipped up his backpack and put it back over his shoulder, calling, "Wherever it is, if you go there in your dreams tonight, take me with you."

As she walked up the path toward her house, she knew Bali would stay sitting on his motorbike, grinning about his gift to her, waiting till she was safely in the door. What was that Gigi song he had been singing after their International Relations class? She sang the chorus to herself: *I'm your guard, I'm your protector, I'm your companion, every step you take.*

If he's still trying to win my heart…God, he's so sweet, so perfect…

She turned on the top step and held up the snow globe in one hand, waved good-bye with the other. The nagging pain in the left part of her chest was still there, she noticed, but the blurry vision and nightmares were less frequent now. *Life looks better looking forward than looking back.*

When she opened her front door, a strange smell, like rained-on laundry, caused her to pause and look around the room for the source. The door closed behind her, revealing a masked man wearing all black. Two more men dressed the same way suddenly stepped out of her kitchen. The snow globe slipped from Sari's hand and she heard it shatter on the wooden floor. The one behind the door lunged toward her and Sari screamed.

A leather glove covered her mouth…strong arms pinned her from behind…the man was saying something about Sari's mother but she couldn't catch all the words. *Scream, just scream.* She tried to wriggle free. The biggest one barked an order she didn't understand. She felt her attacker hesitate and with all her might she twisted free for a moment and screamed again. Then she was on the floor and he was on top of her. She needed air. She needed to breathe so she could scream. All she could produce was a whisper, "Jesus!"

Suddenly she heard the door burst open, someone yelled, and she felt the weight lift from her stomach. Through blurry vision she saw two men fighting, swinging their fists wildly, thudding against her couch, rolling now back toward her. She tried to scoot out of their way but the wall stopped her. Her breath was coming back. *Scream.* She screamed so loud surely her mother could hear it from her grave.

The two black vultures circling, waiting for her death, had disappeared. Her attacker was still thrashing about with…Bali? She heard a crash, a desperate gasp. Through the mist she could make out her glass-topped coffee table was now in pieces at her feet. The last black figure floated like a demon out the door.

Silence. Blinking repeatedly wouldn't uncloud her vision, but she saw no black figures, heard no threats. She peeled her hands off the wall behind her to wrap them around her knees. Soon Bali would come to her and she could rest in his arms. He was her protector. He had saved her.

Bali didn't move.

"Bali?"

Maybe she should try to go to him. Holding her breath, she crawled forward.

The glass in her hands and knees barely registered in her brain. Only one thought found expression in her mind—*Bali!*

Her palm slipped on a pool of blood. Feeling forward she found her best friend lying face down. His leather jacket felt wet and sticky. Her fingers drifted up past his collar to caress his hair, but jerked away at a vicious gash on the back of Bali's head. She gently rolled him over, cradling his head in her lap.

"Bali? Bali?"

His eyelids fluttered, and hope swelled within her. She spoke more urgently, "Bali. Come back. Please, Bali, please!" Her tears splashed on his face. She tried gently slapping his cheek. "Please, God, please."

She stared at the cut above his left eye. His face looked pained, and angry, not the face she loved. She tried to smooth the anger with her fingers to something more peaceful. A grey mist closed in, separating her from his face. *No, not now! I need to see his face. At least one last time, let me see his fa–.*

Just then the front door flew open once again and a large man leaped inside. Sari screamed, then fainted.

Chapter 4

"**A**re you sure it's safe? I don't want anything to happen to my taxi!" The driver's eyes danced from side to side watching for signs of danger as he crept down Kelayan B Street.

"It's time for the *Mahgrib* prayers. Everyone's at the mosque or at home. You'll be fine," Abdullah assured him. He, too, scanned the street ahead, but with a smile. The familiar sights and sounds of one of Southeast Asia's most densely populated neighborhoods had been his home now for, well, since Bali had started school. Amongst Kelayan's vices of alcohol, gambling and violent crime, Abdullah had found it easy to hide from his past, and from those who could use it against him. He'd never once thought of trying to stop a gang war, or of becoming a mediator between angry neighbors. For fifteen years he'd kept his head down, avoiding ever getting involved in someone else's business. And now he was flying around the country doing peacemaking for a living.

Six months of travel with presidential hopeful M. Ramadani to some of the toughest conflicts in Indonesia, trying to make peace… He thought about his last assignment in Poso, Sulawesi, where the beheading of three Christian teenage girls in 2005, among other atrocities, still hampered the Christians and Muslims in the community from trusting each other. They had made some progress with a few Christian pastors and Muslim *ustads*, but they had a long way to go.

It's nice to come home to a city at relative peace.

He maneuvered to stretch his athletic six-foot frame across the back seat and took out his smart phone to reread Bali's latest e-mail. After what had happened to his younger son Syukran, and his wife subsequently leaving him, Abdullah was grateful that his older son still wanted to communicate with him. Bali was all he had left. Well, and Sari.

Two years ago if Bali had said he wanted to date a Christian girl, Abdullah would have insisted she change her religion first. But after meeting Sari's extraordinary mother, after all that had happened, he had started to wonder whether he was the one who needed to change.

He read the e-mail for the fourth time today:

HEY DAD, HOW ARE YOU? I GOT THE PACKAGE—YOU'RE THE BEST! SARI WILL FLIP OVER IT.

YOU'RE STILL COMING HOME NEXT MONTH, RIGHT? TELL ME YOUR FLIGHT AND I'LL PICK YOU UP AT THE AIRPORT. SARI SAID SHE'D LIKE TO MAKE A SPECIAL DINNER FOR YOU.

COLLEGE IS GREAT. I DIDN'T KNOW IF I'D LIKE POLITICAL SCIENCE, BUT I DO. SARI HAS ALL THESE IDEAS ABOUT CHANGING THE JUSTICE SYSTEM, MINORITY EMPOWERMENT, YOU KNOW HER! SHE STILL ISN'T READY TO MARRY ME THOUGH—I HATE HOW OUR DIFFERENT RELIGIONS KEEP US APART. MAYBE YOU CAN HELP US FIND A WAY. ANYWAY, CAN'T WAIT TO HEAR YOUR STORIES, AND YOU BETTER BRING ME A BETTER GIFT THIS TIME—NO MORE SHRIMP CHIPS OR ETHNIC FOODS, YOU HEAR ME? ☺

BALI

Surprising Bali and Sari would be sweet—he knew how much both of them loved surprises!

The taxi turned down Abdullah's alley, *Gang Hanyar,* past the half-dozen or so of his neighbors praying at the *musholla,* and stopped in front of his house. He grabbed his small carry-on from the trunk and paid the driver, who was reciting some Arabic prayer for protection under his breath, anxious to get out of there. He wondered if Bali and Sari were home from class yet, or if he had time to make himself an iced tea and relax on the porch, watching their faces when they drove up the alley and saw him.

A scream...he thought he heard a scream. Abdullah dropped his bag and looked down the alley toward Sari's house. A motorbike like Bali's was lying on its side by the neighbor's fence. He took a couple steps and then saw two men in black exit Sari's front door, fleeing down the alley the opposite way.

Sari! Now he ran. A third man in black stumbled out of Sari's door and took off down the street. He had an odd gait, reminding Abdullah of someone he'd seen before... But there was no time to give chase. He had to get to Sari.

As he leaped up the stairs to Sari's porch, he braced himself in case more men were inside or about to pour out. Then he hit the door with his shoulder and landed in the room in a defensive martial arts position. As he scanned the room for threats, he heard Sari scream, and saw her faint.

There among broken glass lay Sari, and his son Bali. He immediately reached for Bali's pulse, but knew in his heart that yet again he had arrived too late.

Chapter 5

Hafiz felt the blood rushing through his veins, felt alive like never before. He wanted to celebrate with someone. That wasn't going to happen with the two kill-joys he got stuck with. Neither of them seemed happy but Hafiz couldn't figure out why. He'd put the fear of Allah into that Christian girl.

Achmad was waiting for them in a rundown shack off Banjarmasin's southern ring road. At night, only dump trucks carrying coal would rumble by, as smaller vehicles feared the gangs of "road pirates" who would stop them for money or other rewards. Hafiz had never been here at night before, and he knew he never would again, as Achmad never met him in the same place twice.

Apparently Achmad sensed something was wrong. He rose abruptly from a rickety wooden chair without bothering to greet his ninja-dressed cell members. "What happened, Rio?"

"The kid screwed up. We nearly got caught."

"What?" Hafiz countered. "I was great. I freaked out the chick and I fought off the dude while these two clowns did noth…"

Hafiz felt the sting on his cheek, the jerk of his head, and his face hitting the floor all at once. The rush of anger and adrenaline nearly propelled him onto his feet to fight back, but sensing Khaliq towering over him, he decided to stay put.

"Why did you fail?" Achmad demanded.

From the floor Hafiz answered more cautiously. "The plan was to scare the girl. Then big brother tells me to rape her? We shouldn't have changed the plan."

Pain exploded in Hafiz's side from Khaliq's boot. He curled up to protect himself.

Achmad ignored him. "Rio, what do you mean you nearly got caught?"

"The kid let the girl scream so much some guy rushed in. The neighbors were probably next so we split. But we wore the masks. No one saw our faces."

Achmad squatted next to Hafiz. The younger man glanced up at the chiseled jaw, short-cropped hair and equally trimmed moustache and goatee of his new commander in holy war. Achmad seemed to always look intense, while never flustered. But seeing not even a hint of mercy in his eyes, Hafiz quickly looked back to the ground.

"You failed, number one, because you were over-confident; number two, because you haven't learned to follow orders from your superiors immediately without question; number three, because you're still playing games and haven't learned to be ruthless in this war against evil; number four, because you were discovered. When we do an assignment, we disappear, we don't run—the infidels run away, not us."

Achmad straightened up, then continued, "We can never draw attention to ourselves or our family, because endangering one of us endangers all of us. Better to eliminate the one who risks blowing our cover." He paused, pulling a knife from his belt and examining its blade. "But this is your lucky day. I'm going to let you go back to helping your parents sell cakes, kid. Get out of here before I change my mind." Then he turned away.

"No, wait!" Hafiz scrambled to his feet, watching for Khaliq's retribution as he did. He'd wanted this all his life. He wasn't losing his big break now. "You're right, I messed up. I guarantee it won't happen again. Please, give me another assignment, anything, even if I have to blow myself up I'll do it."

Achmad made scratch-marks with his knife on an old wooden table while he thought. When he looked to his deputies, Rio pushed his glasses up higher on his nose and shrugged, the giant next to him showed no response.

"You had a friend named Syukran, right?"

"Yes," Hafiz answered.

"I heard about what he did. He had the heart of a true *syahidin*. Do you?"

"Yes. I will be even better than Syukran, trust me."

Achmad touched the point of his knife to Hafiz's chest. "All right, little brother, I will give you one more chance. This time you will do your assignment exactly as ordered. Khaliq will go with you to make sure you succeed."

"Thank you."

"And if you screw up this time, Khaliq will kill you."

Chapter 6

*T*his casket may never get underground.

Every time the men dug a shovel-full of mud out of the grave, the swamp oozed back in to fill up the hole. They had been digging for over an hour now at the gravesite behind the elementary school in Teluk Kubur, the closest one to his home. Meanwhile, the *ustad* from the local mosque and the minimum forty other Muslim faithful chanted the Arabic prayers over and over. He had no idea what they meant, except something about praying that Bali would be able to answer the angels' questions well and be quickly admitted to heaven. Surely Allah would accept Bali, an innocent youth, dying to save someone's life.

It may not be so easy for me, with all the blood on my hands.

Abdullah stood motionless by the grave, staring at the casket. The events of the morning were still swirling through his mind. Just after the first *sholat* prayers at sunrise, his neighbor Ibu Aaminah had arrived with the neighborhood matriarchs to ceremonially wash Bali's body first with soapy water, then camphor water, and finally with clean water. They'd wrapped him in a long white cloth and laid him in the casket. Various neighbors and Bali's friends had stopped by to say a prayer or pay their respects. Then he'd joined the local men at the noon *sholat* to pray with his son in the mosque one last time. As was custom, burial had to occur within twenty-four hours of death. Which meant only five more hours to get that grave dug…

More traditions demanded that he host another prayer meeting for Bali at his house tonight and tomorrow night. Most people continued these prayer events, which mostly consisted of reciting the *Surah Yasin* from the Al Qur'an, on the seventh night, twenty-fifth night, fortieth night, hundredth night, and each anniversary of someone's death, but Abdullah knew tomorrow night's would be his last. That wasn't how he wished to remember his son.

An image popped into his head, of three-year-old Syukran wearing his new Superman shirt and red cape, screaming in fear being chased by a duck. He and his wife couldn't help but laugh at the irony, but six-year-old Bali ran straight at the duck to rescue his brother.

He'd finally gotten ahold of his wife late last night, through an old friend in Java. Now she hated him more than ever, never wanted to talk to him again. Well, she had deserved to know.

The men lowered the casket into the shallow grave, making sure Bali would face toward Mecca. Two men pushed down on it while the others tried shoveling around the sides and dumping the mud on top.

Even in death Bali wouldn't go down without a fight.

Two hands grabbed his arm. Abdullah looked down and saw horrific scars on the right hand, and a bracelet that looked familiar—it was Sari. He knew the bracelet was a gift from his son. Bali had told him how she always kept that hand gloved or hidden until last year when her mom died. Now maybe it wasn't so important to her anymore. She rested her head on his biceps.

He looked around at all Sari's and Bali's friends from school, from their Peace Generation Club, kids of different religions and backgrounds. He had assumed she'd find comfort from them. But he would never turn her away, not after he had failed her mother so utterly.

His mind turned back to last night, carrying Sari to her bed, then cleaning her floor of the glass and blood. That hollow ache in his stomach—or was it his heart—that he'd felt when his son Syukran died he felt again when he took Bali's limp body in his arms. *Well, there's nothing left to take from me.*

The casket was hardly visible now, so the men began pressing down fresh topsoil like putting the lid on a container. Ibu Aaminah, the unofficial women's leader of the neighborhood, offered Abdullah some jasmine flowers to lay on the grave. He took enough for both him and Sari in spite of Aaminah's raised eyebrows, and breathed in their fragrant aroma. He and Sari laid the flowers on the dirt, a final parting gift. *For the third time in just over a year, it was too little, too late.*

After the final prayer and the last guest's parting handshake, Abdullah realized Sari was sitting alone by the grave. He moved next to her and waited in silence.

Finally she stood. "I hate death."

"Me, too. Let's get you home."

Back at Sari's house Abdullah entered first and silently checked all the rooms.

"Lock the door. And get some rest."

He shuffled the fifty meters or so down the alley to his own home. Well, it used to be his home. Today it was just an empty house filled with memories of his failures.

He noticed the green paint was peeling off his front door. Bali and Syukran had painted this door last Ramadan. Something inside him knew that he'd never paint this door again.

Abdullah wandered through the house like in a dream. He remembered how just over a year ago his wife and sons were sitting at this very dining table, talking about school, arguing about chores. Sari's mother, Ibu Kristyana, had sat on this sofa thanking him for saving her life. Then his *jihad* ghosts reappeared, ripping from him everyone he cared about, just as he had done to others.

For the past six months he had been trying to right those wrongs, to change his *nasib*, his fate. Apparently it wasn't enough. What was his new life worth without any children to pass it on to?

Abdullah stumbled into his bedroom and lay back on his bed wishing with all his heart he were in the grave instead of his son.

Chapter 7

The Teluk Dalam Prison in Banjarmasin smelled of mold, smelled of sewage, but most of all it smelled of filthy human flesh. Built to house roughly five hundred prisoners, the current residents numbered over two thousand. Cells three meters across by four meters long held twenty to thirty criminals at a time. It was so crowded that his dad told him he had to sleep sitting up.

I don't know how my dad can survive in the same room as murderers, rapists, God-knows what else. I'd rather kill myself.

Hidayat showed the prison guard the cake he'd brought for his father, wrapped in paper, and slipped the guard a pack of L.A. Lights cigarettes. He had an extra pack anyway. The guard stamped the back of his hand, then waved him through to the visitors' room with a gruff, "Thirty minutes."

The tiny room was nearly full already. Crying women, restless children, Hidayat didn't have time for this, but since his mom had stopped coming to visit several months ago, he was all his father had left.

His father entered through a door on the far wall. He was wearing the orange jumpsuit of those who'd already been sentenced, while several other prisoners in the room still wore the blue jumpsuits of those whose cases were in process. The blue was probably supposed to give them a false hope of getting out of here. But the way the system was, they would all be wearing orange soon, unless they were rich enough to bribe their way out. *Like we used to be.*

Hidayat shook his father's hand. "Hey, Dad, you look good," he lied. His father had lost so much weight. No telling what he was eating in this place. But the graying hair around the sides of his head was combed and there was still a light in his eyes.

"Son, I'm so glad to see you." His smile gave way to concern. "What happened to your nose?"

Hidayat's finger involuntarily felt the bandage across the bridge of his nose. "Nothing. I fell. Can we sit down?"

He looked around the room and pointed to an empty space on the floor. He didn't like getting his new jeans dirty, but what could he do? They sat cross-legged facing each other with the cake on a brown paper between them.

"*Kue lapis*! This reminds me of your mother's cakes. She made the best *kue lapis* during Ramadan, didn't she?"

How can Dad not be angry at her for moving on?

"Well, it's not Mom's, but it's the best I could find. Try it."

They each took a bite of the colorful layered cake. "Delicious," his father gushed. "This is so much better than anything I've eaten here. Sometimes I wish a pastry chef would steal some recipes or something so we could get a decent cook in here, you know what I mean?" He took another bite, closing his eyes to savor it. "This is top of the line…how could you afford this?"

"I've got a new job."

"I'm so proud of you! First graduating from the Antasari Islamic Institute in *Hadith* Interpretation, now a job! Are you teaching? Tell me all about it."

"It's no big deal. The important thing is I'm making good money and may have found a way to get back at that dirtbag who sent you here."

"Dayat, you know I deserve to be here. Corruption isn't any better than any of the other crimes these guys have done." He waved his hand around the room.

"Come on, Dad," Hidayat scowled.

"It's true."

"But it's not fair! That Chinese scum set you up, and now he's still living in his mansion and you're living here in this..." Hidayat's eyes roved across the room of broken people. "He's going to pay, Dad, I can promise you that! I found some new friends who..."

"Hold on there, Son, I knew selling him the government subsidized rice for the poor was wrong. It's my fault our family is bankrupt and I'm in here. I dishonored my family and my country. Now I have to pay the price. But don't you take vengeance into your own hands. Enduring this is nothing compared to what I'd suffer if you ended up in here with me."

"But I'm talking about justice, Dad."

"And I'm talking about honor. The best way to redeem the family name is for you to live an honorable life—no corruption, no revenge or violence. Isn't that what the *Hadith* teaches?"

"Dad, you don't know...I mean, what about in the *Hadith* where it teaches that you can never trust a Jew or a Christian? After what they did to the Prophet? After what that Christian Chinese pig did to you? You think we should put up with that? I don't think so." Hidayat's raised voice was attracting the attention of other visitors and the guard.

His father put his hand on Hidayat's shoulder to rein him in. "Son, please, I have to listen every day to radicals recruiting prisoners for *jihad* when they get out."

Hidayat gritted his teeth and dropped the subject.

His father leaned in closer and spoke softly. "Dayat, where are you getting this money?"

"It doesn't matter. What matters is making things right. And getting you out of here."

His father sat back and sighed deeply. "Don't worry about me, Son, I'll be fine. I've already finished nine months, only three years and three months to go, and perhaps even less. I'll be out before you know it. But when I get out, I want to find that the shame I brought on the family is eclipsed by the honorable man my son has become. Everyone faces a choice between the right way and the easy way. I made the wrong choice.

May Allah strengthen you to follow the true way of the Prophet to make the right choice."

They sat quietly for a moment. Hidayat offered his father another piece of cake, but he just wrapped it up to eat later. Hidayat checked his wispy beard for cake crumbs, then fiddled with the white *kopiah* on his head. His dad had worn the white prayer cap every day during the trial, but had quit wearing it after his sentencing. *Was prison even stealing his father's religion?*

Finally Hidayat broke the silence. "What do you want me to bring you next time I come?"

His father tilted his balding head and glanced at the ceiling. "Hmm. Maybe a photo of your new girlfriend?"

"I don't have a girlfriend, Dad. No one wants to marry into our family." It came out harsher than he meant it.

A cloud momentarily passed over his father's face. "I'm so sorry, Son."

"Forget it, Dad. It'll all work out okay. Just take care of yourself and I'll take care of me and Mom."

"Yes, please send her my love." Both of them knew those days were over, but the memories still connected them.

Hidayat looked at his watch. He was still on the clock, and Achmad needed him to scout a new target. *These guys understand justice, and how power is the path to freedom.*

"I gotta go, Dad. Seriously, what can I bring you?"

They stood up together. "My pillow you brought me was, well, confiscated. Maybe the safest thing is a paperback book? Maybe *Laskar Pelangi* or something else by Andrea Hirata. I liked the movie."

"Sure, Dad, I'll get the book for you. Hang on, okay?" He reached out his hand to shake his father's, but his father ignored it and hugged his son. Hidayat glanced around quickly to see if anyone was watching.

His father released him, then nodded at him twice with glassy eyes, and turned to walk back into hell.

And Hidayat left with hell's fire burning ever brighter in his soul.

Chapter 8

The next morning Abdullah awoke to the sound of a whistling tea kettle. He bolted upright, holding up his hand to block the sunlight from his eyes. He realized he was still wearing yesterday's black slacks and black formal Muslim dress shirt he'd worn to the funeral. But that didn't matter right now.

Who is in my kitchen?

His first thought was Bali... Then memories of the last two days came crashing in on him, like surging waves threatening to pound him on a rocky shoreline. The surf pummeled him; the current dragged him under into its swirling darkness. He flung out his hand for something firm to hold on to and found a thought.

Something woke me up. He remembered the sound of the kettle.

If not Bali, then who? There was no way his wife would have come back, not after what she'd said on the phone. Unless...Sari?

He forced his mind and body to stand up, then nearly tripped over his open carry-on bag in the hallway. "Sari? Is that you?" No answer.

Leaning his head through the kitchen doorway Abdullah noticed the kettle on the gas burner. The fire was off. He silently slipped into the room and touched the kettle, burning his fingertip. The faint smell of coffee lingered in the air.

Someone was here.

Instinctively he reached for a kitchen knife and palmed it hidden behind his forearm. Then he crept toward the living room.

"'Awakening to a new world is just moving from one dream to the next.' Forgive me, I've forgotten who said that." Sitting in the wicker chair across from Abdullah's green couch was an old man. Abdullah quickly sized up this potential threat: the man was extremely thin, with receding white hair, wearing the type of *batik* shirt common to civil servants, with a steaming cup of coffee in one hand and no weapon in the other. In his peripheral vision he saw no one else in the room. Nevertheless, Abdullah kept the knife ready in case he'd missed something.

"Who are you? Why are you here?"

The old man took a sip of coffee. "Pardon my intrusion. I waited on your front porch for nearly an hour and decided if you were planning to sleep all day I'd just have to make the coffee myself." He took another drink. "Not terribly good, but it'll have to do." He set the mug on the coffee table in front of him. "Why don't you have a seat so we can talk?"

"You didn't answer my questions yet." Abdullah remained standing in the kitchen doorway.

"Ah, you're right of course. But first let me ask a more important question—who are you? Are you the one named Sutrisno who trained under Mullah Omar and fought with Al Qaidah in Afghanistan?" He paused, one eyebrow raised.

Abdullah's muscles went on high alert, even as his face remained passive. "You've come to the wrong house."

"Or have you changed your name to Abdullah, and changed your circles to now include a certain prominent politician running on a platform of religious tolerance and peacemaking? Jihadist or peacemaker—which one are you?" He paused again, but this time Abdullah gave no answer.

"By the way, I was so sorry to hear about your son Iqbal's death. Tragic. Your younger son, Syukran, as well. Terrible, terrible blows for a father to face. My condolences." He took another drink of coffee.

"You seem to know a lot about me. I'd prefer you start talking about yourself or find someone else's house to break into."

"We have much to discuss, you and I. Sure you don't want to get some coffee for yourself and have a seat?" Abdullah remained motionless.

"Very well. Let me explain. My name is Joko. I work for the National Intelligence Agency, or BIN. I know much more about you than you can imagine. And I am convinced that you may be the only person who can help us with a very desperate situation." Joko leaned forward. "I'm here to ask for your help, not to hurt you. So if you could please leave your weapons in the kitchen and come sit down?" He motioned to the couch and waited.

Abdullah lay the knife back on the kitchen counter and stepped fully into the living room but didn't sit down. "My son just died. I'm tired. I can't help you. I'd appreciate it if you'd leave now."

Joko pursed his lips. Abdullah noticed a tic in the old man's left eye. But he kept sipping the coffee and made no effort to leave.

"I understand this is a bad time for you. Arriving too late to save your son must weigh heavy on your heart. But let me ask you, how do you know those men won't come back to Sari's house to finish what Iqbal interrupted? Do you want to be late again? Or would you like to do something that could potentially save Sari's life and thousands of other innocents like her? We can help each other get what we both want—I am confident that you would do anything to protect Sari, am I right? And I want to protect the thousands of other Saris out there while we're at it."

Once again Abdullah felt Sari's head leaning against his upper arm, how tightly she clung to him. After all that she had suffered because of his failures, he knew he couldn't let anything happen to her. His legs moved of their own accord and he felt himself sliding onto the vinyl couch.

"Do you know who did this to my son?" he croaked out.

"That's why I need your help. Our intelligence network has recently picked up an alarming amount of chatter about a group called ISIS moving into Indonesia. This jihadist group began in Iraq and Syria with the goal of creating a new Islamic State that encompasses a large portion of the Middle East. However, as their size has increased, it seems their goals have grown more ambitious. With vast resources of both finances and weaponry, they are establishing bases in several Muslim nations outside the Middle East. It seems they want to create instability that fundamentalists can take advantage of in order to bring the entire Muslim world under unified caliphate leadership.

"There are several suspected cells in Indonesia now. We don't know what they're planning yet, but we believe it will happen soon. ISIS is different—most of the jihadists in Indonesia have been happy to take a shot at a Western hotel or night club until now. But ISIS wants to rule territory. Their attacks will be destructive and catalyze such chaos that the government is shown to be ineffective. Their code for this 'event' is 'Five Five.' We haven't deciphered what that refers to. But what we do know is that one city mentioned multiple times is Banjarmasin."

"And you think the men who killed Bali are with ISIS?"

"Truthfully, we don't know that. It could be an isolated event. Ever since your son Syukran's recruitment and subsequently Sari's mother's death thwarting that terrorist attack last year, we've been keeping an eye on things here, particularly on potential revenge attacks against you or Sari, and this event troubles me. From what you saw, do you think they were your neighborhood's normal hooligans? What if they were part of something more sinister? Do you see now why I think Sari could be a flashpoint of something larger?"

As Abdullah reflected on what happened, he knew Joko was right. He had initially wondered, 'Why Sari?' but he already knew the answer—it could be connected to her mother, or worse, connected to him. He couldn't take a chance this was just a prank. He had to protect her at any cost.

"Ah, I see you agree," Joko continued. "Shall we make some more coffee?"

"Just tell me what you want me to do." Abdullah braced himself for the worst.

The Intelligence agent leaned back in the chair with his hands pressed together tapping his lips. "If ISIS is indeed here, I want you to find their terrorist cell and take it down. And I want you to do this…" he paused, "…non-violently."

Was this old guy insane? "How am I supposed to do that?" Abdullah asked.

"I can't tell you who they are and I can't tell you how to stop them non-violently, though I have some ideas I'll share with you as we go along. But I can tell you why—because taking them down violently isn't working. If we kill them, the radicals' anger grows, and ten more volunteer in their place. If we capture them, our prisons become fertile ground for *jihad* recruitment. There has to be a better way."

Abdullah's mind was spinning. "Has anyone ever tried this before?"

"Actually, yes," Joko answered. "While our American counterpart, the CIA, with its inhumane prisons and interrogations, has created one of the most effective marketing campaigns for terrorist recruiters in history, resulting in an over fifty percent increase in radical groups since 2010, there are a few dissenting voices, and the FBI has tried some softer tactics with cells in America and had some success. I'll share the ideas I'm gleaning from them at another time."

Joko tipped his cup to drain the last coffee drop before continuing.

"Here in Indonesia we have a similar conundrum: the more 'hard power' the Detachment 88 Special Forces use in combating terrorism, the harder it is for the moderate majority to discern who are the good guys and who are the bad guys. Well, eventually Detachment 88 will get access to the intelligence we have, and they'll show up in Banjarmasin, guns blazing. I'm sure you've seen the footage of Israeli soldiers combing Gaza for Hamas fighters? If ISIS is truly here and planning something, Detachment 88 could turn this city into a war zone where both sides cause civilian casualties. This is not the Middle East yet, where defeating ISIS requires all-out war. ISIS is just beginning their invasion of Indonesia. We have a limited window here, to find these groups and motivate them to disband before they feel it's 'kill or be killed.'

"That's why we need you. You know this city. You have the background to understand what motivates these men. You speak their language.

You're also committed to non-violent resolutions to problems. You're our best chance for peace."

Abdullah shook his head and ran both hands through his short-cropped hair. "I still think it's crazy. So are you offering me a job under BIN?"

"Actually, no. My theories are still unproven, so I have limited official resources here. I'm asking you to do this as a civilian. You need to understand that you're basically on your own—I can't call in Special Ops to rescue you. But I will give you all the intelligence leaks I can, and maybe a foot soldier or two if I can wrest them away from other duties."

"On my own," Abdullah mumbled. *What else is new?*

"I've got a flight out at noon." Joko glanced at his watch. "We've got intel hotspots popping up all around the country. I'm trying to figure out which threats are real, and which are imminent. I believe the threat here is both. I'll try to get back here to you as soon as I can."

Abdullah's hesitation seemed to send Joko's eye tic into near spasms. Joko looked into his empty coffee mug, then back up at Abdullah. "Because of what Sari's mother did, Sari may be a very specifically chosen target. She will never sleep soundly, and neither will you, unless you succeed."

"But how am I supposed to even find this cell? Where do I start?"

"I'm going to give you a name and address of a local expert on Islamic groups. I suggest you start there. And here's my phone number, call me anytime, day or night. But do not tell anyone about me, or about BIN being involved. Oh, and one more thing…"

"Yes?"

"I would keep a closer eye on Sari if I were you."

Chapter 9

The long, curved knife swung wildly in the air. Instinctively, Amat slid between the knife and his little brother, not quite afraid, but wondering if he should be.

It wasn't the first time Amat had seen his uncle wield a *keris,* the traditional short sword of the Javanese, though many Banjar families like Amat's kept one on the wall to protect the home from evil spirits. He'd seen his uncle kill a man with that very knife. But that time his uncle was drunk, and the man he killed was a *preman,* a low-life thug who intimidated small business owners for protection money.

This time his uncle seemed moderately sober, and he was swinging his *keris* angrily in the small confines of Amat's living room.

"Calm down, older brother," Amat's father pleaded, hands outstretched with palms down. "Please sit down and let's talk about this before we do anything we might regret."

"Regret? Regret? If she's not dead by morning, that I will regret!"

"Please, sit down. You're scaring my little boy." Amat's father spoke quietly but urgently.

For the first time since Uncle Surya had burst into the front door, he stopped waving the *keris* and looked around. He noticed eight-year-old Adi peeking around Amat's waist, his arms clenched around Amat's thigh, his curiosity overcoming his fear. Uncle Surya sat down with the knife stretched across his lap.

"Adi, let's go get Uncle some tea." Amat tried to pry Adi's hands off his soccer shorts and usher his little brother safely off to the kitchen.

"Wait," called Uncle Surya. "Adi can go, but I want you to hear this, Amat."

Amat handed off Adi to his mother and returned to the living room. He pulled a chair next to his father, facing his uncle who was on their couch.

"Tell us the whole story," Amat's father said. His father leaned back in the chair, legs crossed, in sharp contrast to his crazy uncle's knees bouncing the knife up and down as he gestured wildly with his hands.

"It's Lani. You know, our sister's daughter. She's gone *murtad*. She converted to Christianity and shamed our family. She has to die!"

Amat's mind went back to his childhood when he and Lani had been close. He remembered the rope he'd tied to a tree branch over the river so he and Lani could swing out and jump off. In high school they had compared notes on homework and about potential dates. She always cheered for him at school soccer matches. Lani had never caused her family any trouble. They'd been together all through school, only drifting apart as Amat did his degree in Islamic Studies at the Antasari Islamic Institute, while Lani had graduated with an accounting degree from the secular government university, UNLAM. They stayed in touch through Facebook. He didn't remember anything about her dating a Christian guy, so how was this possible?

"Amat, you know anything about this?" his father asked.

"No, Dad, this is crazy. Are you sure?" he asked his uncle.

"Of course I'm sure! Someone saw her going into a church!"

"But that doesn't mean she converted. Maybe she was meeting someone. Maybe she…" Amat noticed his father's glare and stopped talking.

"What's the difference?" his uncle pointed at him. "SHE WENT IN A CHURCH! No Muslim, no Banjar should ever do that. Does she want the Christian *jinn* to jump on her and confuse her about what's true? Does she want to dishonor our family and our faith? I'm going to kill her and any Christian who lured her over to their side with money or sex or whatever!"

It looked like his uncle was about to jump up and decapitate their lamp when Amat's father spoke. Amat was always proud of how his father was the one everyone in the family looked to for guidance, even if they rarely saw him since he'd become the representative for their region in the national parliament.

"This is a very serious situation indeed." His father spoke slowly and deliberately. "It would be best if we collected some more information to see just how deep her betrayal goes, and how wide is the net which drew her in. There may be more here than just the visit to the church, and we need to get to the bottom of this."

"Yes, yes, you're right," Uncle Surya eagerly agreed. "There could be more."

"If the appropriate punishment is death, we'll need to have the whole family understand why death is the only option. You know, some, like our sister, may propose sending her to an Islamic boarding school up in the jungle to restore her to sanity. Having more information will aid us in discussing with the family the most appropriate solution."

"But what if she runs? We must act before she disappears!"

"That's a good point, older brother. We don't want her to run. If she hears you're carrying your *keris* everywhere you go, she might get spooked and bolt. I suggest you keep your weapon nearby for the proper moment, but hidden. Meanwhile, I'll send Amat to visit her and collect more information. She'll never suspect him." His father turned to Amat. "You two are still close, right?"

"Yes, Dad." Amat didn't like where this was going. He had a lot on his plate right now, and he knew Achmad didn't want him to have any distractions. But he did want to know if the rumor was true. "Sure, I'll go visit her and find out the truth."

"Good idea," smiled Uncle Surya. "You're the most educated one in our family in religion. You won't be fooled by her Christian double-talk."

"Or maybe if she's confused I can help her see the light," Amat argued.

"Oh, she'll see the light all right, on the Judgment Day." Uncle Surya stood, sword at his side. Amat and his father stood as well.

"Don't you want to stay for some tea?"

"No, thank you, brother." His uncle shook his father's hand. "I need to go. I'll wait for your news."

"Yes, we'll call you."

When Uncle Surya shook Amat's hand, he had a parting thought. "Amat, when we do kill Lani, I want you to do it with me, for the glory of Islam."

Amat couldn't come up with a fitting response.

Chapter 10

Ya Allah, what are you doing to me? You give me an impossible task—"find a terrorist cell"—and if I'm so lucky as to find them, they'll kill me. And I can't fight back? This makes no sense.

Abdullah had finally unpacked his carry-on and cleaned the dirty laundry off his bedroom floor in an effort to force some order into the chaos. He was seated on his *sejadah* carpet with the *Al Qur'an* lying open on a pillow in front of him. Growing up, his teachers had quoted many verses about responding to violence with violence; travelling with M. Ramadani he'd heard several other verses for the first time, verses about peacemaking, restraint and forgiveness. He needed a sign, so he was looking for a verse that Ramadani had shared with him last month. If he were going to attempt this fool's mission, he needed to know Allah would smile upon him.

After flipping through several *surah*, he found what he was looking for in the forty-first *surah* called *Fussilat* verse 34:

> *And not equal are the good deed and the bad. Repel [evil] by that [deed] which is better; and thereupon the one whom between you and him is enmity [will become] as though he was a devoted friend.*

Repel evil with good deeds… Abdullah wasn't sure this would work in Afghanistan, or Palestine, why would he think it would work here?

But for Sari's sake, and for all the other potential victims in the city, he would try. Bali had given his life to save her, and he wouldn't let his son's sacrifice be in vain. She was Bali's first love, his joy, his dream. As strange as it sounded, he felt like as long as Sari stayed alive, a part of Bali stayed alive in her.

Abdullah went to check on Sari, and found her door unlocked. "Sari?" he called, swinging the door open cautiously.

"Hi, Bapak!" she called gaily, using the term children use for their father, as she rushed past him and into the kitchen. With a quick glance Abdullah discerned that she was cooking instant noodles on the stove, packing a backpack, and brushing her long silky hair all at the same time.

"What are you doing?" he asked.

"What do you mean?" she answered. "I'm getting ready for class."

"Can you...can we talk for a minute? Sitting down?"

"Sure. You don't mind if I eat my *mie goreng* while we talk, do you?" Sari strained the noodles onto her plate and mixed in some soy sauce and chili spice, then brought it into the living room. She sat on one end of the couch and motioned for Abdullah to sit on the other. The smell of the warm noodles reminded Abdullah that he'd skipped breakfast. *Come to think of it, I skipped dinner last night too.*

Abdullah began cautiously, "So...how are you doing?"

"I guess I'm doing as well as can be expected. Like I learned from my mother's death, life has to go on, right?" Sari's voice sounded a bit high-pitched to him. She stuffed her mouth with noodles.

Abdullah was beginning to doubt if coming over was a good idea. He was a man of action, not wisdom. Maybe someone else should be handling this role.

"Do you have anyone you could, you know, talk to?"

Sari swallowed, then offered, "I wish I could talk to my church friends, but I feel like an outcast. Maybe one of my school friends? We'll see."

Another lull while Sari gulped down her food.

"Um, I've been thinking. Maybe you should take some time off from school and go visit your father in Jakarta. I remember you told me that someday you wanted to meet him, right? Maybe now is a good time to just, well, get away for a while." *Get away from terrorists. And get away from me, the death-magnet.*

"I'll be fine. I have you! This last year you've become more of a father to me than he ever was anyway. I don't want to let the evil in the world rob me of my dreams."

"But I'm…worried about you." Abdullah wanted to tell her why, but didn't want to scare her.

"You're so good to me." Sari patted his knee. "Now I really have to get going or I'll be late for class." She whisked her plate and fork off to the kitchen, then headed for her toothbrush.

This talk hadn't gone at all as Abdullah had hoped it would. He wondered how much to tell her.

"Sari, please be vigilant, lock your door and windows, strange things are going on these days. I don't want you to worry, though. I'm going to be keeping an eye on you. I'm also going to look for the men who killed Bali."

"Oh! But…won't the police do that?" Sari's forehead wrinkled. "I'm sure you wouldn't, you know, take revenge, right?"

"No, no, not at all. No revenge. I would like to stop what they're doing, non-violently…" *It sounded even crazier now than when the old man said it.*

Sari actually stood still, psychology textbook in one hand and open backpack in the other, and stared at Abdullah. After a moment she spoke thoughtfully, "Okay. You know that kind of sounds like, well, Jesus. Huh." Then the book was in the backpack and she was ushering him out the door.

After she locked it, she turned to Abdullah on the porch and took his right hand in hers, lifting the back of his hand to touch her bowed forehead in *sungkan*, the cultural sign of honor children give to their parents.

He stood on the porch and watched her drive away on her motorcycle. If anyone ever threatened a single hair on her lovely head, he doubted there'd be any trace of "non-violence" in his response.

Chapter 11

As Sari turned the corner from her alley onto Kelayan B Street, a white mini-van nearly side-swiped her, horn blaring, driving her off the side of the street into a neighbor's wooden fence. She managed to stay upright, and since the fence did too, no harm done. She turned the motorbike back toward the street and looked more cautiously both directions before pulling out.

Her heart was racing, but what was worse, her eyesight was blurring again. *Am I stressed? There's nothing to be stressed about. Calm down and go to school.*

She decided to keep going—when her eyes were blurry she'd slow down, and when they were clear she'd drive at normal speed. Hopefully she wouldn't meet too many cars on this busy, narrow street where motorbikes, bicycles and pedestrians ruled.

"Life must go on. Life must go on." She chanted her mantra out loud inside her motorcycle helmet.

By the time she passed the area's largest outdoor market, *Pasar Baimbai*, or the "Together Market," her heartbeat had returned to normal and she felt sure she'd be okay. She glanced at the smiling women carrying their groceries home, just as her mother used to do.

The fog drifted over her eyes again just as another motorbike zipped out of a side alley without even a pause and cut her off. She jerked on the hand brakes, instinctively leaning away from the impending crash, and laid down her old Yamaha Vega on its right side, her right leg trapped under the bike and sliding along with it. Sari cried out in pain.

A motorbike driving right on her tail swerved to avoid her and nearly caused a head-on collision with oncoming traffic. Horns were blasting, people shouting, and suddenly she was surrounded by people flocking towards her, like ghosts to a grave.

She felt the figures pressing in around her. Their speech was unclear, but she knew they were men, all men. One was taking her motorbike away. She grabbed onto it, afraid he might be stealing it. Someone yelled at her, then bent over her and grabbed her hand to tear it from the bike.

Sari screamed.

She thrashed about, catching the man in the face with her fingernails. He jumped back into the circle of men around her, perhaps waiting for another chance.

"Get away from me! Leave me alone!" she yelled.

At least her eyes could still discern movement, and the figures weren't moving. Her hand bumped into a rectangular object on the ground—her cell phone! She held it close to her face and could see the screen was shattered. She closed her eyes and used her finger muscle memory to hit the speed dial. Bali would come for her. He would protect her. She swung her head side to side watching for any threats as she waited for him to answer.

After several rings, it was him! "Sari?"

"Bali, help me. They're back. The men."

"What? Sari, this is Bali's dad. Where are you?"

"I'm on the street. Where's Bali?"

"Just stay there, I'll find—" Her phone died.

He'll come for me. He'll protect me.

Sari felt an invisible wall of safety around her. The men couldn't touch her. They wouldn't dare. Slowly her eyesight began to return to focus.

Standing around her were the fat man who sells *satay* from a pushcart, an elderly *ustad* from the mosque, a young man she'd seen help his mother shop at the market before, and a man holding the hand of his kindergarten-uniformed daughter. They all looked concerned for her. None of them looked vicious or evil.

Sari tried to say, "I'm sorry," but just ended up sobbing.

Abdullah spotted the commotion in the road not five minutes from home. He breathed a big sigh of relief when he saw Sari sitting on the asphalt crying and realized she was safe. As he approached her, one of the men nearby warned him that she didn't want to be touched. He cautiously squatted next to her.

"Sari? It's Abdullah. Are you okay?"

Sari looked up at him. "I'm sorry. I tried to call Bali…"

"I know. I heard his cell phone. What happened?"

"I crashed. Then I thought…" Sari started crying again.

Abdullah stood and heard three different versions from the bystanders. Then he asked someone to drive Sari's motorbike home for her. He helped her to her feet and put her behind him on his motorbike and slowly drove home.

When they entered *Gang Hanyar*, Sari spoke. "I don't want to go home. Can I go to your house?"

"Sure, for now."

Sari stretched out on Abdullah's couch. First he brought her some water. Then he found his first aid kit and cleaned and treated the scrapes on her right leg and elbow. Soon she was calm enough to talk.

"Thank you," Sari began. "I'm so stupid. You know, sometimes my vision is fuzzy. I shouldn't have tried to drive. I could have hurt someone. And then…people came to help me but I thought they were…and I called Bali…I'm such a mess. And I think my cell phone is broken too. I'm so glad you came."

"Don't worry about it. You'll be fine. When you're ready to go home, I'll walk over with you."

"I don't want to be alone."

Gone was the bustling Sari of just an hour earlier. This girl looked shattered. Abdullah didn't know what to do. He rubbed his forehead with his hand. Keeping her in his house was bound to start some salacious neighborhood gossip as well—too many of his Muslim neighbors were taking much younger second wives. This obviously was a bad idea.

"I need to go meet with someone." Abdullah saw the tears welling up in her eyes. He sighed. "But I guess I could go tomorrow."

Sari smiled weakly. That smile tugged at something inside him, calling what was dead back to life.

That night Sari slept soundly on Abdullah's couch. Abdullah slept much less soundly, alert for any noise, with a knife under what used to be his wife's pillow and a two-by-four leaning next to his open bedroom door.

Chapter 12

A s Abdullah drove off the next morning, he hoped Sari wouldn't panic when she woke up and found herself alone. He hadn't had the heart to wake her, so he left her a note that he'd be back before lunch.

He had to carefully weave through the crowds of college students at the Antasari Islamic Institute, or IAIN. He remembered reading that the school had accepted roughly two thousand new students this semester, making them the second largest university in the province, behind UNLAM, where Bali and Sari went. Even though IAIN was founded as a religious studies school, it had evolved to where English and Information Technology were now the most popular majors. Bali got introduced to the Peace Generation Club here, so Abdullah figured they must have some very moderate Islamic thinkers. He hoped the professor Joko had recommended would be able to help him.

He parked his motorbike outside the library and asked a student for directions to the *Ushuluddin* department, which he knew covered Comparative Religions, *Hadith* Interpretation, and Philosophy. Then he walked across campus, carefully avoiding the mud in the streets by staying on the wooden planks thrown seemingly at random, but actually strategically positioned for that very purpose, until he was swept along with a group of students also headed for class.

Professor Ardiansyah's office was on the second floor, but no one was inside. Maybe he was teaching a class. Abdullah kept peeking in doors until he found another professor to ask for Ardiansyah's whereabouts.

Apparently, Ardiansyah had a home on campus and usually kept his office hours there.

Eventually Abdullah found Ardiansyah's home. It wasn't large, but it was in much better condition than some of the classrooms and dormitories he had passed. Like all buildings in Banjarmasin, it stood on dozens of ironwood stilts above the marshland, holding up a wooden platform. This home had a thin layer of cement covering the wood, with eighteen-inch square white ceramic tiles for the floor, white cement walls, and a steeply sloping dark green tile roof much like the other campus buildings.

He climbed the steps to the front porch and called loudly, "*Assalamu alaikum.*" From inside he heard someone answer, "*Wa alaikum assalam.*" A much younger man opened the door than Abdullah had expected.

"Pak Guru?" the boy asked. "What are you doing here?"

"Fani?" Abdullah was surprised to see his former student. "What are you doing here? Shouldn't you be at school?"

"I quit school after you left, Pak Guru. Then I met Pak Ardi. He said I could come live with him. You know how my dad gets when he's drunk."

"Fani," called a deep, booming voice from farther in the house. "Let our visitor in."

"Oh yeah, sorry. Come on in, Pak." Fani opened the door fully and motioned for Abdullah to follow him.

At the end of the hall they walked through an open door into what looked like a library. Every wall was covered from floor to ceiling in books, surrounding a large and ornately decorated teak desk with a tall black leather office chair behind it, and two matching teak wooden chairs in front of it. Abdullah assumed the man striding toward him, hand outstretched, must be the one he was looking for.

"Gusti Mohammad Ardiansyah, but just call me Ardi. What can I do for you?"

Abdullah felt the man's firm grip. Ardi was as tall as he was, though much rounder, balding with small, circular wire rim glasses over narrow eyes. He hardly knew how to start.

"I'm Abdullah. Sorry to bother you, I'm looking for some information. I was given your name as a local expert on fundamentalist groups. Do you have a few minutes to talk?"

"That depends…are you planning to join one?" Ardi paused, and Abdullah wasn't sure how to answer.

"Just kidding!" Ardi clapped him on the shoulder. "Fani, could you fix our guest a cup of tea? Have a seat." Ardi motioned to one of the wooden chairs and Abdullah sat. Rather than sitting next to him, Ardi pushed some papers away and leaned back on the desk.

"How did you meet Fani?" Abdullah asked.

"Oh, so you know he's not my son?" Ardi lowered his chin to peer at Abdullah over his spectacles. "It's true. I have only one child, a grown daughter who lives with her mother in Jakarta. I'm nearly fifty now, and need the help. One of my students from Kelayan told me about Fani's home situation, so I invited him to live with me. Perhaps I can get him in college someday. How do you know him?"

"He was my student at the *Al-Mustaqiim Pesantren* in Kelayan for the last several years."

"But you no longer teach there. What do you do now?"

"I've been working with M. Ramadani, I'm sure you've heard of him, in peacemaking efforts around the country."

"Yes, of course I've heard of Ramadani." Ardi removed his glasses and began wiping them with a white cloth. "But we have no conflicts here in Banjarmasin, so why are you here?"

"That's why I need to talk to you. There are rumors, and I'm afraid I'm not at liberty to mention the source, rumors of impending attack by a jihadist cell here in Banjarmasin. I am hoping to find this cell and meet with the members, and persuade them not to go through with it."

Ardi's eyebrows shot up. He cocked his head to look at Abdullah from another angle. "You are either an extraordinarily brave man or a blithering idiot, or maybe both. But why come to me? If this so-called rumor is true, why talk to a simple professor of comparative religions?"

"I was told you have studied abroad at Al-Azhar University in Egypt, where you got your masters in Islamic History, and that you have researched many of the local and national hardline Muslim organizations. My source suggested that I could learn a lot from you, and maybe get pointed in the right direction."

Ardi began to pace around the room, letting his fingers lightly caress some of his books as he thought. Fani entered with two cups of tea, handing one to Abdullah and setting one on Ardi's desk, then he backed out and closed the door.

Finally Ardi spoke. "You had best weigh very carefully what you're about to undertake. Do you have anyone you care about? Any family?"

"Both my sons were killed by terrorists. My wife left me. The only person I care about is actually a Christian girl who is like a daughter to me."

"A Muslim man adopting a Christian daughter? You are a bigger fool than I thought. Such a relationship is not meant to be. Especially if you stay on this path you've chosen. The more successful you are at locating the *mujahidin*, the more attention they will give you. When they find out there's a Christian in your home... Perhaps you should rethink this fool's quest."

Chapter 13

Abdullah felt a gnawing in the pit of his stomach. He shouldn't have left Sari alone. And this professor offered disbelief rather than help. He stood to go.

"I'm sorry to have bothered you."

"Sit down, my friend!" Ardi smiled. "I'm afraid I have a flair for the dramatic. I'll be happy to tell you what I know, provided when you are captured and tortured, you tell them your information came from Professor Syaiffudin over in the English department. He's always correcting my English in such a condescending way, so annoying!" Ardi laughed. Abdullah managed a smile and sat down again.

Ardi continued pacing, straightening out books on his shelves as he spoke. "*Al Azhar*—those were good times. In those days the Muslim Brotherhood was more idealistic, less political. Many of us Indonesian students attended their public meetings, but I was one of the few invited behind the curtain, so to speak. My interest in research matched their desire to be understood by the worldwide *ummah*.

"In those days many Indonesian students went on to join the PLO in Palestine or the Taliban freedom fighters in Afghanistan. These young men had a zeal for the faith, and clear enemies to fight—namely the Jews and the Soviets—but lacked coordinated leadership. Osama Bin Laden provided that.

"In 1998 Bin Laden merged the Egyptian Islamic Jihad with Al Qaeda and declared 'The World Islamic Front.' This was a global war now directed toward America and the West. Al Qaeda began to expand into Eastern Europe and North Africa, through Central Asia, then into Southeast Asia; so recruiting and training Indonesians became essential to jihadist operations in this arena."

Abdullah's thoughts drifted to how he was recruited just a year after he married, how he excitedly joined the training camp in Afghanistan, and how he eventually escaped and made the long journey home. *I may have escaped Afghanistan, but jihad is my ever present shadow.*

Ardi continued lecturing. "Many jihadists today were trained years ago by Al Qaeda-related groups in Afghanistan, or perhaps in Mindanao. If these are the people you are up against, they are well-indoctrinated, skillful in weaponry, and at least in the past they were well-organized. Al Qaeda's Indonesian arm, called *Jemaah Islamiyah,* was the major player here at the turn of the century. In fact, one of the leaders named Hambali was said to have arranged the meeting in Malaysia in January 2001 between two of the 9/11 hijackers, though his primary focus was on our region. Singapore reported that they arrested fifteen JI members before they could strike that city; the Indonesian intelligence network wasn't nearly so prepared. And so, I'm sure you remember, we suffered through the first Bali bombing just a year after 9/11, then the second Bali bombing in 2005, the Marriott and Ritz-Carlton bombings, even last year's attack on the Bellagio—all of these were planned and executed by JI-connected cells, some with funding from Al Qaeda. Despite what the government claims, there are still JI cells in Indonesia, but their funding and organization has significantly crumbled. They are more likely to act independently than..."

Ardi abruptly stopped both talk and walk. Then he slowly moved behind Abdullah and laid his hands on the back of Abdullah's chair. "Abdullah...yes, of course, Abdullah...forgive me, you must know all this. The Bellagio—that was you, wasn't it, who tried to stop the bombing?"

"Yes, it was. But please continue. There's much I need to learn if I don't want to fail the next time."

Ardi resumed his pacing. "I see. Yes, I remember your face now from the news reports. I am honored to have a national hero as my guest. Where was I? Currently, there doesn't seem to be much coordinated movement among the traditional jihad groups such as *Kompak, Darul Islam, Negara Islam Indonesia,* etcetera. Meanwhile, in the past few years several new fundamentalist groups have arisen, some with potentially violent tendencies. The vigilante ones you see on the evening news, like the Islamic Defenders Front, or FPI, and the *Hizbut Tahrir Indonesia,* or HTI, talk loudly, but use mob violence rather than technical or technological skill. They are unlikely to plan a bombing; however, the cell members planning an attack may be part of organizations like FPI in order to gain a media platform for their ideology. So those groups are certainly a potential ocean in which you may luckily catch your intended fish, as are universities and the hundreds of Islamic *pesantren* schools like your own.

"The most recent attacks against police or government targets, Western targets or Christian targets, however, seem to be coming from small cells of fundamentalists who are not connected globally or even nationally, except that they may be in personal relationship with someone from another cell. Thus, their attacks are not coordinated, and are not on the same grand scale as, say, 9/11. This makes it infinitely harder for the authorities to anticipate their activities and circumvent the tragic loss of life. If the cell you are looking for fits this profile, good luck, my friend. You will find them only when their deed is done."

Abdullah asked, "What about some of the newer jihadist groups in the Middle East such as ISIS—any chance they would select targets in Banjarmasin?"

Again Ardi removed his glasses and wiped the lenses with a cloth. "Why would ISIS be here? Of course their sympathizers bombed the Sarinah district in Jakarta not long ago, but so few people died I doubt ISIS had any actual part in it. Their stated goal is an Iraq-Syria Islamic state. Have you heard something I don't know?" Ardi leaned forward expectantly.

What am I allowed to say? Why would Joko send me to this man if he didn't trust him?

"I've just heard how ISIS has such strong financial backing and weapons access. If they were here, wouldn't that affect how the Detachment 88, for example, chooses to respond to a terrorist threat?"

"Detachment 88 has few friends among Muslims anymore because of their Israeli tactics. But I would be quite interested to know if ISIS has truly entered Banjarmasin. Please stay in touch with me."

Abdullah stood and the two men exchanged cell phone numbers. "At least the calling and texting work for me," Abdullah added. "This smart phone is supposed to send and receive photos too, but I haven't figured out how yet."

"Then you probably don't know how to set off a bomb with a cell phone either? Just kidding. You seem to be a peaceful man. Why get involved in this? Why not leave it to the authorities?"

"As I said, both my sons were killed by terrorists. The next generation doesn't deserve to inherit this mess. Our generation needs to do something about it."

Ardi put his hand on Abdullah's shoulder. "I wish I could have been more help. Good luck in your fishing expedition. Let me know if you catch anything. Assuming you're still alive." Ardi laughed.

"Thanks for your time. I'll be in touch."

Abdullah headed home feeling further from his goal than when he'd left that morning.

Chapter 14

Baqri never minded the three-plus hours on his motorcycle when he visited his family up in the village. Especially now that he could afford the powerful 200 cc Honda Tiger, the miles of asphalt and potholes flew right by.

It was refreshing to him to get out of Banjarmasin, a colorless city of gray cement crisscrossed by dozens of chocolate rivers. His parents still lived out in the world's oldest tropical rainforest, where a thousand shades of rich, lush green welcomed him. He'd once read that the Borneo rainforest boasted over 400 species of birds and over 15,000 species of flowering plants. His parents lived too close to the mangrove swamp to see any orangutans swinging in the trees, but occasionally he'd see a monitor lizard or better yet a water buffalo swimming by. No, he didn't mind the drive. It always served to clear his head from the stress of city life.

The final vestiges of civilization appeared as he came down the hill into the town of Negara. Looking down at this backward, glorified village, he imagined what it must have been like over 500 years ago when Negara was the capital of the Banjar kingdom. Those vain Americans hadn't even discovered their New World yet, he thought, while Negara was a prosperous Hindu kingdom. Then in the early 1500s the Banjar had aligned themselves with Islam, a more politically powerful force from Java. Nevertheless, the Banjar had kept many of their Hindu and even previous animistic practices, so that especially in the interior of Borneo, their Muslim faith was so syncretistic he wasn't sure the Prophet would call them Muslims at all. Even with the light of Islam, all his parents seemed concerned about was preparing offerings to appease all the local spirits that lived in the river, in the forest, or in the mango tree behind his house.

When the kingdom had embraced Islam, the capital was moved to the port city of Banjarmasin. Now Negara was nothing but an unimportant town on the unremarkable Negara River, forgotten by the turning wheels of modern progress. Sometimes he wondered if Allah had forgotten about them too.

After cruising through Negara, he turned his motorbike north toward the swamps. Another twenty minutes on a red clay road barely wide enough for two bikes and he was home. Well, he was at the house he used to call home.

Baqri had been raised in this two-room shack with thin wooden slats for walls and a tin roof. During dry season, the roof soaked up so much heat it felt like a sauna inside. He remembered sleeping many sweaty nights out on the small wooden front porch. He wouldn't sleep alone though, with hundreds of mosquitoes to keep him company. But in the rainy season the roof leaked, the walls leaked, and during flood season, water would fill the house up to their ankles or even knees. Though he loved the jungle, Baqri hated this house with a passion. He had begged his parents to send him to an Islamic boarding school when he was just ten years old to get out of this place. Now he was an Information Technology major at STIMIK in Banjarmasin. And he was making a bundle off his current, uh, endeavor. Finally he had a chance to get his parents out of here.

No one answered when he knocked at the door, so he opened it and walked right in. His elderly mother was sitting on the floor assembling a bracelet out of strips of rattan. Her face lit up when she saw him, and she struggled to her feet to give him a kiss on each cheek.

"My son, my son, my son! We haven't seen you in so long! Oh, just look at you!" She stepped back to examine him from his fresh pomp hairstyle to his sky blue Giordano polo to his skinny black corduroy pants and his black Andre Valentino loafers. "My, aren't you a city boy, a real city boy," she beamed.

"Where's Dad?" Baqri asked.

"What?"

He leaned in to her better right ear and asked again.

"You know, he's out fishing on the swamp. If the fish are biting, he'll be out there all day. If they're not biting he'll be out there till they do."

"Sit down, Mom, I have some good news for you."

While she sat on the floor, she asked, "Did you sell the bracelets I gave you last time?"

"Yes, Mom. But that's what I want to tell you. You don't need to make bracelets or bags or any of those handicrafts anymore."

His mother looked confused.

"Mom, I found a…a way to make a lot of money. Enough money to get you and Dad out of this dump and rent a nice place with a tiled floor and a real ceiling and electricity and running water in the city, a house that doesn't leak or flood or have bugs everywhere. You can move to the city with me!"

His mother still looked confused. "Did you say you want us to move to the city? Why?"

"Mom!" Baqri felt exasperated. "Look around you. I've worked hard all my life so I can get you out of this place. Maybe we could even have a doctor check your ears and fix your hearing. You and Dad could have a whole new life. He wouldn't have to fish all day and night just to eat, and you wouldn't work your fingers to the bone making these bracelets."

She looked down at the unfinished rattan bracelet. "You don't like my bracelets?"

"Mom…"

"It's a burden on you to sell bracelets for me, isn't it? I shouldn't ask that of you. You're so busy with school. Your girlfriend probably thinks selling bracelets is—"

"No, Mom! Stop. That's not what I'm saying. Your bracelets are great. I just want something better for you. I have enough money right now for two months' rent on a house, and in a few days I'll be getting a lot more money, enough to take care of you and Dad for a long time."

Baqri's mother was silent, her eyes darting side to side as if she wished there were someone else to step in and rescue her.

"You can ask your father about it tonight, I guess. If he wants to move... I... I don't know what I'd do in a city. What would I do in a city?"

"Anything you want. You could go shopping at the outdoor market, or at the mall. You could go to a salon and get your hair done. I could even take you to a movie theater. The city is an amazing place, Mom, you've got to give it a try. I know you'll like it."

She stood up. "Let me cook you some rice. You must be hungry." She filled a small aluminum pan with a tiny cup of rice, added water from a bucket, then struck a match to light her portable kerosene burner and put the pan on top. She swung open a small wooden window above the burner to let the smoke out of the house.

When Baqri was younger, he'd come home some weekends and spend the night, but not anymore. Between school, his girlfriend, and now this windfall he had stumbled across, he was the man-in-demand. He decided he'd stay for a small plate of rice and dried salty fish, then he'd better get back to the city in case Achmad needed him.

He'd lived his whole life for this moment. Somehow he had to convince his mom to leave this squalor behind and let him take care of them in their old age down in the city.

Chapter 15

"**P**astor, more are coming, and they're getting louder!"

Pastor Christianto heard his elderly secretary's urgent whisper in his ear even while directing the choir practice for Easter Sunday. The music crescendoed in the triumphant "He is risen!" He raised his hands to extend the final note, finally touching thumb to forefinger, and the sanctuary swelled with reverent silence.

After the moment had passed, he stepped away from his music stand. "Take a breather everyone. I'll be back shortly."

He followed his thin, silver-haired assistant to the back of the sanctuary where she had cracked open an opaque white window. Peeking through the slit, he could see about thirty men gathered inside the church yard. They didn't look like any of the neighborhood men. But these unfamiliar faces were definitely angry about something.

The police are always after terrorists, they're happy to sweep our church for bombs, but where are they when a violent mob shows up?

"Do you think I should go talk to them? Find out what they want?"

"No, Pastor! They don't want to talk. They're animals! We've got to get out of here!" The woman's voice sounded even raspier than usual. The wrinkled hands she waved about were trembling.

"Maybe I should invite them in. Perhaps the choir singing will calm them."

"Are you crazy? Come on, Pastor, let's go!" The secretary began pulling his arm. He walked a couple steps with her, then turned back.

"I'm going to talk with them." As he strode toward the door, he heard the elderly woman scurrying toward the dozen choir members and shooing them out the back.

Christianto took a deep breath, then pulled the door handle. The brilliance of the sun and the darkness of hate invaded his sanctuary.

"Good afternoon, my friends. Why have..." was all he could get out before the mob rushed him. They pushed him backwards and surged through the open church door shouting, *"Allah Akbar! Allah Akbar!"*

Someone punched his face, and his knees crumbled. The words of Jesus flashed through his mind: *turn the other cheek,* but he decided keeping his other cheek intact by pressing it to the hard wood floor might be wiser.

There were insults flying: "pig," "drunkard," "womanizer," "infidel," among others. He heard the scraping of wooden pews being dragged outside. Then he felt a kick in his side. *Jesus, is this what you felt?* Though today happened to be Good Friday, he didn't want to be Jesus at this moment. Christianto didn't want to die.

One of the men grabbed the hair on the back of Christianto's head and got in his face. "You criminal! You have no permit for this building! We've put up with you long enough. We're locking the doors of this church. If you try to worship here again with no permit, we'll be back to burn it down! Understand?"

Christianto tried to nod but had no control of his head, so he squeaked out a feeble "Yes."

The man then dragged him by his hair outside into the small fenced-in courtyard, where he smelled smoke. *Had they set the church on fire already?* When the man let him go, Christianto rolled over to see his church pews in a bonfire. He heard a crash as someone heaved a brick through a window, then another. *At least our windows aren't stained glass... Oh God, don't let them burn our church down while it's under my care!*

Someone grabbed his arm and he looked around to find one of his parishioners, the ancient Mr. Barnabas. With help, he managed to stand

and stumble around to the back of the church where a few of the faithful were waiting to whisk him to safety.

His last glance back revealed the same man who had threatened him putting a chain around the handles of the church's front door.

Chapter 16

Saturday's *Banjarmasin Post* claimed the "sealing" of the church was the work of a new organization similar to FPI, but calling itself "Pasukan Tauhid," or the "One-God Army." The article included the threat to burn down the church on Easter Sunday if the Christians continued to use it without a city permit for worship.

That night Abdullah told Sari this might be a part of the terrorists' plan, and he needed to be at the church on Sunday morning in case anything happened. All she said was that she would pray for him. She'd been pretty quiet the last two days, and spent a lot of time sleeping. Abdullah worried about her, but it would have to wait.

The next morning he parked his motorcycle half a block from the church in case things got ugly. When he took off his helmet he could hear the church music blasting over the whole neighborhood. *Why do the Christians always make things worse for themselves?*

He half ran down the street toward the gathering crowd. At least fifty or sixty Muslims were demonstrating outside the church fence. Some were college students waving signs for the television cameras, proclaiming ISLAM—MY WAY MY BLOOD, and CHRISTIANS WORSHIP 3 GODS=AMERICA, ISRAEL AND SATAN, and HELL WILL BE FULL OF THE INFIDELS. Others looked like hired muscle from Abdullah's part of town, carrying long knives and clubs. Inside the church fence stood six police officers. Abdullah noticed the chain was still on the front door, but judging by the music, the entire congregation must have entered through a back door.

Who is pulling the strings? He let his eyes rove the crowd trying to discern who was really in charge. If he could get to the influencer, perhaps he had a chance to stop whatever was planned here today.

His eyes settled on a tall, thin man near the back of the crowd with the long hair of a rock star. When the man turned, Abdullah recognized him immediately—David, the youth pastor from Sari's church. As he approached the younger man, David met his eyes, smiled and started toward Abdullah as well.

"Pak Abdullah!" David exclaimed and surprised him with a hug. "So good to see you! What are you doing here?"

"I was worried we'd have another church burning, thought I might help. What about you?"

Abdullah couldn't help but cringe as the words left his mouth. It was Abdullah's *pesantren* students who had burned down Sari's church not that long ago. Thankfully the church had agreed not to press charges if the boys would help David's construction crew rebuild the house of worship. Their friendship had been born out of that tragedy.

"Same. I know some people in this church, good people. I just don't want to see anyone get hurt."

They were yelling over the blaring music and angry chants of the crowd.

"Hey, you still see Sari, right?" David asked. "Tell her I'm available if there's anything I can do."

"Sure." Abdullah pointed to the policemen. "Do you think they'll do anything if the crowd breaks through that fence?"

"Six guys against this mob? I doubt it. You're the peacemaker, what do we do?"

Yeah, Abdullah, you're the peacemaker, what do we do? His eyes kept searching the crowd. "We need to find who is behind this."

"Maybe we could ask?" David reached out to the nearest man in the crowd, a young father carrying his toddler on his shoulders. "Excuse me, who's in charge here?"

"I don't know," the man replied. "I just came when I got the text message. Did you get one too?"

"What did it say?"

The man took his cell phone back from his son, who was resting it on his dad's head while playing a game. The boy protested loudly, adding his discontent to the general clamor. He opened to the text message and showed David and Abdullah.

Sunday at 9 a.m., join the Faithful to protest criminal Jew-supporting, American-funded Christianizers who are meeting illegally, ignoring our city laws, spreading their blasphemies, buying off poor Muslims to leave the true religion, kidnapping Muslim girls and converting them to be Christian brides. They must be stopped! *Allah Akbar.* Send this to all your friends. Following the message was the church address.

Abdullah and David just stared at each other for a moment. When they looked at the crowd again, it had grown in just the last few minutes. Some were whacking the fence with clubs or pushing against it. The Christians sang even louder, if that were possible. Abdullah knew the crowd was approaching the threshold of mayhem, when six policemen or even sixty couldn't control them.

Someone threw a sandal over the fence at the police. Abdullah looked for the thrower, and spotted...Hafiz? His former student? What was he doing mixed up in something like this?

He tried to push through the crowd toward Hafiz, with David hanging on to his shirttails. Now everyone was bending to take off their sandals and shower the policemen. It seemed the slogans started on Hafiz's side of the crowd then were echoed by those around Abdullah. He was just a few meters from Hafiz when a young man next to Hafiz changed the chant from Arabic to Indonesian, shouting, "The fires of Hell! The fires of Hell!" Then all hell broke loose.

The fence collapsed. The crowd surged forward. The policemen ran for their lives. Abdullah saw men with gasoline cans running around the base of the church building, but the sea of people kept him from getting close enough to do anything. Then a man in a white turban stepped forward with a cigarette lighter, shouted, "*Allah Akbar!*" and touched it to the gas-soaked front door of the church.

Whoosh! As the flames shot upward the crowd threw their hands in the air in ecstasy. Some began dancing around. At the same moment, screaming burst through the church speakers heard throughout the neighborhood. Then a gunshot exploded, and everything was pandemonium.

Abdullah couldn't see the policeman who'd fired the shot, but it did get most of the mob to run in full retreat, their mission accomplished. Abdullah and David ran with their hands in the air toward the back of the church hoping to help get people out without getting shot themselves.

The flames were less around the back. People were pouring out of the door crying, coughing, some heading for their cars or motorbikes, others standing by the back fence hugging each other and watching the flames. Frantic mothers were trying to locate their children. The police were moving people from the door to a safe spot away from the flames.

Abdullah and David managed to squeeze past the flow of people to get into the church, where they searched the sanctuary to make sure everyone got out. When the last person was evacuated from the building, they told the police, who made one final peek through the door, then closed it and moved everyone away from the building.

The fire was really blazing now. Even at a distance of ten meters Abdullah's skin was painfully hot. His eyes and nostrils burned from the smoke. He could hear the sirens of the volunteer fire department on its way.

He turned to David. The profound sadness in the young man's face cut him to the heart.

"I'm sorry—" he stammered, turning in shame to stare into the flames. David didn't answer.

He had no idea if this tragedy was connected to Joko's terrorists or just the age-old prejudice between religions in Banjarmasin.

The fire roared louder and the flames increased in brightness, but Abdullah was still in the dark.

Chapter 17

Sari opened her eyes and immediately wondered where she was. *This isn't my room. This isn't even a bed. Why am I sleeping on a couch?*

Within moments her memory caught up and she recognized Bali's living room—the family photo on the wall, the Arabic script on a white paper above the front door, the small TV, the wicker chair, and the green couch she lay on. The clock on the wall behind her told her it was after eleven. She tried to remember what day it was—Sunday? Was she late for church?

The pain started again in the left side of her chest. Sometimes she couldn't tell if it was closer to her chest or her back, it seemed to stab straight through. More memories surfaced, telling her why she wasn't going to church, why she wasn't sleeping at home, why her mother wasn't...

Better to think of something else.

She slowly stood up and wandered to the kitchen. She knew she should eat, but nothing Abdullah stocked looked appealing to her.

Next she thought about a shower. Her hair was a tangled mess. Had she really worn these same clothes for two days? Maybe she should walk home and at least pack a few things if she was going to be here anther day or two.

The front door creaked as she opened it to the bright sunlight. The alley was quiet except for her neighbor's gray cat across the street. He looked up from the gecko under his paw to see what Sari would do next.

Sari patted down her hair, searched for some flip-flops near the door, and started down the front steps. When her feet touched the narrow brick path between door and gate, her legs began to wobble. She kept walking slowly, as if in a trance, until her fingers reached to open the gate. Then her whole body began to shake.

Her eyes scanned the street for threats. There were none. She knew this fear was unreasonable, but there was no way she was going out that gate. She turned and hurried back into the house, locked the door, and collapsed on the couch gasping for breath.

It took several minutes before her body stopped shaking. *So I can't go home. No big deal. Quit beating yourself up, Sari.*

She decided to search for a Sunday morning Christian program on TV to get her thoughts back to a good place.

As she flipped through the channels, she paused on *Metro TV* where they were reporting breaking news from Makassar. The headline read, "Mall bombed—441 dead." She saw the images of people searching through the rubble for survivors, and more images of the injured being carried off towards ambulances. They replayed a cell phone video of the blast. Screams of terror leaped out from the TV assaulting her ears, trying to get their evil clutches on her mind. She covered her ears. Her vision began to blur. The trembling started again. She felt the tears hot on her cheeks. It was like a vortex of swirling darkness had opened below her and was sucking her in.

Sari curled up on the couch and pulled the blanket over her eyes and ears to block out the world.

She awoke again with a start at the sound of the front door opening.

"Sari? I'm home," a comforting voice called. Abdullah entered and plopped down in the wicker chair. "How are you doing?"

She still had the blanket wrapped around her. The clock read 11:45. She once again attempted to pat down her wild hair. "I'm sorry. I overslept."

"That's okay. What are you watching?" Abdullah's attention was drawn to the continued coverage of the Makassar bombing on TV. "*Ya Allah…*" he said.

Sari fumbled in the blanket for the remote, and when she found it, turned off the TV. "I don't want to watch anymore." Her eyes began to well up again.

"I'm worried about you." Abdullah moved to the edge of his seat. "Can you tell me what you're going through, or is it too hard to talk about?"

"Ah," she sighed and shook her head. Her mouth opened, but closed again and she turned away.

His voice caught in his throat. "Just pick one thing you feel, and start with that."

His concern gave her a faint spark of courage. She steadied herself with a deep breath. "Okay. My body is doing weird things. It freaks me out sometimes."

He nodded sympathetically and waited several seconds for her to continue.

Finally the words began to pour out of Sari. "I don't feel like eating. I cry a lot. I want to sleep, but I'm bothered by nightmares… I wish God would speak to me in dreams like He used to. I tried reading my Bible, but it's like the words don't get through to me. I don't want to see anyone, but I'm afraid when I'm alone. I was never like this. Why am I like this? Why can't I just be stronger and live a normal life?"

"I went through similar things when I came home from Afghanistan. I know it's brutal for you. But I can promise you that you will come through this."

"I feel bad for you, Bapak, that I'm sleeping on your couch and bothering you, and I'm no help at all around the house. I should go home. But I…I can't just yet. I'm sorry."

"Don't worry about that, you can stay as long as you like. In fact, why don't we get you off this couch and you can have Bali's bed. Maybe you'll sleep better in a real bed."

"Oh no, I couldn't," Sari protested.

It looked like Abdullah had made up his mind. "Do you think Bali wouldn't give you all he could? Even now, I know he'd offer his bed, his room, anything for you, Sari. I'll clean his room a bit, put his things in my room, then I'll go get what you need from your bedroom at home and bring them..."

"No, wait, you don't need to move his things. I need to miss him. I don't want to forget a single thing about him. Please."

Abdullah smiled. "I know what you mean...about not wanting to forget." His brow wrinkled in pain, and he turned toward the window. "After I get your things, I'll make us some fried rice for lunch. We'll eat once you get a shower and put on some clean clothes, okay?"

I must look horrible, or maybe smell horrible! I guess a shower would feel good.

"After my shower, you'll see a new me, I promise." Sari tried to smile. "And then I want you to tell me about what you did this morning. Tell me how you're going to find Bali's killers and stop them from killing again."

Chapter 18

Abdullah knew that a reconciliation meeting between the church leaders and the One-God Army leaders was unlikely, but he tried to set one up anyway. This was the strategy Ramadani had taught him, and they had been at least partially successful in Sulawesi, Ambon, West Java and South Sumatra. Of course, success depended on both sides coming to the table and being willing to listen to the other. As he feared, no one from the One-God Army would agree to show up. They seemed to feel a protest outside the police department was more important.

With no One-God Army coming, Abdullah saw no reason to even have a meeting, as his mission was to find the terrorist cell. However, David had begged him for help to keep the Christians from looking for revenge. He owed a debt to David for his help with Abdullah's *pesantren* students, so he agreed.

David had found it difficult to convince the church leaders to meet with Abdullah, but in the end he succeeded. David had hoped to host the meeting in his church, but his senior pastor "didn't want to get mixed up with any more Muslim anarchy." So they met in David's house.

It was the first time for Abdullah to meet David's wife Angelina and their baby girl, Josie. Seeing David and Angelina dote over their cute infant reminded him of happier days, when he saw Bali for the first time after coming home from Afghanistan. *If only I had never left my family, maybe they'd all be alive today.*

When the five leaders from the church arrived, David ushered them all into the living room. Where Abdullah imagined the sofa and coffee table should be, he found a beautiful lunch laid in the middle of a large Persian carpet. All the men sat cross-legged on the floor in a circle, and David formally welcomed everyone, then said a prayer before they ate.

Abdullah scooped some rice onto his plate, then passed the rice bowl around. Next he added some beef covered in West Sumatra's famous spicy red *rendang* sauce, some tiny pickled cucumbers, carrots and shallots, and some fried noodles. No pork, thank Allah, though he'd felt sure David would take pains to accommodate his Muslim dietary restrictions. While he ate, he acquainted himself with the other men around the circle.

To his right he recognized Pastor Christianto, who looked younger than Abdullah, thin with an unusually hooked nose for an Indonesian, still exhibiting some residual bruising under his right eye. The pastor slumped over his food, avoiding eye contact with everyone, like he'd been beaten down on the inside more than the outside.

Next to Christianto was Rudi, a lawyer. Abdullah noticed Rudi's smile to Angelina was bordering on flirtatious, but with the men his smile tended to slip down one side of his face almost like a sneer. During the meal Rudi would whisper into the pastor's ear, but Abdullah never saw the pastor respond.

Next to Rudi was an older Chinese man, who explained that his name was Lang Jingjing but everyone called him Stephen. He owned one of the four-star hotels in Banjarmasin, as well as a significant amount of prime real estate along the main boulevard called A. Yani Street. He was the chairman of the church's board.

Across from Abdullah sat Dr. Widartono, an eye specialist. The way he tore the *rendang* in his teeth reminded Abdullah of watching hyenas fight over scraps. *Was the doctor looking for a fight?*

The oldest and calmest of the group was next, Barnabas, a retired banker. He was the only one of the five to greet Abdullah with a genuine smile.

Between Barnabas and Abdullah sat David, the youngest man in the group. Abdullah hoped the older men would be willing to listen to someone younger than them. This was a real challenge in the Indonesian culture of honoring elders, especially if the elders were religious leaders. But he appreciated David's shrewd tactic of having them eat together first. He knew that Indonesian culture made it harder to attack someone after they'd eaten a meal together.

When everyone had eaten enough of the main course, Angelina brought out sliced watermelon. The chilled, juicy fruit was a perfect dessert in such humid weather. David waited until everyone had eaten their fill, then cleared his throat.

"All right everyone, I want to say again how much I appreciate your willingness to come here and discuss what to do about the situation the church is facing. I especially want to thank my dear Muslim friend and personal guest, Pak Abdullah, an experienced peacemaker in such cases, for coming to share his perspective with us. Now, who would like to share first?"

Abdullah noticed the doctor's twitching face, biting his tongue like his appendix was about to burst, but his money was on the chairman of the board going first, and he was correct.

"This is a horrible tragedy," Stephen began, "one that never should have happened. My sources in the church tell me that these criminals warned the pastor not to hold the Easter service in the church, but he didn't listen. His foolishness has now cost us a very expensive building." Pastor Christianto kept his eyes down.

"We have insurance on the building," Rudi interrupted.

"That's not the point. The point is we can't fight these people with bravado and presumption. We need to fight smart, avoid direct conflict and live to fight another day," the chairman declared.

"For how long? How long do we have to defer to these thugs? They only speak one language—intimidation. And you want us to give in?" The doctor jumped in, clearly agitated. "Next time we get the police to stand guard. Or the military. Or if they won't help, we hire the same roughnecks everyone hires during election season, and we make a statement—we will not be intimidated." He pounded his fist on his hand with each of the last five words.

"You're a fool if you want to go toe-to-toe with the Muslims," Stephen argued. "See where that got the Christians in Ambon? They didn't just burn the churches, whole villages were burned to the ground."

Abdullah had been to Ambon and seen the destruction. Many people from both religions had lost their homes and worse, family members, in the sectarian violence.

"We could sue," Rudi offered.

"Sue who?" the doctor countered.

"Well, the One-God Army for starters. Then the police department for inadequate protection. Then the city government for delaying our permit which would have made this whole protest moot. And if we think of anyone else, we'll sue them too."

Stephen, Dr. Widartono and Rudi all started talking at once, each getting louder to get the others to listen. David gave Abdullah a worried glance, but Abdullah mouthed, "It's okay," in return.

After giving them a few moments, David tried to interrupt. "Excuse me, guys, we haven't heard from our elder Pak Barnabas yet." The three men quieted down to show their respect, and everyone looked at Barnabas.

Barnabas smiled. His smile seemed to gently blow the charged atmosphere out the window. "My friends, we have endured much injustice for the sake of our faith in Jesus, who also endured much injustice. Remember his words on the cross: 'Father, forgive them, for they know not what they do.' This is the response I have chosen. It is a difficult path to walk. But I believe God has sent us a guide to help us on this path, our new friend Pak Abdullah. I'd like to hear his counsel to us."

Abdullah was stunned. He'd heard Sari's mother talk like this, and David, but the way Barnabas said it, not just the words he chose, but his countenance, it seemed as natural to him as breathing.

Now everyone was looking to Abdullah. Even Christianto's eyes were raised, maybe even hopeful? Then the pastor spoke.

"Please, Pak Abdullah, we need your help. Tell us what to do."

Chapter 19

Abdullah silently mouthed the briefest of Muslim prayers—"*Bismillah*"—and with a soft, calm voice entered once again the arena of waging peace on his enemies.

"I want to thank my friend David for inviting me to join you all today, and thank you for giving me a few minutes to share from my heart.

"I was there with David yesterday trying to rescue people from the church fire. I agree with my brother Pak Barnabas that this was a horrible injustice. I am ashamed that these criminals perpetrate such atrocities under the banner of the religion that I love. They are fools. Not only will they suffer ultimate failure in pursuing their wayward goals by such evil means, but they will also suffer Allah's judgment in the afterlife. It is not our duty to punish them. They have already chosen a path that leads to their own destruction.

"Sadly, I was once deceived as they are. I believed that the most noble thing I could do was to give my life in the defense of the Faith, and become an instrument of Allah's judgment. I killed those who were innocent. But in His great mercy, He allowed me to see the error of my ways. I fled that life to start a new life here in Banjarmasin.

"But now I have reaped what I sowed. Because of *jihad*, both of my sons are dead, and my wife has left me. I am alone, wishing that I had died and they had lived. My life means nothing to me now, unless it can be useful to stop the hatred and violence around me, that I may in some small measure atone for my sins."

The room was deathly quiet. Even Angelina in the doorway stood transfixed by Abdullah's words. *Now comes the hard part.*

"I will tell you what I tell my Muslim brothers, exactly the same thing. The only true and lasting change happens when men's hearts, like my own, are changed. And men's hearts are never changed by fear, intimidation, control, threats, or violence. All of these only succeed in reproducing themselves in those we want to change. Fear produces hatred; hatred produces threats; threats produce violence; violence produces anger; anger produces more hatred, then more violence, and the cycle never ends.

"The only way toward true peace is to stop that cycle and start a new one. There is another cycle we can choose, as Pak Barnabas pointed out. It starts with forgiveness; forgiveness opens one's heart, and into that open place can flood understanding, empathy, peace and love. Isn't this what your Prophet 'Isa said, to 'love your enemies'?

"When I left *jihad*, it was because I finally realized that it was the wrong path. But it took a Christian woman who laid down her life for others to show me what the right path was. This path may not change your enemies' hearts overnight, but it stops one cycle that leads to death and invites them into a new cycle that leads to life.

"Sometimes our best chance for true peace emerges from a tragedy such as this one. I hope you'll take the chance that is before you today to become true peacemakers."

Abdullah scanned the men's faces. The doctor and lawyer were looking down. Stephen's eyes were locked on Abdullah's. The pastor was looking at Barnabas, who had silent tears running down his cheeks.

Rudi mumbled, "That's all fine and good, but what about our church?"

"We are the church, not some building." Pastor Christianto had finally found his voice. "Pak Abdullah's right. If we can't learn to love, what's the point of singing and preaching anyway?"

"I'm with you." Stephen was still staring at Abdullah. "I agree that fighting back would be idiotic. We have to respond in a merciful way. Pak Abdullah, can you tell us what a merciful response might look like?"

So many memories of conversations like these working with Ramadani rushed through Abdullah's mind. "Each situation is different, but I can tell you what others around Indonesia have tried, and some have seen encouraging results. If you have a friend in the media, making a public declaration of forgiveness shows the community which cycle you're supporting. This can turn public opinion against the One-God Army and other vigilante groups. I also suggest you publically appeal to the mayor's office to bring a quick resolution to your building permit problem, either approving a permit for that land or providing a new plot of land and a permit. Finally, I think it's good in your public statement to recognize that you don't blame Islam for the actions of one radical group, and invite any Muslim friends and neighbors who would like to be involved in the rebuilding of your church to join you. I, for one, will come, and will try to bring others. When the radicals see that every time they try to marginalize Christians it results in Muslims and Christians coming closer together, perhaps they'll rethink their tactics.

"I also hope that in the future your church members will make it a priority to build friendships with their Muslim neighbors, co-workers, and especially the neighborhood around the church. We've seen in other parts of the country that when radicals came to attack a church, local Muslim neighbors would defend the church. Those who want peace in both camps need to build bridges for their communities to walk across. I can share more ideas about building bridges at another time.

"For now, I'll leave you to discuss among yourselves how best to respond to this opportunity. Peace be upon you."

From experience, Abdullah knew it could be difficult for their true feelings to be expressed with him in the room. He leaned forward on his knees to shake hands with each man before standing and heading to the door with David. He thanked Angelina for the delicious dinner. Once outside, David gripped Abdullah's right hand tightly with both of his.

"Pak Abdullah, I'll never forget this moment. Gracious encounters like these are the best chance our nation has for true peace. I'm so grateful you came."

"Anytime, David. I may be needing you soon to speak to the Muslims, so be ready." Abdullah smiled.

"When this is all over, would you be willing to share with my church youth group?" David asked. "And maybe you could bring Sari with you? They all want to see her."

"Sure, I'd love to. After we find out who's behind all this and…and get a few good nights' sleep."

Chapter 20

On the way home Abdullah stopped at a mini-mart for some groceries. Besides his staple of instant noodles, he tried to pick out some potato chips and cookies for Sari, hoping he could get her to at least eat something. She couldn't afford to get much thinner.

He was stepping onto his porch when someone called to him from down the street.

"Pak Abdullah! Pak Abdullah, could you wait just a moment?"

It was that busy-body Ibu Aaminah. He knew she meant well, and she had been kind to Sari's mother, but Abdullah's wife had never liked her and he found that over the years he'd been swayed to his wife's predilection.

"Hello, Ibu Aaminah. How are you and your husband?" He spoke loudly as it was taking the woman an eternity to walk toward him. He realized he'd get this over with much faster if he went to her, so he set his groceries on the porch and covered in a few long strides the distance between them.

"We're well, thank you, though my hip has been slowing me down lately. My husband and I have been thinking about you. How are you coping?"

"As well as I can, thanks for asking." He knew she'd never be satisfied with such a short answer, but what else was there to say?

"If you ever need someone to talk to, my husband would happily come over." It was true, everyone knew Pak Zaini must be a good listener since Ibu Aaminah was such a good talker.

"Thank you again."

Aaminah paused, then glanced at his house as she spoke. "Or maybe you've found someone else to share your pain with?"

He hadn't wanted to face this moment, but he'd known it would come. He hoped his answer didn't sound like he'd been practicing it for days: "Sari was attacked while alone in her home. She feels safer staying with me for a few days. She was like a sister to my son Bali, and she's like a daughter to me."

Aaminah seemed to be considering his response, but perhaps he'd not been the only one preparing for this confrontation. "Of course, Pak Abdullah, I'm sure all the neighbors want Sari to be safe. Why don't you send her to stay with me, and that will avoid anyone being confused about your intentions. She is a vulnerable young orphan, after all, and we all have a duty to take care of her."

He couldn't tell anyone yet about the potential threat of terrorists, nor did he want to risk them being killed if anyone came after Sari again. He'd have to stall.

"Let me talk with Sari about it when she's feeling up to it and see what she says." Abdullah tried to smile.

His smile was not quite returned. "You do that, Pak Abdullah. I expect to see Sari soon, or I will be back."

And with that the elderly woman pushed her cane into the dirt to help her spin slowly, then lumbered home.

Sari wasn't the least bit interested in moving to Ibu Aaminah's house, nor could she understand why Aaminah would object to her staying with Abdullah.

He tried to explain. "She's worried about gossip. And she's worried that I'll...take advantage of you."

"That's the stupidest thing I've heard since my pastor told my mom not to spend time with the Muslim women of this neighborhood! Christians don't trust Muslims, women don't trust men...how can we ever build godly relationships if we're always assuming the worst about everyone and keeping our distance?"

This girl sounds like Ramadani. Where did she learn to think like this?

Abdullah finished putting the groceries away and held out some cookies and chips to Sari, who waved them away.

"You'd definitely eat better at her house."

"No I wouldn't. It's not the taste that's the problem. I'm just not hungry."

"What about staying with David and Angelina? They speak very highly of you. I'm sure they'd take better care of you than I could." Abdullah thought she might be safer far from this neighborhood where no one would look for her.

Sari was quiet for a moment. She pulled her knees up under her chin on the couch. "My being here is making a problem for you, isn't it? I should go."

"No!" Abdullah quickly came out of the kitchen to face her. "No, your being here is not a problem. You can stay here as long as you like, no matter what the wagging tongues say. I just want you to know that you have choices. You don't have to stay with me if you'd be better off somewhere else."

Sari relaxed her grip on her knees and brushed her hair back off her face. Then she closed her eyes. "When I'm here, I feel…I feel close to Bali. And I feel safe." She opened her eyes to look at Abdullah. "And I know someone is coming home for me, bringing me cookies I don't want to eat and gossip I don't want to hear, but it's for *me*, and that means, you know I'm…here."

Abdullah didn't know what to say, so said nothing.

"But I'll think about Ibu Aaminah's offer," Sari added. "Just give me a few days, okay?" She smiled.

Abdullah nodded and smiled back. "Fair enough, but if you stay here, my house rules say you have to eat. You can have anything in the house, and if you think of something I don't have, I'll go get it. Just please eat."

"Okay, I'll try some instant noodles. And Bapak?"

"Yes?"

"Thanks for letting me stay."

Chapter 21

*B**ite your tongue. Don't screw this up.*

Amat had just insulted him again, trying to provoke Hafiz to lose his temper. But a lost temper might mean a lost opportunity to prove himself. Or worse, the wrong reaction could cost him his life.

Hafiz was thrilled to even be invited to this dinner. It was rare for Achmad to gather this many of the group together in one place, and Hafiz had never even met Hidayat and Baqri. He was starting to feel accepted by them, and he knew their teasing of him as the youngest was part of that initiation.

They were seated in one of many small bamboo huts at a well-known restaurant named Pawon Tlogo on the north edge of Banjarmasin. Their hut was the farthest from the kitchen and other customers, affording them enough privacy to talk without being heard. Plus there was the white noise of the paddle wheel turning in the canal that ran through the middle of the restaurant grounds, and the rumbling traffic passing just outside on the main road from South Kalimantan to the jungle interior of Central Kalimantan.

Hafiz had never been to Pawon Tlogo before. He marveled at this large oasis of pine trees, palms, and sweet-smelling frangipani trees, with hibiscus, dahlia and bougainvillea all around. Each hut sat eight to twenty people on a raised platform floor around one or two short tables. Their group was in one of the smaller huts since there were only seven of them.

He'd never seen a menu this expensive before either. Achmad must be independently wealthy or have a generous backer to cover such a spread.

As the waitress brought their food, Hafiz noticed Achmad had ordered a Javanese dish, *nasi pecel,* while most of the others had ordered more local dishes such as the sour vegetable fish head soup, chicken satay, barbecued catfish, barbecued whole shrimp on a stick, or fried rice. Baqri had even added a tall glass of avocado juice with chocolate syrup, while he and the others all drank sweet Banjar tea or water.

As they dug into their food, he wanted to ask Hidayat why he had a bandage on his nose, but hesitated. He whispered the question to Amat next to him.

"Hafiz wants to know what happened to your nose," Amat announced. Hafiz cringed.

"Got in a fight." Hidayat glared at Hafiz, who focused intently on his catfish.

"Hafiz says it makes you look like a wuss," Amat lied. Hafiz waved his hands in protest while showing that his mouthful of fish surely proved him innocent. Hidayat ignored the dig, causing Amat to aim his humor elsewhere.

"Hey, Achmad," Amat joked. "That waitress kept trying to make eye contact with you. Why don't you give her your phone number?"

Achmad rolled his eyes. "The last time I looked at a girl was before Afghanistan. Don't lose your focus now, when we're this close."

"I'm just saying, you're a good-looking guy for your age. You got to think about getting married sometime, right?"

Achmad's jaw clenched and his eyes visibly narrowed.

Baqri lifted the tension in the air. "No worries, boss, I'll give her my number." Though he was the shortest, he was the best dressed of the group, in a fake Calvin Klein checkered button-down, khaki slacks and shiny black dress shoes, unlike the sandals most of them wore. He was texting on one cell phone when a second phone rang and he started to answer it.

"Put your phones away, Techno-genius. We need to talk." *Is Achmad always this uptight? Probably.*

Achmad raised his glass of tea. "Congratulations on a successful first assignment. Now let's talk about the second," Achmad began.

"What?" Amat interrupted. "No 'thank you, Amat'? No 'good job, Amat'? That church was up in flames faster than you could say, '*Al Fatihah*.'"

Achmad glanced around to make sure no one could hear them. "You'll get your thank you, and your reward, when all our assignments are successfully accomplished, assuming you're still alive. Now on to task number two. Rio and Baqri, you have everything you need for the job? Is everything ready?"

"Sure, boss," Baqri answered, then looked over at Rio. He'd hardly eaten any of his fried rice. "Rio, are you okay?"

"Yeah, I'm just tired." Rio took his glasses off and set them on the table, then rubbed his eyes.

Hafiz saw his chance and took it. "If Rio's not feeling well, I could take his place. I helped Amat at the church. Give me something to do."

"This task is…delicate. Better leave it to the big boys. But don't worry, you're playing a major role in task number three," Achmad answered.

"What is it? When is it? What do I get to do?"

"He sounds like a mosquito," Amat joked. He mimed with his thumb and forefinger a bug flying around Hidayat's ear. "Bzzzzzzzzzzzzzzzz." Hidayat mockingly slapped his hand against his white skull cap, took a drag on his cigarette and exhaled in Amat's face.

"Patience, kid," Achmad took control again. "If all goes well tonight, Rio will be busy tomorrow and Wednesday getting the package ready for you to deliver on Thursday. Khaliq will go over the plans with you. He'll make sure you perform your role perfectly. Three more days till your shot at glory."

Hafiz glanced over at Khaliq. The big man was dressed in his usual ragged t-shirt, his hair long and unkempt. Most of the group were nearly done eating and Khaliq was watching to see if there'd be any leftovers.

"Is Thursday my last job?" Rio asked softly, looking down. Everyone stared at him. Hidayat even put down his cigarette.

"What are you trying to say?" Achmad's voice had a hint of cold steel.

"Nothing. I'm just tired. I brought you all the materials you need. Couldn't I train someone else how to assemble the packages?"

Hafiz raised his hand slightly. "I want to learn."

"Shut up." Achmad glared at Hafiz, then turned back to Rio. "We couldn't do this without you, brother. We need you to stay till the last assignment, then I promise you can walk away. It's just a few more days now. No turning back."

Rio was silent. Hafiz couldn't understand why everyone wasn't volunteering to learn how to make bombs from Rio. Amat had whispered to him that Rio had learned from Abu Musa, who had trained at the Al Jamaah Military Academy in Mindanao and had bombed the Australian Embassy in Jakarta. *What an awesome skill that would be! It would really make me someone essential to the cause.*

The waitress was approaching with the bill. Achmad ignored her, so Baqri reached out his hand to accept it. As he did, he said, "Hey, Beautiful, that guy over there with the Ronaldo haircut and Real Madrid jersey wants your phone number." Amat's face turned bright red. The waitress smiled at him then walked away. Hidayat, Baqri and Hafiz all jeered at Amat, "Hoooooooooooo." Achmad's lip gave a slight twitch, not quite a smile, but close.

Baqri handed the bill to Achmad, then checked one of his cell phones. "Sorry, bros, got a night class, I'm out of here. Rio, see you at midnight." Rio nodded. Hafiz noticed Rio's plate of half-eaten fried rice was now in front of Khaliq and almost gone.

Achmad and Khaliq went to pay the bill. Hafiz left with Amat for Amat's motorcycle in the parking lot, Hidayat walking with them. Rio had said he'd find his own way home, and was staring into the dredges of his tea glass when they left him.

If only Syukran and the gang could see me now...

Chapter 22

The party crowd was in full force at the Nashville Pub & Café when Baqri arrived just after midnight. This was the most famous night club in Banjarmasin. The parking lot of Hotel Banjarmasin International, which operated the club, was full of skimpily-clad young girls, metro boys, expensively dressed older men, and even a few in modest Muslim outfits and head coverings. Baqri had rented a small pickup truck with a driver and his teenage son to help deliver the package. It took them several minutes to inch the truck through the crowd to the service entrance, but with all the girls to check out, the other two were content moving slowly.

He desperately needed to pee, but that wasn't going to happen anywhere near here.

There were six boxes for delivery. Each man grabbed two boxes at a time. Baqri made sure that he carried the one that would make this delivery worthwhile.

They took the elevator up to the night club, then stacked the boxes carefully in front of the bar, the special box in the middle of the pile.

The bartender protested loudly, "Hey, what do you think you're doing? You can't leave those boxes here."

Baqri yelled over the deafening house music, "Pak Fauzi told me he'd pay me Rp.500,000 a box for these. It's Foster's, from Australia. Got it from a boat. You owe me Rp.3,000,000."

"Pak Fauzi's only here in the day, you get your money from him. Now get these boxes out of here."

Baqri told the driver and his son to wait in the truck. He opened the top box and took out a bottle of Foster's Lager. "This is premium stuff." He turned to a passing businessman and held out the bottle. "Australian beer, you want to try it?" The man nodded and Baqri shrugged and grinned as he passed the bottle to the bartender. The bartender scowled. "You'll sell it all tonight, and I'll bring the invoice to Pak Fauzi tomorrow, okay?" He started walking away.

The bartender called after him, gesturing to the boxes, but Baqri mimed that he couldn't hear and kept walking to the elevator.

Back in the parking lot, he paid the truck driver and his son and sent them home. Then he tried to walk nonchalantly out to the street where Rio was waiting on his motorbike, face covered with a black helmet.

"How'd it go?" Rio asked.

"Like feeding a monkey bananas," Baqri replied. He took the spare helmet from Rio and put it on. "Let's get out of here. I really gotta pee." Now that he was on the motorbike his knees felt like jelly.

They drove to a parking lot two buildings away with a clear view of the night club. Baqri took out a cell phone that looked much simpler than the two he usually used.

"Hold on, I gotta pee first." Baqri rushed to some bushes behind the building. When he came back, his knees were still weak, but the adrenaline was pumping through his temples making him hyperaware of everything.

"This is your first time to detonate something using a cell phone, right?" he asked Rio.

"Yeah. Let's hope it works."

Baqri punched the phone number while explaining. "Just like we tested with the fireworks, when this call goes through, the electric current passing through the phone's vibrator into the wires that connect to the bomb should set it off...and here we go." He hit CALL.

They felt the earth shudder even before they heard the blast. From their vantage point, they could safely watch the west wall about six stories up explode outward sending chunks of cement raining down on the cars and motorcycles parked below. Next came the sound waves of smashing metal and glass mixed with the screams and shrieks of those outside the building running for cover. As they watched, the roof began to slowly crumble in on itself, dropping tons of steel and cement through the disco floor and each succeeding floor, until the entire building was rubble.

Baqri was in awe. "Dude, I've never seen anything like that. How many times have you done this before?"

Rio sighed. "Believe me, it gets old fast. Let's go."

A few more seconds passed as Baqri soaked it all in—the rubble, the smoke, the screaming, the people all around them rushing toward the hotel to see what had happened.

"Whoa, that's...that's insane. That's freaking...insane. Bam!" Baqri punched the air. Then he closed the visor on his helmet and climbed on the bike behind Rio. His knees were visibly shaking now, but the job was done.

They headed back to bring Achmad the good news.

Chapter 23

At five in the morning, Abdullah's cell phone rang.

He bolted upright, scanning the room for threats, his hand unconsciously reaching for the knife under his wife's pillow. He saw no one.

His phone rang again.

He took a deep breath and returned the knife, then checked his phone to see who would be so rude as to interrupt his troubled dreams. The cell phone showed the name JOKO.

"Morning Pak Joko."

"Pak Abdullah. Sorry to call so early. I hope I didn't interrupt your *Subuh* prayers?"

It had been many years since Abdullah had gotten up before dawn to do the first of the five daily Islamic prayers. "No. It's fine. What's up?"

"Did you hear about the night club bombing?"

"Where? Here in Banjar?"

"Yes, at the Hotel Banjarmasin International, at around 12:30 a.m. From the intelligence I've gathered so far, this is the real deal. This isn't some vigilante group burning a church, this feels like the terrorist cell we've been hearing about. So tell me, are you making any progress in finding them?"

Abdullah ran his fingers through his hair. "No, sir, I'm afraid I've found nothing. Maybe I'm not the right man for this job." He paused. "Were there a lot of casualties?"

"Preliminary estimations are at least a hundred dead, but it will take time to clear the rubble."

"Ya Allah. Please, Pak Joko, send in your trained guys. Don't let my city get blown apart like this."

"It's not just your city, Abdullah. I'm calling you this early because I'm planning to stop by Banjar for a few hours today. Can we meet?"

"I guess so. When and where?"

"Can you come out to the airport to meet me, say at eleven o'clock? You know the Heroes' Cemetery across the street? That'll afford us the privacy we need."

"I'll be there." Abdullah hung up and lay back on his bed.

And maybe I'll talk some sense into this delusional fool for thinking I could ever do what he asks.

The Bumi Kencana Heroes' Cemetery Park had beautifully manicured green grass, hundreds of well-kept tombstones, many with fresh flowers on them, all guarded by three imposing gray obelisks at the far end of the park away from the street. When Abdullah pulled up on his motorbike, he saw a short, elderly man standing alone in the shade of the central obelisk and figured it had to be Joko.

As he crossed the park to join Joko, he couldn't help but glance at the tombstones. Most of these were military men who had died in the war for independence from Holland. His grandfather was killed in the Battle of Surabaya, the bloodiest conflict of the war, and though the vastly outmanned and outgunned Republican troops lost that battle, it rallied the nation to come together. His family was still very proud of their grandfather's sacrifice, because after centuries of resisting European oppression, Indonesia had finally won her freedom. Now a new type of oppression was threatening, this time originating in the Middle East. He wondered how many more would die in resistance before his country would be free from the terror of *jihad*.

Joko shook his hand warmly. "Abdullah, my friend, I was worried you might not come. But you are here, so let us talk. By now you've probably caught the local news about the night club."

"Yes. It's horrific. But you said this is happening in other cities too?"

"That's right. In Makassar, a bomb went off at a McDonalds in the mall. In Solo, a car bomb exploded at the police academy, and when investigators and public officials gathered to investigate, a suicide bomber ran in and killed some significant leaders of the community. In Banda Aceh, a Western NGO doing rebuilding work after the tsunami, but long suspected by locals of being a front for Christian proselytizing, had their headquarters bombed, with much of the debris destroying a poor elementary school next door. Many of the kids were injured; twenty-six children and one teacher were reported dead."

"Ya Allah." Abdullah felt his stomach drop right through the grass he stood on.

"And the chatter is that Jakarta is next. Everyone there is on high alert, trying to anticipate what the target or targets might be, and find some way to circumvent the attack. My department is working twenty-four hours a day right now. The Detachment 88 Special Forces are unable to respond to any of these regional conflicts in case they need to be mobilized to protect federal government buildings, the president, etcetera. But if this is not the end, if this is only the first wave, eventually Detachment 88 will come. Until then, we still have a window of time to find this cell and bring it down ourselves."

"Non-violently?"

"Non-violently." Joko held Abdullah's gaze. The eye tic was still there, but not as pronounced today.

"So tell me," Joko continued. "Tell me everything you've learned so far, leave out no details, no matter how small."

Joko began strolling between the grave sites, so Abdullah walked at his side. There were no other visitors at this hot time of the day. Abdullah spoke in normal tones about his visit to the pessimistic professor Ardi, then told the story of the church being sealed and subsequently burned, and mentioned his meeting with the Christian leaders. He told Joko about trying unsuccessfully to meet with the leaders of the FPI, the One-God Army, and the Hizbut Tahrir, as well as his visits to four Islamic *pesantren* boarding schools that although they talked like radicals, they didn't seem to be inclined to action. In summary, though the bomb proved the cell was out there, Abdullah didn't have a clue who they were or how to find them.

"So you see, Pak Joko, I'm not the man for this job. I don't have spy training. And even if I found them, I don't know how to stop them."

Joko paused his stroll, crossed his arms, then rubbed his chin. "From what you've told me, I think you're exactly the man for the job."

Abdullah's hands opened out wide. "And why is that?"

"You've approached this challenge in the only way that brings true peace—relationally. What you did with those Christian leaders, that's what you have to do with the radicals in our religion. Right now you're getting to know all the local players—be on the lookout for those who aren't local, who don't speak the Banjar dialect. You hid here successfully for many years—look for those who would hide like you.

"I suggest sharing what you've learned with Pak Ardi again. Maybe he'll have a new idea now that he's had a few days to think about it.

"Also, try to anticipate. If the cell is not done here yet, what might be their next target? Watch for public events that attract politicians, police, military, or especially Westerners."

Joko ran his hand along the top of a tombstone. "Our heroes are buried here. They're remembered not for their victories, but for their sacrifices. Most of them died having never seen our nation's independence. But what a debt we owe them."

Joko laid his hand on Abdullah's shoulder. "And now it is our time to sacrifice."

Chapter 24

"So why did you want us to come over?" Udin asked Hafiz. "And what's with the black eye?"

Udin and Juki had just arrived and plopped down on Hafiz's rickety porch, carefully avoiding the loose plank that had once sent their friend Kiki stepping into the muddy marsh below the porch.

Hafiz touched his cheek gingerly. "Hey guys, what's up?"

Juki lit a cigarette. "Seriously, who hit you? You call us here to get them back or something?"

"No, man, nothing like that. It's no big deal. You should see the other guy," Hafiz joked to his former classmates and martial arts comrades. "What going on with you guys?"

Udin answered first. "Nothing, man. No job, no money, no girl, and I never see you guys anymore. Life sucks."

Hafiz looked at Juki. "Since we graduated, I've been going out to Martapura to study religion every day."

"Didn't you get enough at the *pesantren?*"

"They have some cool speakers out there. Hard-core dudes. Talking about us joining the *caliphate*, you know, the whole world united under one strong Muslim leader. You should come."

"Not if the chicks are wearing those black sacks," Udin protested. "If you ask me, covering up a beautiful girl is a worse crime than anything going on here in Kelayan."

"Sorry, bro," Hafiz told Juki, "I got other stuff going. Big stuff. That's why I wanted to see you."

Udin looked around at the empty space on the porch. "You invite the others? Where's Kiki?"

"Yeah," Juki added, "and Fani?"

"Fani's disappeared, man," Udin said. "I asked his dad the other day, but he was too drunk to answer. No one's seen Fani for weeks."

"I called Kiki, but he said his parents needed him today."

Juki touched his cigarette to a passing ant and watched him burn. "It's not the same without Syuk and the others."

"Yeah, I know what you mean," Hafiz nodded. "But stuff happens, and we got to be ready to let go." He paused. "You guys need to know that...I mean...I'm glad you're my friends."

"Dude, what's up? You leaving us too?" Udin asked.

"Let's just say, I'm part of something big, real big. Big as Syukran big, maybe bigger."

"No way!" Udin leaned forward. "You join the *mujahidin?*"

Hafiz couldn't hide the grin.

Udin slapped the wooden floor. "You did! You found a group like Syuk did, didn't you? Come on, you can get us in too, right?"

"Is it ISIS?" Juki wondered. "In Martapura they keep saying ISIS is coming."

It took all Hafiz's will-power to keep his secret. "I wish I could say more. Just watch the news, boys. Syuk won't be the most famous Banjar martyr for long."

Both boys started asking Hafiz questions at once, but they were interrupted by the front door banging open.

"Hafiz? Where have you been? You never came home last night!" Hafiz's mother noticed his bruised cheek. "*Ya Allah*, what happened to you?"

"It's nothing, Mom. We're busy." He waved for her to go back inside.

"Have you been in a fight again? Are you in trouble? Hafiz, you tell me what's going on right now."

"I said it's nothing." Hafiz turned away hoping she'd back off.

"When your father gets home, we'll have a talk young man. And tomorrow I need you to help me bake cakes. We got a huge order for—"

"I can't, Mom, I'm busy tomorrow." Hafiz noticed his friends were watching the traffic, pretending not to hear this embarrassing dialogue.

"But we need the money. I don't see you getting a job. All you do is—"

Hafiz stood up and glared down at his shorter mother. "Mom, chill out! I stayed in school till graduation like you asked. Now it's my life. I got bigger things to do than bake cakes." He whipped out his wallet and thrust Rp.500,000 into her hand. "Here, now leave me alone." He spun around and sat on the farthest end of the porch with a scowl.

His mother's eyes nearly popped out of their sockets as she counted the money. "Oh dear, oh dear, are you selling drugs? You better not be selling drugs! Your father will beat the crap out of you if—"

"Mom! I'm not selling drugs! I'll explain later. My friends are here, give us some space!" He glared at her until she looked down again at the money.

His mother glanced up and down the street as though someone might be watching her take the dirty money, then bustled into the house muttering to herself.

When she'd gone, Hafiz stood up and slammed the front door closed, then returned to his seat.

Udin's eyebrows were raised. "Dude, you rob a jewelry store and don't invite us? That's not cool."

"Relax, guys. You know I'd get you in if I could. But I'm on the edge as it is. I get one shot to prove myself. If it goes well, maybe I'll move up and can get you guys in. Or maybe you'll be reading about me in the Banjarmasin Post. Just give me a couple days, okay?"

Juki frowned. "You shouldn't treat your mother like that. You know the *Hadith* as well as I do, that 'heaven is under your mother's feet.'"

"There's more than one way to heaven," Hafiz argued. "Besides, my parents are stuck in the past. They only want me to earn money for them, they don't care about my dreams."

"But they're your parents," Juki countered.

"In a few days it won't matter anyway. Like the man said, the time for my glory has come."

Chapter 25

Seven nights. One full week of life, lost, never to be experienced again. One full week wasted on sleeping, crying, staring at the wall, and wondering when real life would return to this mortal body once again.

Sari was losing her connectedness to living. Beginning with her church, then her mother, then Bali, even her best friend Nina had married and moved away, she was losing touch with people.

But beyond that, she was losing touch with music, with dance, with food, with color, with all that makes living feel alive.

Worst of all, she was losing touch with God.

Each day she still tried to open her Bible at least once and read something. Reading David's *Psalms* brought a little comfort, knowing she had a fellow-sufferer. But there was no tender whisper in her spirit, no light to illuminate a path for her. All was darkness and silence and unanswered tears.

It was after ten at night, but Sari wasn't sleepy yet. She stared at Bali's poster of Liverpool's former captain Steven Gerrard opposite her bed.

"Have you ever been afraid?" she asked the man on the wall. "What would you do?"

He didn't answer. He seemed more interested in kicking a soccer ball than talking to her.

Bali's room never talked to her. She missed her own bedroom. Her walls were covered with Bible verses, poems she had written, and inspirational posters. She remembered one of a cat chasing a lizard up a palm tree. It said, *Chase your dreams till they have no more place to run.*

How am I going to ever chase my dreams again when I can't even walk out the front door?

Practically the only thing familiar in Bali's room was her Bible on the nightstand. Sari picked it up again, not knowing what else to do. She flipped through the pages randomly, with honestly no desire to read it, and stumbled upon a folded up homemade card.

The front of the card said, "Happy Birthday Sari!" and had some hand-drawn balloons. She knew right away who had given her this card and why she'd kept it. She raised it to her lips and kissed it, then opened it and read the words that had pulled her out of despair so many times.

> *My dearest daughter,*
>
> *Sixteen years old! And look at you—you're beautiful, you're smart, and so very strong.*
>
> *When you were a baby I used to worry that without a father, living where we live, you'd grow up angry or lonely or fearful like me. But somehow you didn't. You're like a songbird that, even if it's a rainy day, even if some greedy housing developer cuts down her jungle trees, she can't help but sing.*
>
> *I tell you all the time that you mean everything to me. Today I want you to know what "everything" means:*
> *—your laughter lifts my heavy burdens*
> *—your song calls my heart back to the One who loves me*
> *—your dance inspires me to dance on my problems*
> *—your dreams give me hope that nothing is impossible with God*
> *I don't know where I'd be without you, and I never want to find out. You're the greatest gift I could ever have. There's nothing I wouldn't give you.*
>
> *All my love on your birthday,*
> *Mom*

Sari kissed the card again, refolded it and returned it to her Bible. Normally, reading this card would bring tears to her eyes, but not today. Maybe she'd already cried all her tears for one day and had none left.

If the card wasn't enough to break through her darkness, maybe she needed to do something more. Like the card said, what helped her mom was Sari's laughter. Maybe if she could think of something to make herself laugh…

Sari had to concentrate hard to recall humorous events from happier days.

She remembered when she was six she got to play the role of Mary in the church children's Christmas program. She had a doll stuffed inside her dress, riding on the back of a high school boy who played the role of the donkey, when the donkey lost his balance and she fell off, the baby falling out of her dress and rolling across the stage. Everyone laughed. She told her "husband Joseph" to get the baby, but he just whacked the donkey with his staff. An "angel" had to bring her the baby and help her get back on the donkey's back to finish the trip to Bethlehem. At the time she'd been mortified, but looking back it always made her chuckle.

Until today. All she managed was a wry half-smile.

Maybe she could sing. If her cell phone were fixed she could open a Misty Edwards worship album she'd downloaded. She imagined Misty was there in her room playing the keyboard, and she quietly hummed along with the song. The house was quiet. Abdullah had shared with her briefly over a late dinner about his fruitless search for clues at the bomb site and gone to bed early. For a few moments she just let the soothing adoration music wash over her. She made it through one song and tried to hum another. But after a couple lines, her voice quit working. She ordered it to sing, but there was no authority behind her demand and her voice refused. The keyboard music grew fainter in her head, and then Misty disappeared and she was alone again.

How will I ever climb out of this pit?

The card held one more idea for her. Maybe she could dance. Worship dance had always been her most intimate connection place with God. If she could force her legs and arms to move, perhaps they'd carry her into His presence, the place where she always felt His joy over her.

She stood by Bali's bed. There was very little room between his bed and his brother Syukran's, but it was enough. She pulled the scrunchie from her hair and let it flow in its own dance. Her body began to sway with the music in her head, then her feet started to tiptoe in a rotating triangular pattern, then she added the arms first lifting her offering to God, then miming His love showering over her like rain.

She felt nothing at first, but she kept dancing. She tried to imagine all her problems underneath her feet. She danced on grief. She danced on pain. She danced on loneliness. She danced on fear. She danced on depression.

Above her she imagined God's cascading waterfalls of love pouring over her. She imagined His strong and gentle hands lifting her high above the earth. She tried to imagine His face smiling upon her.

Except she couldn't see His face. The dark cloud was still there.

She felt a new song filling her heart, "*When I can't see, when I can't hear, when I can't feel your presence near...*" She mouthed the words as she continued her dance, and the dam broke. Great sobs erupted from her chest. Rivers of tears poured down her face.

Still she danced. The song continued forming inside her, "*Still I will hope, I will hope in you...*"

At last she heard something in her spirit—it was her mother's voice: "There's always hope."

Sari collapsed on her bed weeping until there were no more tears.

Eventually she crawled into bed, the music gone from her head. The room was silent once again.

So silent she could hear the leaves rustling outside her window. She heard twigs crack; a louder rustling of leaves; what sounded like a scratching finger on her window pane. She sat up in time to see a ghostly shape retreat from her view back into the shadows.

Sari screamed.

Chapter 26

A piercing scream jerked Abdullah from his dream. *Sari!*

In two seconds he had the knife in his left hand and the two-by-four in his right and was standing in Bali's bedroom doorway.

He found Sari cowering on the floor against the wall opposite the window. She pointed at it. Without a word Abdullah turned and slipped silently out the front door.

The alley was quiet. Most of his neighbors' indoor lights were turned off. There were no motorcycles or cars parked on the street. If anyone was lurking in the dark, they had come on foot.

He crept down the stairs and dropped to his hands and knees beside the porch. Like everyone else in Banjarmasin, his house was built on stilts over the swamp. Near the front right corner of the house there was a gap between the floor and the swamp large enough for a man to crawl into. If someone was outside and had been discovered, that might be his first hiding place.

It took only a few moments for his eyes to adjust to the darkness. Then he craned his neck around the corner at ground level to search for any shadows under the house that didn't belong there.

Nothing.

Next he stood and moved to the side of the house with Bali's window. Back there, the marshlands sunk two to three feet deep in mud and murky water, depending on the tide. It was unlikely anyone would try to climb into a window from there. But there was a mango tree on his neighbor's side of the fence with branches that reached toward the window. Perhaps someone was hiding in the tree. He examined it from several angles, but saw nothing the size of a man hiding there.

Suddenly a branch moved and Abdullah jumped back into a defensive position. From a low branch near the window a small figure had leaped to a higher branch, then an even higher one, then it was gone.

A monkey.

Abdullah let out a sigh of relief and relaxed his taut muscles. He headed back inside, returned his weapons, and went to check on Sari.

"I found the intruder. It was just a monkey."

Sari was still sitting on the floor with her knees curled up under her chin, crying.

In between sobs she managed to choke out, "I'm sorry."

Abdullah wasn't sure what to do. He sat down beside her on the floor and put his hand gently on her arm.

Immediately Sari shifted her head to his chest, her folded knees leaning on his thigh. He extended his arms around her, locking his fingers together to clearly communicate his intentions. She continued to cry, but softer now.

"You're safe," he spoke softly. "I won't let anything happen to you."

They stayed like that for a while, Sari crying softly, Abdullah not knowing what to say. He'd never had this experience with his two sons, and was surprised at how he ached to hold them both now. His memory wandered back to the last person he had held like this.

Siti. He remembered the day twenty years ago that his girlfriend, Siti, had come to him in tears. Her parents had refused to let her attend college, preferring she marry quickly and get a job to help support them. After all, she was seventeen and most of her friends were already married. He remembered wiping the tears from her cheeks, then holding her much like this. Her hair had smelled like jasmine. She was so beautiful. He had promised her that day that if one dream was taken away from her, Allah would give them a new one even more wonderful. She trusted him, followed her parents' wishes, and they were married just three months later. She got a sales job in a department store, and he volunteered to join the *mujahidin* in Afghanistan.

Of all the people he'd failed, he wondered if his failure to his wife was the worst. *And here I am making promises to this girl that I may not be able to keep. I never learn, do I?*

Abdullah realized how much he missed his wife. Though their last year together was hell, he had always imagined that no matter what they went through, they'd still grow old together. Yet he couldn't blame her for leaving him. And if she were here right now, there was no way Sari would be allowed in their home, considering the prejudice Siti had felt toward Sari's mother.

But Siti was gone, and Sari was here now, in his home, in his arms. She had stopped crying, and her breathing was slowing, maybe she was asleep.

Am I in over my head? Was Ibu Aaminah right?

He looked down at Sari, an orphan, scared, traumatized, needing to feel safe and loved, and looking to him.

He promised himself once again to do everything in his power to protect Sari from harm, even if it meant protecting her from himself.

And he decided to let her sleep in his arms as long as she liked. And that having someone that close to him, a daughter to love, was worth enjoying every moment.

Because considering the task he was undertaking, every day might be his last.

Chapter 27

It was nearly nine a.m. and Abdullah was about to head out on his haystack-needle-hunt when Sari finally emerged from the bedroom. Her long black hair was brushed, she'd changed her clothes—apparently the terrors of the night had fled with the dawn. Abdullah smiled at her over his coffee cup, and she returned the smile.

There was an awkward silence until Sari blurted out, "I hate monkeys!" She giggled, and Abdullah couldn't help but laugh too.

"Can I make you some eggs?" he asked, standing.

"No, sit down, Bapak," she replied. "Eggs sound good. But I can make them for myself. What are you up to today?"

"I'm hoping to check in with Professor Ardiansyah at IAIN and see if he has any more ideas for where I can look. I'm worried that this isn't over yet, and the jihadists could strike again."

"Okay, I'll pray that God will guide you and protect you."

"Thanks." He'd never imagined in a million years that one day he'd feel grateful for the prayers of a Christian.

"Uh, can I ask you a question?" Sari twisted her fingers through her hair. "You don't have to answer it if you don't want to."

"What is it?" Abdullah answered cautiously.

"Why did you become a terrorist?"

Abdullah leaned back in his seat and smiled. "Oh, I thought you might ask me a hard question! I was a teenager. I liked martial arts. All my friends were Muslims, and the coolest Muslims were the ones who went abroad to do *jihad.* I told my family and friends I was doing it for

Allah, for the *ummah*. But looking back, I think I just wanted people to think I was manly and cool."

He gazed quietly into another world. Sari continued.

"Did you, you know, uh, hate Christians?"

"I was taught to hate all Christians and Westerners, but the truth was, I'd never met either one. If I'd grown up living next door to you or your mother maybe things would have turned out different."

"So why did you leave *jihad*?"

"I didn't handle death as well as I thought I would."

"Did that happen to a lot of terrorists you knew?"

"I wouldn't say a lot, but yeah, people join for all kinds of reasons, and it doesn't always turn out like they thought it would."

"I've been thinking," Sari leaned forward across the table, "that we should be praying for these terrorists too. If we do, maybe when you find them you'll discover that God has already changed their hearts."

"Okay, Sari, if you say so." He hoped that didn't sound condescending. "I guess it is possible." *Look at me.*

It was good to hear Sari talk about prayer again. It was something about her that had impressed Bali. And now it was at least a small sign of life.

He put down his empty cup. "Have you thought more about moving to David's house for your protection? Once this group finds out I'm looking for them, I don't want them to come here looking for me and find you alone."

He saw what looked like a shudder pass over Sari's eyes. Soberly, she responded. "Yeah, I've thought about it. I'm still afraid. I'm afraid of like…seeing people, of people seeing me like this. Please, just a little while longer…?"

"Of course, you're welcome here as long as you like. You're the closest I have to family." He smiled. She breathed a sigh of relief and half-smiled too.

"However," Abdullah continued, "I am concerned about you being alone. While I'm out scouring the city for these guys, can we have someone else here to keep an eye on you? Is there anyone you'd feel comfortable with?"

She thought for a moment. "The only person I could handle seeing me like this is Nina, but she married and moved to Rantau. Before my phone broke, I was trying to text her, but she never answered. Probably she can't get service up there surrounded by jungle." She twisted her hair in her fingers pensively, then abruptly turned toward the kitchen.

"Let me cook you some eggs." Sari grabbed two eggs from the fridge and moved to the stove.

Abdullah scanned through a list of faces in his mind. All those years of hiding from his past hadn't afforded him a lot of close friends. The elderly headmaster at the *pesantren* where he had taught English and martial arts, his always-busy neighbor Darsuni...surprisingly, the next person on his list would probably be the Christian youth pastor, David. All of these men worked during the day.

His mind turned to his former students. The most recent graduates who had also been in his *silat* martial arts class were Juki, Hafiz, Udin... He decided to make some calls and see who might be available to keep an eye on Sari.

A few minutes later he had a winner: Juki was off in Martapura taking more religion classes, Hafiz didn't answer his phone, but Udin said he'd be glad to help and was on his way over. While he'd been making the calls, he noticed Sari had her Bible open on the kitchen counter and was copying some words onto a small paper, then she posted it with magnets on the fridge. After he hung up, he went to take a look at it.

"What's this?" he asked.

"This morning I finally found something in the Bible that seemed to be speaking directly to me. These are words of Jesus. Do you mind if I put them here where I can think about them when I'm cooking or washing dishes?"

Cooking and washing dishes? Now those sounded like very healthy and normal activities.

"Sure, no problem. Can I read them too?"

Sari giggled. "Of course."
Abdullah read the posted words aloud:

You're blessed when you're at the end of your rope. With less of you there is more of God and his rule.

You're blessed when you feel you've lost what is most dear to you. Only then can you be embraced by the one most dear to you.

"Hmm. What do you think that means?" he asked her.

"I want to think about it for a few days, you know, like meditate on it. Then I'll tell you what I learn. But for now, it's giving me hope that I'm not outside of God's blessing even in what I'm going through. He has something special for me even here. I want to find out what that is."

"Then it sounds like we both have secrets to search out today." Abdullah grinned. "You go deeper, and I'll go wider. Hopefully at least one of us will find what we're looking for."

He picked up his motorcycle keys and headed out the door. It strengthened his heart to know that Sari was once again pursuing life while he was out there chasing the very thing he hated most—death.

Chapter 28

Lani's house was locked up tight when Amat arrived. He saw no motor-bikes in the driveway, no sandals on the front porch, and was about to turn around and head back home when he noticed the tiniest wisp of smoke coming from the kitchen in the back of the house. He parked his new Shogun motorcycle, walked around to the back and peeked in a window. Sure enough, there was Lani's mother moving around the kitchen.

"Aunty!" he called into the window. "It's me, Amat."

He heard the clang of something metal hitting the floor, then silence. Surely she'd heard him—why didn't she answer?

"Aunty, it's me, Amat. Open the door. I need to talk to Lani."

Silence.

"I know you're in there and I'm not going away till I get to talk to Lani."

Suddenly a pair of eyes popped up in the window apparently checking to see that Amat was alone. Then he heard the lock clicking on the back door, and it cracked open. He entered the house through the storage room where he passed a pile of sandals and two motorbikes.

"Amat! I'm so happy to see you." She accepted her right hand being raised to her nephew's forehead in *sungkan*. She was wearing a Winnie-the-Pooh cotton *daster*—an unflattering pajama-like top and bottom outfit comfortable for women to wear indoors, revealing to Amat that she hadn't been outside all day. She didn't wear the head covering at home, and it looked like she hadn't combed her long grey hair either.

She added, "But you can't stay long. If my brother Surya sees a motorbike in the yard, he might barge in and...well, I'm assuming you've heard by now what a terrible mess we're in."

"Yes, Aunty. Uncle Surya's pretty upset about Lani. Is it true she's forsaken Islam and become a Christian?"

"I'll let you talk to her about it just for a few minutes. Please, Amat, try to help her see reason before something unfortunate happens."

"I'll try." She led him not to the front sitting room, but to an inner room with no windows and motioned for him to sit on the Persian carpet, then she went to fetch Lani. While he waited he looked around the room, his eyes drawn to a family photo on the wall. His aunt, uncle, and Lani were at the beach, arm in arm, laughing. He wondered how his aunt and uncle could stand looking at that photo if Lani were dead. Then he tried to put himself in Lani's shoes, wondering how scared he would be if he knew Uncle Surya was coming to kill him.

Within moments Lani appeared, flashed him the same grin he knew so well, and sat on the floor cross-legged facing him. In sharp contrast to her mother, Lani looked relaxed, no different than the last time he'd seen her. She had makeup on, her long hair had a small braid resting delicately on her right cheek, she wore blue jeans and a navy blue and maroon Barcelona FC t-shirt. Typical Lani–she'd probably put it on just to bug him, knowing he was a diehard Real Madrid fan.

"Hey, Amat, how's it going?" She smiled warmly at him.

"I'm doing well," he answered. He wasn't sure how to proceed. "I'm sorry to cut to the point, Lani, but I came because I, uh, I heard some rumors about you and I didn't want to believe them until I could hear it straight from you." He waited.

She sighed. "Yeah, I wish we didn't have to talk about that. I'd rather hear about your life."

He didn't answer.

A slight shadow passed over her face. "Okay. I guess you can see life isn't exactly normal here. My parents are afraid to let me outside for fear I'll run away, and they're afraid to let anyone know we're home in case

Uncle Surya comes to kill me. So for the moment it feels like I'm waiting on death row."

"Is it true you became a Christian?"

"I honestly don't know. I do know something is going on inside of me that is fresh and exciting and new. I feel more alive than I ever have. It's hard to explain."

"But I don't understand how this could happen. Do you have a Christian boyfriend? Did someone put a spell on you? My teacher says their falsified holy books can sound true—have you been reading a Bible?"

"No, none of those."

Amat scratched his head. "Then how? What deception has come over you that could pull you from the truth into the fires of hell?"

Lani smiled wistfully. "It's hard to explain."

"I'm not leaving till you tell me."

She paused for a while, playing with her braid. Amat noticed her fingernails were painted a pretty pink, and he realized he'd never seen Lani's fingernails painted before.

"I'm hesitant to tell anyone, you know, because if my story gets back to Uncle Surya, he'll turn it against me."

Amat let his finger gently rest on her knee. "I promise I won't tell a soul. But I need to know for me. If you consider me your friend, please tell me."

Lani's head tilted, seemingly considering. Finally she spoke. "Actually, it might feel good to tell someone in my own family. I do trust you, Amat, you've always been a good friend.

"It really started with a dream. In the dream I was standing in a grassy field when I heard someone call my name. I turned to look, and there was an Arab-looking man in a radiant white robe. Somehow in the dream I knew it was the Prophet 'Isa. He called my name again, holding out his hand, and added, 'Follow me.'

"Then I heard another voice call my name from the opposite side of the field. It was my Islamic religion teacher from elementary school.

Next to him stood Uncle Surya, looking furious. My teacher wasn't angry, but looked concerned. He called to me, 'Don't go, Lani. That's not our prophet. He's unclean for us Muslims.' He also stretched out his hand and added, 'Come with us.'

"In the dream I remember thinking it odd how he had called the Prophet 'Isa 'unclean.' That didn't sound right to me. But I didn't want to make a wrong choice, so I hesitated.

"At that moment, my teacher and my uncle grabbed my arm and started to pull me toward them. I took a step or two, then cried out for help, and suddenly they had fallen to the ground and I was free. I heard 'Isa's voice, 'You must choose.'

"Then I looked past my teacher and uncle and I could see far into the distance, that their path led to a swamp filled with thorns and crocodiles. I looked back toward 'Isa and I couldn't see past him, the light around him was too bright. Again he stretched his hand out toward me.

"This time I stepped toward him and took his hand. He led me down his path to a beautiful sparkling river where he washed me. I've never felt so clean. It was as though the water penetrated my skin and washed my soul. When I woke up I still had the most amazing feeling of being clean, almost like being a new person.

"I didn't know who to tell about my dream. I didn't want my family to freak out about the 'Isa part. So I told a Christian friend from college, and she took me to a church to learn more about 'Isa.

"And that's my story." Lani leaned forward, forehead wrinkled, searching Amat's eyes for something.

But for some reason he couldn't endure her gaze. Amat looked at the ceiling, running his hand vigorously on the back of his head. Then he wiped the sweat beads that had formed on his upper lip. His body rocked forward and back a few times. He really didn't know what to say or what to do.

"That's pretty...uh, intense, Lani. I've never heard anything like it. But I still don't fully understand. Did you become a Christian? Did you renounce Islam? Did you get baptized?"

"I haven't renounced Islam or gotten baptized. But I don't know if I'm a Christian or not. I thought the Prophet 'Isa was for us Muslims too, right? All I know is, I don't want to go where my teacher and uncle are going. I want to follow 'Isa." She paused. "Look, I didn't ask for this dream, but I can't ignore it. Do you think because I made this choice I deserve to die?"

Ah, that was the question.

"Honestly, I don't know what to think, Lani. I gotta go." Amat abruptly stood up. Lani stood too. "I wish…I don't know. Just take care of yourself, okay?" He called out a good-bye to his aunt and nearly sprinted out the back door.

Instead of going directly home to report to his father, Amat decided to drive out of town to the north and head for the Barito Bridge, the "Golden Gate" of Banjar, a place he'd gone many times before to sort things out.

In just ten minutes his entire world had been rocked to the core.

Chapter 29

As soon as Udin arrived, Abdullah headed for IAIN.

Fani met him at Professor Ardiansyah's door. *"Assalamu alaikum."*

"Wa alaikum assalam." Abdullah answered. "Is Pak Ardi here?"

"Sorry, Pak Abdullah, he's teaching a class right now."

"Can you tell me where on campus to look?"

"Sorry, I don't know. You'd have to check at his office for his teaching schedule. Sorry, Pak."

Abdullah smiled. "That's okay, Fani. How are you doing?"

Fani brightened up. "Really good, Pak. I can eat all I want. Nobody's fighting. And Pak Ardi is teaching me from the *Qur'an* every night. I feel like I'm just discovering what being a Muslim is all about."

"And what is it all about?"

"Well it's, you know, about surrender. It's about doing good. This week we read in the *Qur'an* how Allah loves those who do good and who don't reject their faith. So maybe…" Fani stopped.

"Maybe what?" Abdullah prompted.

"Maybe…Allah will love me?" It came out more like a question.

Abdullah laid his hand on Fani's shoulder. "I'm sure Allah already loves you. The *Qur'an* also says he loves the pure in heart, and I know that's talking about you." He smiled. "I need to find Pak Ardi. You take care, Fani."

"Yes, sir."

Abdullah headed back to campus to Ardi's office. As he neared the building, he was fortunate to see Ardi just leaving with a briefcase under his arm. When he called out to Ardi, the man glanced back briefly but kept walking. Abdullah had to push his way through the crowd of students at a jog to catch up.

When he finally pulled up alongside the professor, Ardi continued walking, speaking to the air ahead of him. "Ah, the delusional demon-chaser has returned. I'm glad to see you're still alive. Wise of you to give up your night-clubbing for the moment. So are you here to tell me you found the evildoers?"

"Actually, no, I haven't. I came with some more questions, and wondered if you'd found out anything?"

They passed through a crowd of students heading the opposite way. Girls whispering to each other, guys joking around, they all looked carefree and happy. Abdullah couldn't help but imagine Sari and Bali being part of the scene. His heart ached.

"I've asked around, but none of the groups I'm in contact with claim any knowledge of the bombing. How about you?" Ardi shot him a quick glance as they navigated a narrow board over the mud.

"Nothing. I've been to schools, mosques, everywhere I can think of, but though I meet angry people, or idealists, no one fits the profile of a bomber of this magnitude."

"Well, in most cases around the nation, bombs are a one-and-done. It's probably over. This cell will head deep underground and you'll never find them. I'd be surprised if they're even in the city any more. They're probably holed up in Java."

"But what if that's not the case? What if they strike again?"

"Then my advice is to be there to catch them in the act. That's the only way you'll find them." Ardi got some mud on his black dress shoe and paused to wipe it off in the grass. He muttered, "'No money for sidewalks,' our fat chancellor claims…"

"Can you at least give me somewhere new to look?"

"There is one group I've heard about but haven't met anyone personally there yet. In the back of Sungai Andai just outside of town there are rumors of a new mosque that is following a strict form of *syariah* law.

I'll text you the directions. They meet every night between the *Mahgrib* and *'Isya'* prayers."

They had arrived outside a classroom, with students already streaming inside. Abdullah glanced through the window slats to see roughly thirty chairs with attached writing tables and a whiteboard. Bali's descriptions of his classrooms at UNLAM sounded more modern—this looked exceedingly simple. *Still, it's not the quality of the furniture, but the teaching that counts.* He imagined Ardi was probably an entertaining, if not overly sagacious lecturer.

"Thank you. I'll let you know what I find out."

Ardi leaned in and spoke softly. "My guess is you'll find out nothing and this drama will be filed in the unsolved cases of general discontent. But just in case you do find a terrorist cell, I'd rather not have you lead them to me. All those near to you will be endangered. So next time, call me, don't just drop by."

With that Ardiansyah turned and joined the final stragglers entering his class, then pointedly closed the door.

Chapter 30

Sari had hardly seen anyone but Abdullah for several days, and a part of her wanted to engage her adopted father's former student Udin through the front window, but another part of her that seemed to be centered in her stomach felt apprehensive. For nearly half an hour she wrestled back and forth, even praying to ask God what to do. Finally she decided to take this baby step in reengaging with the outside world.

She made a glass of iced jasmine tea and handed it through the open front window to Udin who was seated on the front porch. When he accepted it their eyes met and the recognition was immediate.

"Hey, you're that chick with the freaky hand." Udin looked at Sari's burn scars on the hand that offered him tea. She quickly released the tea and pulled her hand back inside the window.

"You're that guy who was trying to hit on my friend last year."

"Yup, I have an unforgettable face, don't I?" Udin grinned. Sari didn't consider him ugly, his eyes just seemed a little too flirtatious and his smile too close to a smirk. He kind of reminded her of the character Chris Pine played in a Star Trek movie Bali had taken her to see, the guy who tried to steal his best friend's girlfriend. *Why would Pak Abdullah ask this self-absorbed Romeo for help?*

"I wish I could forget. Are you such a jerk to all the girls, or just me and my friend?"

"Most girls find me irresistible. Your friend must have, or she wouldn't have given me her phone number."

"That's not how I remember it," Sari countered. "We left you begging for her phone number and walked away."

"Well, I may have lost it. Could you give it to me again? What was her name anyway?"

"Not gonna happen," Sari willed herself to give him another chance. "So tell me, Udin, what are you doing now?"

"Oh, all kinds of things. Sometimes I help my parents, or my former teachers like Pak Abdullah. I'm a helpful guy, lots of people rely on me. What do you do, besides flirt with the handsome babysitter?"

"I'm a Poli-Sci major at UNLAM. I just haven't been to class for a while, well...since Bali died."

"That was crazy, huh? I heard some ninja dudes jumped him. Were you there? Did you see it?"

Sari pushed the memory back into its locked box. "Uh, did you know Bali?"

"Of course I knew him. Went to school with him when we were kids. But mostly I hung with his brother Syukran. Remember the guys with me that day we met? That was my gang. But I never see them anymore," Udin frowned. "Syukran went and blew himself up. Hafiz said he joined some *jihad* group too, probably gonna end up like Syukran. Juki's in Martapura studying more religion. Wouldn't be surprised if they all die in the struggle for the Faith. Could be a shortage of available men—you better grab one soon." He cocked his head and arched his eyebrows at her.

Sari made a mental note about Hafiz—maybe Abdullah could ask him for help finding the terrorist cell.

"Aren't you interested in, uh, *jihad* too?" she asked.

"Nah, I've got my whole life ahead of me. Why would I want to throw it away? I mean, it's cool that Syuk became a martyr and all that, but it's just not for me, know what I mean?"

"Does it bother you all the innocent people that died?" Sari was thinking of her mother, of course.

"People live. People die. That's the way it goes. Just make sure you're the one who lives, not the one who dies, that's how I see it." Udin grinned at her and took another swig of the iced tea, with seemingly not a care in the world.

"I really don't know why Pak Abdullah thinks we need someone here to watch the house while he's gone, and I really don't know why he'd pick someone like you. If anyone tried to attack us, would you even do anything, or just run away?"

"Hey, just because I like living doesn't mean I don't know how to fight! I was part of Pak Abdullah's martial arts class for three years. I was one of the best fighters, too. Except for maybe Syukran and Hafiz, I could beat anyone else. If Pak Abdullah trusts me to protect his house, you can be sure nothing will happen while I'm on the job."

Sari wondered how much of Udin's claim was empty bravado. But if Pak Abdullah trusted him, maybe she should too.

"Anyway, thanks for being here," she added. "When you feel weak, it's nice to know there's someone stronger than you nearby when you need it. I think I'll take a rest now, but it was nice to meet you—well, I guess nicer to meet you this time than last time."

"Sure, you too. Get your beauty sleep. The Awesome Udin is on the job." Udin flexed his biceps while putting his hands behind his head, stretched his feet out in front of him, and looked equally ready to get his nap as Sari turned and headed for her bedroom.

Chapter 31

The directions from Professor Ardiansyah's text led Abdullah to a small, blue mosque at the outer edge of Sungai Andai named *Mesjid Attaqwa*. Abdullah knew the Arabic concept of "taqwa" meant "fearing God." It seemed like a perfectly normal name for a mosque, but if what Pak Ardi had said was true, this group's exclusivity and insistence on an ultra-conservative interpretation of Islam was definitely not normal for Indonesians.

By the time he parked his motorcycle it was 6:45 p.m. The sun had been down for half an hour, and the *Mahgrib* prayers should have already ended. He had expected to see a stream of worshippers exiting the mosque, giving him a chance to talk to some people before the *'Isya* prayers started in about forty-five minutes.

But no one exited the mosque.

He could see through one of the tall windows the men sitting on the floor in the front, and a few women, covered head-to-toe in the black *burqa* common in Saudi Arabia but rarely seen in Indonesia, sitting behind a screen in the back of the mosque. It looked like Ardi was right, and they were having a teaching session between the evening prayers. Perhaps he could slip in to do his own *Mahgrib sholat* and eavesdrop on what was being said.

An overweight man wearing a navy blue security uniform stood at the mosque's entrance.

"*Assalamu alaikum,*" Abdullah greeted him. "Where is the washing place for my *wudlu*? I'm running late for my *Mahgrib* prayers."

"*Wa alaikum assalam.*" The man didn't answer right away. He angled his head and looked closely at Abdullah. Abdullah smiled back.

"What's your name?" the security guard asked.

"Abdullah. And yours?" He held out his hand, but the guard didn't reciprocate.

"Who invited you to our group?"

Abdullah hesitated to mention Ardi's name after the warning he'd received. He answered vaguely, "A friend told me to check it out. Do you mind if I do my *sholat* and then sit in for a few minutes and learn from you?"

The guard wasn't budging. "Are you police? Are you MUI?"

It was common knowledge that the *Majelis Ulama Indonesia*, the self-appointed watchdogs of Muslim orthodoxy, had been trying to flush out and shut down any group they considered heretical. If this guy was worried about MUI, they could definitely be considered extreme. But they might also just be loopy.

He raised his hands in innocence. "No, brother, I'm just a fellow Muslim who needs a place to fulfill my Islamic duty. But if you're not sure, call your *imam* and let me talk to him for a moment and I'm sure he'll let me in."

"Wait here." The guard waddled up the stairs into the mosque. Through the window Abdullah could see the *imam* rise from his position seated in the front and head to the door. Then every person in the mosque turned as if on cue to look out the window at him. Their glares didn't seem too friendly.

The *imam* stopped halfway down the steps. "*Assalamu alaikum.*"

"*Wa alaikum assalam.*" Abdullah answered. "I came to do my *Mahgrib* prayers. May I come in?"

"*Mahgrib* has passed, my son, I'm sorry but you're too late."

"It looks like you're having an event tonight, I'm sorry to interrupt. What's it about? Perhaps I could join you until the *'Isya* prayers?"

"This time is reserved for me to teach my followers. If you want to join us, you need to be introduced to me by one of my followers directly. Did one of them invite you tonight?"

Abdullah wasn't getting anywhere so he thought he'd try a new approach. "Or maybe you could just answer one question for me: Are you training your students for a *jihad* that includes burning churches and bombing night clubs?"

The *imam's* eyes widened momentarily, then narrowed. Through pursed lips he staccatoed, "The answer is 'No.' Now leave."

The burly guard stepped toward Abdullah and brought his hand up towards Abdullah's chest. Two seconds would be more than enough to pin this fat bully to the ground and break both his arms, but Abdullah stepped backwards instead. The response from the *imam* and the laughableness of his security staff told him all he needed to know.

"All right, I'm going." Abdullah said. He jumped on his motorcycle and roared away. There were no police posts in Sungai Andai, so he left his helmet off and enjoyed the wind blowing over his short hair.

Night and day, from end to end, I roam the city, chasing the wind.

Chapter 32

"Let this be the day my father Abdullah finally gets his breakthrough," Sari prayed aloud. "Turn the terrorists' hearts to peace and restore peace to our city. Amen."

"Amen." Abdullah echoed. It had been a week since Joko had warned him of ISIS invading his city. So far he'd watched a church burn down, counted bodies at the night club bombing, and found not even the faintest scent of who was behind it. He was truly in need of divine intervention.

Sari got up from the breakfast table and whisked away their empty plates. She'd made him a fried egg and fried up a small fish for him to eat with his rice, and she'd fixed the coffee. It still felt strange to see her every day in his house. But if she weren't here, he'd be stuck talking with the ghosts of his past.

"What are you going to do today?" he asked her.

"Last night I promised myself that I'd go back to college today, but when I woke up, I, uh, started shaking so badly, I just can't do it yet," Sari answered. "I was so looking forward to it because at my campus they're having a study abroad festival. Several colleges from overseas will have booths, and there will be a presentation about how to get scholarships—you know that's one of my dreams, right?"

"Yeah, Bali told me. I hate for you to miss it."

"Me too," she looked devastated. So much of her lively spark had gone into hiding, he felt a pain stab at his heart just watching her. She turned to wash the dishes.

"Tell you what, why don't I swing by UNLAM and at least collect some brochures for you. Then you can follow up with the schools online."

She brightened up immediately. "Really? You would do that for me?" She left the dishes and came up behind him at the table and threw her arms around him, nearly spilling the coffee in his hand.

"Okay, okay!" he laughed. "At least that'll keep you busy instead of reorganizing my kitchen again. My neighbor Pak Darsuni said he'll be home today, so I asked him to keep an eye on you." He pushed back from the table. "I better get going."

"Thanks so much, Bapak," Sari said, touching his hand to her forehead in *sungkan*. "Be safe."

Two brochures from Australian universities, one from an American university, and one from a Singaporean university later, Abdullah was smiling broadly. He had forgotten how much he enjoyed speaking English, and this was one of those rare opportunities in Banjarmasin to actually talk with native speakers. It made him miss those days of teaching English and martial arts at the *Al Mustaqiim* Islamic school.

Perhaps it was because he was thinking about his former students that he spotted Hafiz exiting the main door of UNLAM's large multipurpose building used for assemblies, weddings, and events like today, where presentations took place inside and booths filled the parking lot. He headed toward him to say hello. Hafiz was in a hurry, glancing nervously side to side, and didn't notice Abdullah until they almost bumped into each other.

"Hafiz! So good to see you."

The teenager nearly jumped out of his skin.

"Pak Guru! What are you doing here?"

"I just dropped by to pick up some information on studying abroad for Sari. Are you interested in studying abroad? You never told me that."

Hafiz shifted uncomfortably. "No...I mean, yeah, why not? Look, I gotta go. You really should, too." He started to step around Abdullah.

"All right, but I should say hello to your parents before I go. I just saw them carrying some cakes in the side door over there. What a blessing to get the contract to feed all these participants, eh?"

But Hafiz missed the last sentence because he had spun around and set off running for the building's side door, screaming, "Dad! Mom! Get out of there! There's a bomb!"

Abdullah tried to make sense of what Hafiz was yelling, but he was distracted by watching him run with that odd gait...

A large Australian man stepped out of the booth nearest the building to see what the commotion was just as Hafiz was sprinting past. They collided, knocking Hafiz backwards into the booth.

A deafening explosion split the air. Abdullah watched the blue tile roof of the building disintegrate as orange flame erupted violently upward, much like he imagined a volcano might look. Chunks of white cement from the nearest wall came flying towards him. As he dove for cover the last thing he saw was a four-foot-wide cement missile hammer the Australian in the side of the head, snapping his neck instantly.

After a few seconds Abdullah lifted his arms from covering his head and looked up toward the wreckage. Through the smoke he saw only the far corner of the building was still standing, and it was on fire. All the booths had either been blown over by the shockwave or knocked down by the debris. He saw some people farthest from the blast begin to scramble to their feet and check themselves for injuries. It was eerily silent for a moment. Then little by little the sobs began, then the calling out for missing loved ones.

Closer to the building none of the bodies were moving. Abdullah figured they must all be dead. His eyes were drawn to several white bodies now covered red in their own blood. He'd never seen this many white people in one place, and this was how Banjarmasin showed hospitality to their guests.

I'm such a fool. Joko told me to check out public events with Westerners.

Then he remembered Hafiz.

He crouched on his knees, then stood slowly to his feet. He felt his muscles begin to tremble, but then his training kicked in. *Focus on the mission at hand.* He used the large Australian's corpse as his signpost to guide him to Hafiz.

"Hafiz! Hafiz!" he called, pulling the rubble of cement and the flimsy wooden booth off of the spot where he thought he'd seen Hafiz fall.

Sure enough, there was Hafiz underneath a couple four-by-six wooden beams, some smaller cement chunks and a pile of ashes. His forehead was bleeding badly and Abdullah wasn't sure if he was dead or just unconscious. He pinched Hafiz on the cheek. "Hafiz, wake up!"

Eyelashes fluttered, then a faint groan escaped Hafiz's lips. He forced one eye partly open, then closed it again. *Alhamdulillah, at least he's alive.*

A noise behind Abdullah startled him, and he looked around. There was one of the largest men Abdullah had ever seen. He had long, straggly hair and hardly a hint of dust or debris on him. The man seemed to be looking at Hafiz, maybe they knew each other?

"Hey, give me a hand with this mess and we can get my friend out, okay?" Abdullah figured with that guy's muscles they'd dig Hafiz out in no time.

The giant looked one last time at Hafiz, who was groaning again, then stared at Abdullah for a moment before turning and walking away. Abdullah watched him curiously. The man wasn't going to assist other victims; he just walked past everyone heading for the street. *Maybe he's in shock. Don't blame him.*

Abdullah glanced down at his arm and noticed it was bleeding. He had no recollection of how or why.

It didn't take long to clear the rubble and examine Hafiz. He had multiple scrapes and bruises, the worst being the one above his left eye—that would leave a nasty scar. But he hadn't broken his arms or legs, maybe a rib or two. He told Hafiz he'd take him to the hospital.

"No!" Hafiz grunted, eyes now open, pupils flitting back and forth wildly. "No hospital! They'll find me!"

"What? You need a doctor," Abdullah argued.

Hafiz gripped Abdullah's arm. "No, please no! Hide me. They'll kill me." Then he passed out.

Abdullah began to wonder if his former student had played a role in this tragedy. Either way, Abdullah wasn't about to let him die. He straightened up and pulled out his cell phone to call home.

"Hi, Pak Abdullah, did you get the brochures?" Sari asked excitedly.

Reflexively he looked at his empty hands. Where were the brochures? An immense sadness settled into his soul making it hard to speak.

After a moment, he tried, his voice breaking. "Sari, I'm sorry, something's happened."

"Are you okay, Bapak?" Sari asked worriedly.

"Yes, I'm fine." He told her about the bomb. As he described the destruction, the thought occurred to him that Sari was planning to be in that building listening to the presentation. He shuddered, terror and gratefulness swirling through his mind.

"One of the victims is my former student. He's going to be okay, but he won't let me take him to the hospital. How would you feel if I brought him home and we try to nurse him back to health?"

"Of course! Bring him here. I'll help."

He swallowed. "The only thing is, I think he may know something about the bombing. I don't want you to get mixed up in—"

"Just bring him, Bapak. We should do all we can to help him."

"Okay, why don't you get the couch ready for him. I'll be home soon."

Chapter 33

The large parking lot of the 17 May Soccer Stadium, where the local professional team Barito Putera had thrilled Banjar fans for years before the timber company sponsoring them had to lay off workers including the entire soccer team, was completely deserted, save for one man sitting on his parked motorcycle, enjoying a cigarette and staring at his cell phone. Achmad checked again, but no message had come in. Khaliq was late.

Finally he saw the big man turn into the parking lot, and he breathed a sigh of relief.

Khaliq drove up and parked next to him, then took off his helmet.

"Success?" Achmad asked, stroking his goatee.

"The bomb exploded as planned. Many people died, including all the foreign dogs. But..."

"But what?"

"The kid never made it to the microphone to make his statement. He knew the timing on the bomb, and he just threw it inside the door and tried to get away."

Achmad cursed. "He said he was ready to die. We recruited him precisely for this suicide mission." He cursed again, then looked back at his lieutenant. "So you had to kill him."

Khaliq looked away. "I started toward him, but right before the bomb exploded, the kid tried to run back into the building. It's crazy. He's crazy." Khaliq waved his hands above his head in disbelief.

"Why?"

"I don't know why. He stopped to talk to a man, then he just ran toward the bomb. He was hurt in the blast, but not killed."

"So then you killed him."

"I couldn't. The other man got to him first. I'd have had to kill them both, and there were too many witnesses."

"You left him alive?" Achmad's voice rose in anger. He flung his cigarette in Khaliq's face. "You idiot! You did this to me in Poso, now you've done it again. No loose ends!"

Khaliq didn't flinch, nor did he look away from Achmad's gaze. "I'll find him. And I'll kill him."

"Yes, you will, before he talks. Time is running out. Rio should have the rest of the bomb materials in a day or two. You will visit the bus driver tonight to remind him what is at stake. Then you will devote the rest of your days and nights to finding Hafiz and killing him. Do you understand?"

Khaliq nodded. Achmad knew the best medicine for Khaliq's embarrassment was a chance to kill someone. For Achmad, killing was what he was trained to do in Afghanistan, and here in Indonesia, he was paid well for it. But for Khaliq, he knew the big man's reason for killing had nothing to do with money or religion or fame. Something much darker boiled constantly inside of him. Achmad was fortunate to have been one of the first to see it, and harness it to a noble purpose.

His mind drifted back to Poso and the many Christians they had killed together. They had a much better team back then, before the police were paying such close attention. Then Khaliq made a mistake. Their team of six, led by Hasanuddin, attacked four Christian girls on their way to school. They beheaded three of them, but one girl got away. She remembered the faces of some of the attackers, and Hasanuddin and two others were caught. Khaliq's role had been to ensure no one could identify them, but he had failed. Not knowing if the police would torture his colleagues and get them to talk, he and Khaliq had to flee the island of Sulawesi for Kalimantan, and after a few years of laying low, start all over again recruiting and training operatives, and delicately searching for new benefactors.

Achmad had almost been caught in Sulawesi. He wasn't going to get caught this time.

"Just a few more days," he said to the dark clouds above. Khaliq quietly waited for his dismissal. "When the last attack is over, I'm taking my reward and disappearing again. If any of our team gets caught, I'll be long gone."

"Khaliq will go with you," the giant stated.

"Of course, Khaliq, just you and me." Achmad wanted to reassure his partner, though he hadn't decided yet if he'd take Khaliq with him this time. *Let's see how this plays out first.*

He looked back at Khaliq while lighting another cigarette. "Well, what are you waiting for? Go clean up your mess."

Khaliq roared away on the motorbike. Lightning flashed in the distance. Could be a heavy rain coming.

Achmad took a long drag on the Marlboro. For an evil empire, the Americans did make excellent cigarettes.

Just a few more days...

Chapter 34

Sari opened the door for Abdullah to carry in an unconscious young man. Abdullah laid him on the green vinyl couch that Sari had covered with a white sheet. She already had rummaged up some pain pills and a few first aid supplies and immediately took over washing the boy's wounds with hydrogen peroxide.

"So tell me everything," she said.

Abdullah paced around the living room while telling her the story. When he finished, he pointed down at the probable bomber. "I've known this kid since he was little. Now he might be a mass murderer. What's more, he's an orphan. His parents were both in the building when the bomb went off. He's an orphan and it's my fault. Joko warned me and I...I can't do this anymore. They're killing everyone around me and I...can't...stop it."

He grabbed off the wall a plaque that stated "Peace Champion," a gift from M. Ramadani, strode to the window, jerked it open, and flung the plaque into the swamp. Then he slammed the window closed and collapsed into the wicker chair, his head in his hands.

"It should have been me who died, not those young kids."

Sari looked up at him and noticed the blood on his arm. "Bapak, you're hurt! Let me clean your arm."

He didn't respond. She took a fresh piece of cotton soaked in peroxide and knelt on the floor beside him. Then she took his hand in hers to hold the arm steady, and began to cleanse the wound. When she finished, she asked if there were any other wounds. He shook his head, silent tears dropping from his cheeks. She squeezed his hand, then moved back to continue working on the boy.

"This cut above his eye is pretty bad. I wish you could get a doctor to stitch it up."

"He said, 'No doctors,'" came the mumbled reply.

She cleaned in silence for a while. The boy's face looked familiar, but she couldn't match it with a name yet. She was about to ask when Abdullah spoke.

"When you finish, pack your bags, you're going to David's."

His harsh tone startled her.

"I can't go now," she protested. "Who will take care of this poor boy?"

"This poor boy is most likely involved in the bombing. This poor boy and this incompetent fool…" he pointed to himself, "…are going to get you killed. Ibu Aaminah was right. You should stay as far away from me as possible."

Sari wasn't sure how to respond, but she was very sure she wasn't going anywhere. She decided to try a different tack. "Remember those words of Jesus I was meditating on a few days ago, from his Sermon on the Mount? I have a new one for today. Do you want to hear it?"

Abdullah's head dropped back in his hands.

She continued. "Jesus said, 'You're blessed when you care. At the moment of being "care-full," you find yourselves cared for.' Today I feel so blessed. All this time you've taken care of me, and now I have a chance to take care of someone too."

She waited hopefully for a response but none came. She tried to remember what her mother had taught her about using Band-Aids to make a butterfly stitch. What she came up with was crude, but would have to do for now.

Eventually Abdullah stood and moved to face the window again. She barely heard him mutter, "Then maybe it's time we disappeared. The two of us should get out of this city before it's too late."

Sari knew he wouldn't go. He'd saved her mother once, and nearly died doing it. She knew he'd rather die than give up. Surely God would answer their prayers.

She tried to change his focus to the problem at hand. "I've seen this boy before. What did you say his name was?"

Abdullah kept looking out the window. "Hafiz."

The memory flooded back. She was walking through the Ramadan cake fair with Maya when Udin, Hafiz, Syukran and some others started harassing them. Hafiz! Hadn't Udin said something about him?

"Oh, Bapak, I think Udin said that Hafiz had joined a radical group. Do you think it could be the terrorist cell you're looking for? What if God brought Hafiz to us to help us find them?"

Slowly Abdullah turned and stared down at Hafiz, eyes narrowed and jaw clenched.

Finally he spoke. "I'm going to take a shower and lie down for a few minutes. But call me at the first groan from that kid's lips. He's got a lot of deaths to answer for."

Chapter 35

Baqri knocked twice, then twice more on the hotel door. Rio asked who it was, then opened up and let Baqri in. The double bed with a *batik* bedcover, the lamps, the TV—everything looked normal till he peeked in the bathroom. There were mechanical parts, wires and powders spread out all over the place. He put his plastic bag down on the desk and sat on the bed.

"Here's your fried rice."

Rio opened the bag and noticed only one portion was inside. "You're not eating dinner?"

"I had something earlier." Baqri had taken his girlfriend out for Kentucky Fried Chicken at the mall, but no need to make Rio feel like he was missing out.

Rio opened the stapled brown paper which became his plate. He scooped the rice hungrily with his hand to his mouth. "Did you bring the phones?" he asked with his mouth full.

"Yep." Baqri pulled them out of his various pockets. "Five second-hand cell phones complete with SIM cards already registered to the local people who lost them." He set them on the desk. "You're making five separate bombs?"

"That's what Achmad wants. I've collected all the components, just need to start assembling. But I need your help with the detonators."

"Should be the same as the last one we did, right?" Baqri thought back to the night club blast.

"Here's the thing," Rio explained. "Achmad wants all five phones to activate in the proper sequence from only one phone number. I'm worried that someone else will call one of these old numbers once the bomb is armed and set it off too soon. Can you fix that?"

Baqri considered. "If we're wiring the bomb into the phone's vibrator, I can probably set it to vibrate only on one particular number, and not vibrate on the others. Let me take a look."

He picked up one of the phones and began scrolling through the settings. Rio finished his meal and threw the paper and plastic bag into the trash, then went to the bathroom to wash his hands. Baqri could hear him muttering as he moved things out of the sink.

When Rio returned, he sat next to Baqri on the bed.

"Can I ask you something? Why are you doing this?" Rio asked.

Baqri kept searching through the phone. "What do you care?"

"Just curious."

Rio seemed to be waiting for an answer, but Baqri wasn't sure what answer to give.

"I believe in the cause." Rio didn't respond. "What, don't you? Besides, Achmad promised to pay me well."

"Is that all?"

Baqri swallowed hard, his mind spinning for an acceptable answer that wouldn't give too much away. "I like the challenge. I like learning new things. It allows me to get where I want to go in life." Baqri hoped Rio would notice his hairstyle, his designer clothes and shoes, and let it go. He felt too ashamed to tell the truth, that he was fighting to get his parents out of poverty.

"Huh. If you say so." Rio pushed his glasses up on his nose. He didn't sound convinced.

"What about you? Why are you doing this?" Baqri turned the tables on Rio.

Rio lay back on the bed, hands behind his head, and stared at the ceiling. "Lately I've been asking myself that question. It started when I was in high school, a Christian group called the "Red Force" bombed my home while I was out with my friends. Both my parents and my little sister died. So I decided to join the *jihad* training in the Philippines with Abu Sayyaf. I used to be so angry. I figured if I could learn to make bombs, someday I could avenge my family's deaths. I helped the *mujahidin* in Sulawesi for a while. That's where I met Achmad."

Baqri was stunned to hear such personal details, too stunned to speak. Rio continued. "Honestly I don't know why we're here though. There are no Christian militias, no Americans to speak of. Achmad hasn't even told us yet where these bombs are going. Sure a few foreigners died at UNLAM today, but weren't most of the casualties Muslim university students? Sorry, I don't know why I'm telling you this. Don't worry though, I'm loyal to the cause, and I'll see it through to the end."

"Hey, no sweat, we've all got our own stories," Baqri assured him. He was almost afraid to ask, but curiosity got the better of him. "What are Achmad's and Khaliq's stories?"

"I've never asked, and they've never told. I've heard Achmad was trained in Afghanistan. He's from Java. I don't know where Khaliq is from, but I saw him with Achmad in Poso, Sulawesi when I got back from the Philippines. Achmad was a leader in his early twenties. Maybe he's the one who recruited Khaliq.

"I'll tell you one thing though, if you promise not to tell anyone else," Rio added.

"Sure," Baqri nodded eagerly.

"Khaliq can't speak a lick of Arabic. When he does the *sholat*, which isn't often, he just mumbles mumbo-jumbo."

"Ha!" Baqri laughed. "A Muslim *jihadi* who can't even say his prayers. I guess it takes all kinds."

"Yeah," Rio sighed. "I just want to get this over with and get out of here."

"Will you go back to your family?"

Rio sat up abruptly. "Who told you I have a family?" he snapped.

"Rumor is you're married with kids." Baqri put down the first phone and with sweaty palms picked up the second. *Now I've done it—I've said too much.*

Rio hissed, "Keep that rumor to yourself. And get out of this game before Detachment 88 or some Christian extremists find your girlfriend and use her to make you talk."

Baqri stopped working on the phone. He hadn't thought that far ahead. *Could that really happen?*

His phone buzzed, and both he and Rio jumped. It was Achmad.

"Change of plans. The kid didn't die in the blast and now he's missing. Finish your work there as quick as you can, leave your older brother there, and help the others find the kid before he talks. Got it?"

"Got it." Achmad hung up. Baqri passed on the news to Rio. Sweat formed on the older man's forehead almost immediately.

"Crap. If the kid talks... I hate my life." Rio was already off to the bathroom to get back to work.

Baqri attacked the phone again, wondering how they were ever going to find Hafiz. None of them really knew him. None of them really knew each other, for all the "family" or "brother" references Achmad tossed around.

Rio thought it safer if no one knew about his family. Baqri resolved to quit bragging about his girlfriend, and to never, ever talk about his parents.

But if I die, who will tell them?

Forget it. It's better they never know and live.

Chapter 36

The asphalt was wet under Abdullah's running shoes from the previous night's rain. He hoped the starless sky overhead didn't have a second round of showers in mind. It felt good to be up before dawn, running the streets of Kelayan, clearing his head from the nightmares he faced both waking and sleeping.

His upper body felt sore from the blast debris hitting him, but nothing some exercise wouldn't cure.

He passed Ibu Aaminah's husband, Pak Zaini, on his way to the pre-dawn *sholat* at the neighborhood *musholla*. Someone had just turned on the *musholla* lights for those faithful planning to start their day by remembering Allah.

Remembering is not my problem. It's where to go from here.

He turned the corner onto the main drag, Kelayan B, and headed north toward the July 1 Bridge. He knew every home, every mosque, every food stall in a two-mile radius. Those years when he'd been hiding from his past, suffering from what he now realized was depression, running in the dark was his safe place, the only place he felt free. Well, running and reading. Maybe it was time to get back to reading again too.

Bali had warned him before that Hafiz was a bad influence on Syukran. He'd done nothing about it. Now Syukran was dead. Bali was dead. And Hafiz had somehow survived. *What kind of justice was that?*

Hafiz had regained consciousness, but between the moaning and groaning had mumbled nothing useful. He was terrified of something, that much was clear. Even looking at Sari's smiling face seemed to scare him. Sari had given him pain meds and told Abdullah to let him sleep. Abdullah could hardly wait for the kid to wake up so he could beat the truth out of him.

"Stop the terrorists non-violently," Joko had said. In a world full of rapists, arsonists, and bombers, that was impossible. Violence was the only language they spoke. Well, he could speak that language too. As soon as Hafiz could talk...

He crossed the July 1 Bridge and turned south on Kelayan A street, across the river from Kelayan B. Ahead of him he saw another jogger, a young man. Maybe he was training for soccer or basketball. Or maybe he had just stolen something and was fleeing the scene of the crime. Kelayan had significantly more crime than any other district of Banjarmasin. He chided himself for assuming the worst. What would Sari say?

It was still hard for him to understand what motivated Sari to nurse Hafiz. *Jihad* had cost Sari everything. Shouldn't she hate him?

He was closing on the runner ahead, who seemed to be limping a bit. His mind flashed back to UNLAM, to Hafiz shouting and sprinting toward the building. Hafiz definitely had a distinctive style of running, one he'd seen often teaching Hafiz physical education at the *pesantren*.

Suddenly it hit him. That wasn't the only time he'd seen Hafiz run. The day Bali died he'd seen three men run away from Sari's home. The last one out had sprinted away with the exact same distinctive gait.

Abdullah stopped abruptly in the street. He didn't want to believe it. He didn't know for sure.

But he could feel it in his gut. Hafiz had been one of Sari's attackers.

Hafiz had been one of Bali's murderers.

Abdullah spun around and raced back up Kelayan A. He had to get home to Sari before Hafiz woke up.

Twenty minutes later, he burst into Sari's bedroom. She jumped, a scream on her lips, then when she saw it was Abdullah she covered her mouth with a pillow and let out the scream.

"Sari! I'm sorry. I'm sorry. I need to talk to you." Abdullah was out of breath, sweat pouring down his face.

"Bapak, you scared me," Sari whined, eyes wide.

He squatted on the floor next to her bed so they were eye level. "I'm sorry. I needed to tell you something before Hafiz wakes up. I could be wrong about this, but I don't think I am. I think you're right that Hafiz may be mixed up with a terrorist cell. In fact, I don't think this was his first crime."

He paused, catching his breath. Her cobwebs hadn't fully cleared yet from the rude awakening. She yawned. "What are you talking about?"

"I think he may have been one of the three men who…who assaulted you and killed Bali."

Sari gave a sharp gasp, eyes even wider than before. This time she bit the pillow.

"Wait…why do you think that?" she squeaked out.

"I got there just in time to see the three men fleeing your house. One of them had a way of running that looked familiar to me. Yesterday when Hafiz ran to save his parents from the bomb, I saw it again. This morning I just made the connection."

Sari visibly shuddered. Abdullah put his sweaty hand gently on her shoulder.

"Do you think you could identify him by his voice?"

"I…I don't know."

"Don't worry, I'll get him out of here this morning, before I kill him myself. I'll turn him in to the police. Even without being charged for murdering Bali, with any luck they can trace the bomb to him and he'll get the death penalty. I'm done with this whole thing. We'll let the police handle it."

Sari was still shaking, but he withdrew his hand. He couldn't imagine what was going through her mind. She had been doctoring the wounds of one of the very men who had inflicted on her the worst pain possible.

Sari buried her face in her pillow. Abdullah stood and was about to leave her and get a shower when her face resurfaced.

"Bapak, please don't take him to the police." She shook her head.

He was stunned. "Why?"

"He may go to jail, but what about the others? Who will stop them? What if God sent him to us? He's our best chance at stopping the terror, right?" Her soft brown eyes appealed to his.

He just stared at her.

"And besides," Sari added softly, "maybe he can tell us, you know, why."

"No way! Uh-uh." Abdullah shook his head at her. "You...you..."

Then he spun and marched out of the room.

Chapter 37

On his way back to the bombsite, Abdullah noticed that most of the stores downtown were closing, though it was the middle of the day. As he approached the Grand Mosque, police were waving drivers over to the side of the street for random identity checks. He joined the line of motorcycles, ID and registration in hand. While waiting for his turn, he thought of the drugged killer and insane nurse he'd left behind. When he got home he'd have to deal with them both. Soon he was back on the road headed north to the Lambung Mangkurat University.

The main gate to the campus was still open, though there was little traffic. Most likely classes had been canceled for the day and everyone had gone home. The side road toward the multi-purpose building was blocked off by police cruisers and there were police everywhere, sifting through the rubble. Abdullah parked his motorbike and approached an officer, asking who was in charge. The policeman eyed him suspiciously and said nothing. Abdullah dialed Joko's number on his cell phone, then handed it to the policeman, who became instantly more cooperative, and took him to Sergeant Eko.

The sergeant was a good two inches taller than Abdullah, thin but muscular, with a receding hairline and pencil moustache. He looked Javanese, and as soon as he spoke Abdullah could discern the strong accent of East Java.

"Are you an eyewitness?" Sergeant Eko assumed.

The officer answered for him. "Sir, this man is vouched for by Pak Joko of BIN, who has requested we share our findings with him."

One of Eko's eyebrows went up. "You're with Intelligence? Happy to help. I'm Eko Purwanto." He held out his hand.

"Abdullah." They shook hands. "What have you found so far?"

"Death count currently about 120, injured maybe 50-60. We're still combing through the rubble for the dead, though it's barely possible we could find more survivors. The blast epicenter seems to have come from just inside what used to be the front door of the auditorium." The sergeant pointed to where the doorway had been. "It's doubtful that anyone inside the building could have survived the blast, not to mention the collapse of the roof and walls around them. Apparently there was a presentation yesterday about opportunities for study abroad."

Abdullah was unsure about whether to mention his presence there earlier. It could cause unnecessary questions. And it could endanger Hafiz, if he chose not to turn him in to the police, which would of course be considered as obstructing an investigation.

"Any eyewitnesses able to identify the bomber or bombers?" he asked.

"We've taken statements from those who didn't need to be rushed to the hospital, but will have to follow up with all the injured through the next day or two. No one has given us anything concrete yet."

"What about identifying the type of bomb?"

"Still not sure. We're checking for signs of pipe-bomb shrapnel or maybe TNT. We really need some experts from Jakarta out here. You know, until that night club event, we've never had a bomb detonate in Banjarmasin, at least not that I know of. This is above my guys' pay grade." Eko shook his head. "Any BIN resources you could send our way?"

"I'll pass your request on. From what I hear we're not the only part of the country fighting terrorists right now." He handed the sergeant his card. "I'd appreciate it when you find any leads that you keep us in the loop."

"Will do." They shook hands again. Abdullah watched as two cringing policemen lifted the charred corpse of what had probably been a college girl about Sari's age, but was now unrecognizable. His heart ached for the families who would have to closely examine body after body trying to identify which one was their son or daughter, so they could give their child a proper burial.

But what made him feel the sickest was remembering the charred corpses of Afghanis that he had once bombed, and their broken-hearted families he'd left behind.

Chapter 38

Darsuni was perched alertly on his doorstep when Abdullah got home. He thanked his neighbor, then went inside to check on Sari and Hafiz.

Hafiz was half-sitting on the couch with a pillow behind him, holding a glass of iced tea in his hand. He heard someone in the kitchen.

"Sari, you all right?" Abdullah went to the kitchen first. He found Sari chopping cucumbers and tofu in an effort to make *gado-gado*.

"Yes, Bapak. Hafiz is awake. How was it?"

"Grisly. Over a hundred dead and counting. But the police have no idea of who was responsible yet," he added softly so Hafiz wouldn't hear. "I need to talk to Hafiz."

"Let me make you some tea," she offered.

He waved her off. "Later." But she ignored this and made him a glass of sweet jasmine iced tea anyway. He took it with him to the living room and sat in the chair across from Hafiz.

"How are you feeling?"

Hafiz set his tea on the coffee table. "My head hurts. My knee hurts. Actually, my whole body hurts. Trying to get from here to the bathroom was torture."

"You're lucky to be alive."

"You call this lucky?" Hafiz snapped. "My parents are dead, and soon I will be too." He glowered at Abdullah. The chopping sound from the kitchen slowed. Abdullah figured Sari wanted to hear this.

"Who wants to kill you, Hafiz?"

Silence.

"Why do they want to kill you?"

No response.

"You were the bomber, weren't you, Hafiz? Surely your friends would want to congratulate you. They'd probably want to shake your hand, maybe take you out to dinner for killing all those innocent kids. Why would you be afraid?"

Hafiz's face contorted in anger. "You don't know squat."

Abdullah stood, towering over the boy. "I know that you're mixed up in a bad group, Hafiz, a group that's most likely going to end up killed by the Detachment 88, or given the death sentence in prison, or killed by your own kind. Their future is dead, dead, or dead. So is yours, unless you help me stop them."

Hafiz guffawed. "Ha! You? Stop them? Is that why you brought me here, to use me against them? Fool." He turned his face away.

Abdullah's fists clenched. He strode around to the back of the couch and leaned down to look Hafiz in the eye again. "You killed those people, Hafiz. You're a murderer. I'm even starting to wonder if you're the one who murdered my son."

Surprise showed on Hafiz's face. "You know I had nothing to do with Syukran joining those *mujahidin*."

"Not Syukran. Bali. Did you kill Bali?"

Hafiz looked lost. *Maybe I was wrong. But I don't think so.*

"I don't know what you're talking about," he stammered. "Leave me alone." Then Hafiz stumbled from the couch toward the bathroom.

Abdullah yelled after him, "The truth, Hafiz, I want the truth!"

Hafiz slammed and locked the bathroom door.

With a roar, Abdullah punched the wall, putting a hole through the first layer of plywood.

Then Sari was there behind him, her small hands gripping his upper arm, as if that would hold him back. He could toss her off as easily as flicking a mosquito, break down the door and choke the truth out of Hafiz.

Instead, he let her pull him back to the kitchen, let her seat him on a plastic chair. She handed him a stone bowl of peanuts and a pestle.

"Could you grind these peanuts for me? I need them for the *gado-gado* sauce."

Abdullah smashed the peanuts, still boiling inside. Sari needed him to stay under control. He could do it for her. He had to do it for her.

She added bean sprouts to her large bowl of vegetables and tofu. "Give him some time, Bapak," she whispered.

He noticed his teeth were grinding in the same rhythm as his hands. He heard Sari saying something about a broken family, but the peanuts grabbed his attention. One moment they were whole; the next moment they were dust. *Whole, dust. Whole, dust. If Hafiz's head were a peanut…*

The thought startled him. Sari was still talking. "Don't you see, Bapak? You're kind of like *Nabi* Ibrahim; Hafiz is like Ishmael—"

"He's not my son." Abdullah was revolted at the thought.

"Then am I not your daughter?" Sari asked. She smiled at him. There was something about that smile, its innocence, its sincerity. *Maybe I'm the peanut and Sari is the pestle.*

He wasn't ready to return her smile. The demons still raged inside him. But he kept his eyes on Sari's face until their protests dwindled to a wordless whine.

"All right, my daughter, I'll give him some time."

Chapter 39

*H*er wedding dress was beautiful, even better than those she'd seen on television. It was so radiantly white it nearly hurt her eyes to look down at the delicate skirt floating an inch above the floor. Perhaps it was the thin veil she wore over her face that protected her eyes from the dress's glory.

She heard music, and knew it was time. Gripping her bouquet of white roses tightly, she began to march down the church aisle in rhythm to the music.

The building did not look familiar to her, but the people did. On each side of the aisle sat people she knew—Christians on the left, and Muslims on the right. Muslims in a church? And in the front, Bali was waiting for her.

He looked so handsome in his white tuxedo, a huge smile on his face coaxing her forward. Why hadn't she agreed to marry him before? It felt so right.

Someone stood up on her left. It was her old pastor Susanna scowling at her, pointing her finger. "I object!" the pastor exclaimed. "This Christian girl cannot marry that Muslim boy."

Sari stopped walking down the aisle.

Then her mother stood in the front row and turned to face her. "That Muslim boy gave his life to save Sari. He's more like Jesus than you are, Pastor, so hush!" Her mother winked at her and sat down again.

Sari resumed her march.

Suddenly from her right a young man grabbed for her bouquet. It was Hafiz. He snarled at her and pulled on her flowers, but she wouldn't let go. She couldn't get married without the flowers. She watched some of the white petals drift gently to the floor.

"Who let him in here?" boomed Bali's voice from the front. Bali glared at Hafiz with hatred.

"I did," Sari squeaked from behind her veil, but no one heard her.

"Get him out of here!" Bali commanded, and two police officers appeared from behind him.

"Wait! I invited him," Sari finally managed to say. Hafiz was still pulling on the flowers, but her eyes were on Bali.

"Choose him or me." Bali's eyes narrowed, his arms crossed.

This was not the Bali she knew. Sari looked around nervously. It seemed everyone was unhappy with her, both Christians and Muslims. The policemen were getting closer.

She gave a mighty tug and ripped the bouquet out of Hafiz's grasp, but her momentum sent her slipping backwards to the ground. She fell through the floor and kept on falling, falling...

Sari's eyes opened. She was in Bali's bed, the dream still vivid in her mind. She let it wash through her memory again, trying to make sense of it. After a few moments, it hit her—was nursing Hafiz a betrayal of Bali's love?

A wall clock above the bed with a picture of the Muslim faithful circling the Ka'aba in Mecca said it was just past midnight. She knew it would be hard to get back to sleep, so decided to pray. This is what her mom had taught her to do with dreams. Maybe God would guide her in what she should do.

Over and over the word *forgiveness* came to her. Bali, Abdullah, everyone else, they would have their own convictions, but for her, she knew she had to forgive Hafiz. She asked God for grace to follow Jesus, who said, "Love your enemies."

God, would you please show me Hafiz as You see him? Sari waited, eyes closed, until in her imagination a scene appeared.

She was lying on the floor on her back. A man was on top of her, a mask on his face, saying something she couldn't clearly hear. She felt the terror rise within her. *No, God, not this scene!* But the impression only intensified and she couldn't pull away.

In her mind's eye she saw herself rip the mask off her attacker. It was Hafiz, his panicky eyes mirroring her own. He was shaking her by her shoulders. Now she could make out his words: "Help me! Help me!"

Sari remained still, eyes closed, meditating on what God had shown her. The picture faded, but the words continued to reverberate in her brain. "Help me! Help me!"

Until she realized that the words were not inside her mind, but were coming from the living room. Her eyes popped open as she strained to listen. She heard it again.

"Help me! Help me!"

Chapter 40

Sari tiptoed to the bedroom door and gripped the door handle. Her breathing was too loud; surely whoever was out there would hear her. She tried to breathe shallowly. Slowly she pulled down on the handle until the door opened a crack and she could peek out.

There was no one there. Then she heard the "Help me!" again, almost a whimper this time, coming from the couch. She crept forward until she could see Hafiz, eyes still closed, talking in his sleep. He was in a fetal position, his forehead furrowed, his hands balled into fists as though braced to guard his temples.

She sat down on the floor near his head, placing her right hand on his arm.

"Hafiz, wake up," she said gently, then repeated it.

His eyelids fluttered, then opened. His neck jerked left and right looking around the room in abject terror. "Help me!" he cried to Sari. "Hide me!"

Now she added her left hand to his other arm. "Hafiz, you're safe. It was just a dream."

He stared at her wide-eyed for a moment, then slumped back into the couch, shaking her hands off his arms. "Don't touch me. Get away from me."

Sari wasn't sure what to do, but curiosity got the best of her. "You were saying, 'Help me!' in your dream. Why?"

"None of your business."

"Was someone trying to kill you?"

"I said it was none of your business. Leave me alone."

"Why did you say, 'Hide me'? Are you afraid the other cell members are coming for you?"

"Yes, you bleating goat, they're coming for me, and they'll kill me and kill you too. Now shut up and get ready to die."

"Are they still looking for me? What do they want from me?"

"They don't care about you, idiot. You're just another cockroach with a cross on its back." He twisted the heel of one hand against the palm of his other while glaring at her.

Sari felt a weight lift off her knowing the terrorists weren't hunting her down. Although if they were hunting for Hafiz, they'd end up here anyway. Would she ever be free?

It seemed obvious that Hafiz didn't want to talk, but Sari wasn't sleepy anymore and didn't move. She sat quietly for a while pondering what to say next.

"Would you like some tea?"

"Go away," Hafiz growled and rolled over on the couch to face away from her.

She thought some more.

"Why do you hate Christians?" she asked gently.

"'Cuz they're annoying. Especially you," Hafiz answered still facing the sofa rather than her.

Sari kept her tone soft though her heart was pounding loudly. "Why would you want to attack me and kill Bali?"

Hafiz was silent.

"I thought Bali was your friend's brother."

Silence.

"You know it broke my heart to lose Bali, and broke Pak Abdullah's heart too."

Hafiz's breathing grew slower. Was he sleeping or just pretending to sleep? Sari had come this far and wasn't about to stop now.

"Pak Abdullah told me that your parents were killed in the UNLAM bombing. I'm so sorry. I lost my mother in a bombing last year, and I know how it feels. For a long time I wasn't sure I wanted to go on living without her. She was my life, you know? Then I felt that way about Bali, and I lost him too. I hate death, don't you?"

Sari rose to her knees and leaned forward to see Hafiz's face. His cheek looked wet with tears. He looked so lost, so alone, her heart went out to him. She put her hand on his shoulder.

Hafiz brushed her hand off. "Leave me alone," he mumbled.

Her dream flooded back into her mind. There was Bali's face justifying her rejection of Hafiz. But that wasn't how her mother had raised her. It wasn't what she believed in. She knew what she had to do.

"I don't hate you, Hafiz," Sari whispered, partly to him and partly to herself. "Good night."

Sari went back to bed wondering how this boy went from a cute toddler to accidentally killing his own parents with a bomb. Surely there was a story there.

Surely that story wasn't supposed to end with another senseless death.

Chapter 41

The South Kalimantan Regional Library was a beautiful structure, exhibiting the traditional Banjar steeply angled A-frame roof with small decorative wings carved on each corner, and less steeply sloped roofs protruding from the front and back of the A-frame. The building was two stories and housed thousands of books, especially on the history and culture of the region. But Hidayat could understand why Khaliq had chosen the library parking lot as their meeting place this Saturday morning—no one ever used it. Hidayat was nearly as old as the library was, and he'd never been inside, nor had any of his friends. Recently the library had started a mobile library service, driving vans full of books into neighborhoods trying to get the kids to read, but he doubted it would work. If they wanted kids to read they should turn this place into an internet café.

He pulled out his L.A. Lights pack and lit a cigarette. His dad was trying to get him to stop smoking, but it was about the only thing he enjoyed in life anymore. That and imagining the suffering of the man who had ruined his family. Once he finished his assignments for Achmad, he was planning to ask for help in dealing with that Chinese Christian crook. Achmad would owe him one.

Amat was second to arrive. They'd been friends in college and Hidayat had invited Amat into the group. Amat was dressed for a soccer match. He parked his Shogun next to Hidayat's motorbike. Hidayat offered him a cigarette, but Amat waved it away.

"Glad to see that ugly bandage is off your nose. Can't see any scar. What really happened anyway?" Amat wondered.

"Lost my temper." He chose not to say any more. It had been a stupid thing to fight about anyway. He needed to keep his rage under control till this was all over.

"Hmm," Amat grunted, and dropped it. "You find any sign of the kid?"

"Nope. You?"

Amat shook his head. "This is so bogus. I've got other stuff I need to do. I can't spend the whole weekend chasing down this idiot. Who brought him in, anyway?"

"Not me. Do you think he's ratting on us to the cops? Should we be getting out of town instead of looking for him?"

"I don't know, man. I don't see why we can't just let him go. It's not likely he wants to get caught and face a death sentence. "

"But if he's caught, Detachment 88 will torture him. He'll talk." Hidayat tugged at his wispy beard.

"I just hope this is over soon. There are some things that are bugging me... You know, I'm starting to wonder if—" Amat paused his thought as Baqri roared up on his giant Honda Tiger, dressed as if he were headed to a modeling shoot right after.

"Hey guys," Baqri removed his helmet. It looked to Hidayat like he'd gotten another new hair style. "I hope this is quick."

"Just waiting for Khaliq," Amat responded. Hidayat took a drag on his cigarette and checked the clouds for any sign of a coming rain. Baqri whipped out a cell phone and the three of them sat in silence until Khaliq came.

Hidayat wished Achmad had come. Clearly Achmad was the brains and Khaliq was the brawn, why should they take orders from Khaliq? Besides, he was nervous that Khaliq would kill one of them just for looking at him funny.

"Any news to report?" Khaliq began. They all shook their heads.

"That's not good enough," Khaliq reprimanded them. "We find Hafiz or Detachment 88 finds us."

Amat protested, "Look, we have no photo, no address, nothing. How are we supposed to find a guy like that?"

Khaliq glared at him. "We have a name and a face, and a general part of town where he's from. Achmad said to check every place where someone like Hafiz would hang out: schools, mosques, roadside food vendors, whatever till we find him."

"Fine, I'll check the futsal fields. Maybe he played indoor soccer," Amat offered.

"I'll take the food vendors," Baqri chimed in. "If I remember, the kid liked satay."

"You're the one who likes satay, metro boy."

"Enough. You take the mosques, I'll do the schools," Khaliq ordered Hidayat. He could see Amat stifle a laugh. He'd always admired how Amat could think on his feet. Saturday was Amat's futsal practice day, and he'd just manipulated a way to get approval for what he was planning to do anyway.

Now mosques…that was the worst. Banjarmasin had more mosques and *mushollas* per capita than just about any city in Indonesia, and Hafiz's area of the city, Kelayan, had perhaps the most mosques in Banjarmasin. Hidayat berated himself for not handling the situation better. He was supposed to visit his father in jail today. Well, it would have to wait till Monday. He never went on Sunday when the Christians were singing their religious songs there. And there was no way he'd want Khaliq to find out he was shirking his assignment till that prick Hafiz was caught. He wasn't going to risk Khaliq's wrath.

"Anyone spots Hafiz, do not let him know you are there," Khaliq continued. "Contact me with your location, understand? Me."

Khaliq put on his helmet and took off, Baqri right behind him.

"Better look busy," Amat chided, then laughed.

Hidayat wasn't finding this turn of events the least bit amusing.

Chapter 42

Abdullah's stomach growled with hunger, but he had no appetite. He was swishing the last of his coffee around his cup, trying to plan out his day, when his cell phone buzzed. It was a text message from Sergeant Eko. He gulped down the rest of his coffee as he read it. Sari waited quietly across the breakfast table, nearly finished with her rice and scrambled eggs.

"The police know it was Hafiz. I've got to talk to him. Now."

"Be gentle, Bapak, he just lost his parents."

Abdullah stood and headed for the living room where Hafiz still lay on the couch.

"Sit up," Abdullah barked. "We're going to talk. I'm going to talk. Then you're going to talk." He sat in the chair across the coffee table from Hafiz.

After a few seconds Hafiz gingerly moved to a sitting position.

"The police just texted me. They were checking selfies taken by the bomb survivors. One shows you in the background carrying a large box into the UNLAM auditorium two minutes before the blast. Another person's selfie shows you leaving the auditorium one minute before the blast. The police are on to you, and they're looking for you." Actually, the police had the photos with no name yet, but Abdullah decided Hafiz didn't need to know that detail.

Hafiz stared down at the floor sullenly.

"Did you hear me? The police are on to you. Maybe I should text them back and tell them I've found the bomber. What do you think about that?"

Hafiz's eyes widened. "No! Don't do that, they'll find me!"

"Exactly. And they'll lock you up for the rest of your life or maybe—"

"Not the police—*they'll* find me." Abdullah could see the fear in Hafiz's face, just like when he'd first brought him home.

"Give me your phone," he ordered. He held out his hand. Hafiz didn't move.

"You remember that I was your martial arts teacher, don't you? Now give me your phone before my knee comes down on your injured leg."

Sari stood behind the couch where Hafiz couldn't see her, shaking her head vigorously at Abdullah's threat, but he ignored her and stood up menacingly. Hafiz retrieved the phone from under his pillow and reluctantly surrendered it.

Abdullah scrolled through the previous day's text messages. The names of the senders were obviously bogus, but the tone was clear: WHERE ARE YOU? CONTACT US OR WE'LL HAVE NO CHOICE BUT TO KILL YOU.

He started texting on Hafiz's phone.

"What are you doing?" Hafiz asked, alarmed.

"I want to meet these guys, so I'm inviting them here to talk."

"No!" Hafiz fell off the couch grabbing for the phone. He started crying. "O God, no, please, no!"

Abdullah stopped texting and stared down at his former student. "Then you better start talking. How many in the group?"

"I only know four," Hafiz whimpered.

Abdullah returned to his seat, motioning to Sari to get a pen and paper. She did, then sat on a plastic chair behind the couch where Hafiz wouldn't see her taking notes.

"Names," Abdullah demanded.

Hafiz closed his eyes and murmured slowly, "Rio…Baqri…Hidayat… Amat."

Abdullah stared at him for a moment. "Remember that I've been your teacher for many years, Hafiz. I'll know if you lie to me." He paused before his next question. "What organization is behind the group? Is it ISIS? Jemaah Islamiyah?"

"I don't know."

"Who handles the money?"

"I don't know."

"Who's in charge?"

"Rio."

"Who made the bomb?"

"Rio."

"What do the others do?"

"I don't know."

"How did you join?"

Hafiz didn't answer right away. Abdullah waited. "I saw something online. I bragged about...about being Syukran's friend. They emailed me to meet them at the Grand Mosque. I...I wanted to do something big, like Syukran did."

It was like a cobra kick to Abdullah's gut. Not only had he failed his son Syukran, but his failure was inspiring others to become terrorists. He had to push those thoughts down and keep Hafiz talking.

"Where do they meet?"

"It always changes."

"What are they planning next?"

"I don't know."

"There's a lot you don't know, what do you know?" Abdullah was frustrated.

"I know that if they find me, they'll kill me."

"Not if we find them first. Hafiz, help me find them. Are any of them local guys? Do you know where they might hang out?"

"Yeah, a couple of them might be local, but I don't know where to find them."

"Did they go to school here?"

Cautiously Hafiz offered, "I think one of them might be a graduate from IAIN."

"Good! That's what I need. I have a contact there. Listen, either I find them, or I invite them here, so you better hope I find them."

He had Hafiz describe each one as Sari took notes, then he called Joko to pass on what they'd learned.

As he grabbed Sari's page of notes and his motorcycle keys to head out, Sari caught his arm. "Bapak, maybe we should pray over these names, that by the time you find them, God would change their hearts, that they would stop these attacks on their own."

"Fine Sari, you pray. And pray that I can stop them before they strike again."

Sari emerged from praying in her bedroom about a half hour later thinking she should change Hafiz's bandages and then start thinking about what to cook for lunch. She grabbed her gauze and peroxide and knelt down by Hafiz's side. The bandage above his eye was soaked in red and yellow. She wet a piece of cotton and wiped the pus out of the wound as Hafiz squeezed the couch cushion, growling through gritted teeth.

"You did the right thing, you know," she said as she placed a new piece of gauze over the wound and taped it down.

"That old fool is going to get himself killed if he finds them," Hafiz retorted.

"But like he said, better he finds them than they find us, right?" Sari smiled. "Now let's look at your leg."

She was just about to lift the bandage when they heard someone on the front porch. Both of them froze.

Suddenly the door flew open and several figures burst into the room.

Hafiz tried to run but collapsed on top of Sari on the floor, muffling her screams.

Chapter 43

*F*inally a concrete lead to follow!

A faint glimmer of hope rose inside Abdullah as he drove up to Professor Ardiansyah's home on the IAIN campus. With Hafiz's help he could blow this whole search wide open.

If Hafiz wasn't lying.

Abdullah leaped up the steps to Ardi's home calling loudly, *"Assalamu alaikum."* After a few seconds he repeated himself even louder.

The door opened. *"Wa alaikum assalam.* Hi Pak Guru, how are you?" Fani greeted him. "Come in."

"Thanks, Fani, I'm fine, and you?" Abdullah entered the home.

"I'm happy."

"Glad to hear it. Is Pak Ardi here?"

"Sure, come on back to his study."

Fani led Abdullah to the same room where he'd first met Ardiansyah. The big man was sitting at his desk talking on the phone. He gave Abdullah a quizzical look, then murmured, "I'll call you back," and hung up.

"Pak Abdullah!" Ardi smiled and stood, offering his hand. "I had hoped never to see you again."

Since Ardi neither sat nor invited Abdullah to sit, he remained standing. "Pak Ardi, I'm sorry to disturb you, but we've caught a break in our search for the terrorist cell, and once again I'm in need of your help."

"I'm very curious, you must tell me everything." Ardi's left eyebrow lifted over his wire rim glasses. He motioned for Abdullah to sit while he leaned back on his desk.

"Someone has identified a group of men who may be behind all these attacks. I have here a list of their names and descriptions." He handed Sari's notes to Ardi, who studied them for a moment.

"Is this the complete list? Where did you get this?" Ardi asked. "Who is your source?"

"I can't say. As far as I know it's complete. But do you recognize any of these descriptions? My source said that one or more of them were students at IAIN."

Ardi handed the page back to Abdullah, hands waving in the air. "There are thousands of students here! I have hundreds in my classes every year. Do you know how many boys named 'Amat' and 'Hidayat' attend IAIN? I have three Hidayats in my Saturday morning Comparative Religions class alone. This information is useless."

Abdullah wasn't about to give up. "Please, Professor, you're no doubt aware of the desperate situation our nation is in. Right now the Islamic Defenders Front and the Laskar Jihad are flooding their forces into Makassar and Solo for a confrontation with the Detachment 88 Special Forces. You want that here? Think of all the civilians who will get caught up in this, all the tragic loss of life. Think of your students, some of whom will probably volunteer to take up sticks and rocks against the military. We have a very, very slim chance of avoiding a bloodbath in our city if I can find this cell first. Now look at this again and think, which of your current or former students with these names talked publically about *jihad* or joined a radical group on campus or wrote papers for you that were angry against the West. Think!"

Abdullah grabbed Ardi's right hand and thrust the page back into it. Ardi glowered, but looked down at the names again. He scratched his bald head. Abdullah waited quietly.

After what seemed an eternity, Ardi finally spoke. "Have you shown this list to anyone else?"

"No, I got it this morning and came straight to you."

Ardi tapped the paper with his finger three times, then pointed to the name 'Amat.' "I can't be sure of course, but a couple of years ago I taught a young man by this name who always wore soccer jerseys to class and whose hairstyle seemed to follow the most famous soccer stars. He was quite outspoken against Christianity. I suppose it's possible...I have no idea where he lives now." He handed Abdullah the paper. "But even if you found him, what are you planning to do with him?"

"In my peacemaking work with Ramadani, he taught me that there are basically three kinds of men who join *jihad* groups: men of conscience—they have good intentions but wrong information; the self-deceived—they choose this path believing it will ease their personal pain; and men who know the truth but choose evil because of what they can gain, such as power, wealth, fame, the pleasure of seeing others suffer, and so on. Some of these men can be turned. In fact, they may become our nation's future leaders in peace."

"And just how do you propose to turn them?"

"Ramadani and I are working on a plan for a rehabilitation center that's more like a half-way house. If we can deal with the source of their pain, and provide the right information, they'll have a good chance to reintegrate into society."

"Ah! Ever the optimist. I'd have thought after your last encounter facing the terrorist cell in Jakarta that you'd be more of a realist. My word of warning to you—do not engage with a man who wants to kill you unless you are ready to kill him first. Or unless you're ready to die."

Abdullah folded the paper and put it in his pocket. "I guess I'll take this to the school's registrar? Maybe they can get me a home address."

"No, no, no need for that, my friend." Ardi motioned for Abdullah to rise, then directed him toward the door, talking as they walked. "I just remembered...if this is the Amat that I used to know, he was crazy about indoor soccer. He would always skip my Saturday afternoon class to attend his practice at Borneo Futsal. Do you know where that is?"

Abdullah nodded.

"Perhaps he still plays there. Look for him there between, say, five and six o'clock this afternoon. I imagine how he responds to your questions will confirm whether he is or isn't the Amat on this paper."

"Thank you very much, Pak Ardi, I'm indebted to you."

Ardi opened the door. "Always happy to point someone in the right direction."

Chapter 44

Sounds and images swirled around Sari as if from another world. Through blurry eyes she saw the figures surround her, with raised clubs ready to strike. They were demanding something, but she couldn't make it out over her own screams. She clung to Hafiz who was now her human shield. He wrestled with her to escape but there was no way she'd let go.

Her tears gushed out, further blurring her sight. She saw many arms come down and grab Hafiz. They pulled; she dug her nails into Hafiz's back and she heard his cry of pain. It sounded so much like Bali.

For a moment she was back in her living room. A man was on top of her. She pushed him away and screamed. Then a crash, glass and blood everywhere, Bali's face in her lap.

Don't leave me again, Bali.

Someone had pried her fingers loose. She curled up on her side, eyes pinched shut, knowing she was at their mercy. There was no one to save her now. Her fingers brushed against the coffee table. It wasn't broken. Her mind slowly transitioned back into the present.

"Sari, are you okay?"

She hadn't expected to hear her name, so it didn't register at first.

"Sari, you're safe. We caught the kidnapper. Are you okay?"

No hands were grabbing her, and the voice sounded vaguely familiar. Sari turned her neck and opened her eyes. She knew these faces, but from where?

Slowly she rolled onto her back and looked around the circle. Two teenage boys were holding Hafiz by the shoulders. Three other boys had lowered their clubs and one was holding out his hand to her. She stared at him.

"Sari, it's me, Jerry. You're safe now. Take my hand and let's get out of here."

"Jerry?" She didn't take his hand, she just stared.

"Are you okay? Did they hurt you?" asked another voice. She turned to look at the boy next to Jerry.

"Paul?" Sari felt her nerves calming, but couldn't make any sense out of what she was seeing.

Jerry looked at Paul. "She's pretty confused. I wonder if they brainwashed her."

Hafiz started to say something but a slap in the face shut him up.

It was almost like Sari felt the slap herself, and snapped back to the present.

"Don't do that!" she protested. "He's hurt. Put him back on the couch." She sat up, then gripped the coffee table, and on unsteady legs, tried to stand. Jerry reached out to grab her arm. The two boys holding Hafiz didn't move.

"Sari, we need to get out of here now, before the others come back," Jerry urged, trying to pull her toward the door. "We'll take this kidnapper to the police."

She jerked her arm free. "Jerry, stop. He's not a kidnapper. What are you talking about? He's my friend, and he's hurt. Billy, Markus, put him on the couch now!" She glared at the two holding Hafiz and pointed forcefully to the couch. Hesitantly, they sat him down, hands still on his shoulders.

"But I thought..." Jerry struggled for words, "...he looks like one of *them*."

Paul jumped in. "Sari, we heard you were kidnapped by radical Muslims and forced to convert to Islam. We tried calling your cell phone but no one answered. Then someone said they saw you outside this house, so we called the church youth group guys to come rescue you. Is it true? Did you convert? Did they brainwash you?"

Sari was almost too stunned to speak. "That's the most ridiculous thing I ever heard! My cell phone broke. I was never kidnapped, brainwashed, or whatever. My best friend was murdered in my home, so I didn't feel safe there. His father offered me to stay here till I feel safe enough to go home. He's Muslim, but he's been super kind to me. Now I get to pass it on to this injured young man whose cuts I was treating when you barged in and scared me to death! What were you thinking?"

Some of the boys looked down sheepishly. Jerry's face was red, his forehead wrinkled. "Ooooooh," was all he could say.

Paul spoke softly. "We're sorry, but don't be too hard on the guys. It took a lot of courage to come rescue you. We figured some of us might die in the fight, but we had to try."

A moment of silence passed. Sari noticed her hands were still trembling, so she tried to hide them behind her back. *Calm down. Nothing bad happened. You're among friends.*

She inhaled deeply and looked around at her personal Search and Rescue Team. Then she offered solemnly: "You brave, courageous idiots!" and burst out laughing hysterically. Around the circle she went, hugging each of them as she laughed, and soon they were laughing too. She smiled at Hafiz who just rolled his eyes.

Chapter 45

Borneo Futsal was one of the bigger indoor sports arenas in Banjarmasin. Abdullah counted four futsal fields, one basketball court, two badminton courts, and a side area with several table tennis and billiards tables. There was even a space for players waiting for their time slot to sit at tables watching television and enjoying something from the snack bar.

He estimated roughly fifty or sixty young people, only three of which were young women: two were playing badminton, the other was watching indoor soccer—probably there for her boyfriend. That left an awful lot of young men wearing soccer jerseys. *Yet another needle in another haystack...*

Abdullah walked the length of the four futsal fields, serenaded by the squeak of shoes on the rubber turf and players calling for the ball. Bali had been a decent player. He recalled watching one of Bali's games in a high school futsal tournament. With the small indoor soccer field and only five players to a team, the action was fast and furious. Bali had scored four goals but his team had still lost 8-6 and been eliminated. Abdullah smiled at the memory. This is where young men should be testing their prowess—not at a *mujahidin* training camp like he had chosen.

An idea came to him. Back at the front desk, he asked what teams were playing now in the 5:00-6:00 time slot. On field three was a team from IAIN. He asked if that team had a player named "Amat." The staff member replied that Amat was the team leader, always outspoken, and that the team wore white Real Madrid jerseys.

Abdullah headed back to field three and took a seat alone on the one and only bench for spectators. There was no scoreboard, but after watching three goals in three minutes he figured the IAIN team must be winning.

The loudest guy on the team seemed to be their sweeper. He would yell out directions to the others and coordinate the attack from the back. His hairstyle was definitely modern. Hafiz said it looked like Cristiano Ronaldo's hair, but that didn't help Abdullah much as he never had kept up with the soccer world.

The loudmouth stole the ball near his own goal, faked out an opponent, and launched a powerful shot from the half-way line into the top corner of the goal. He performed a couple salsa steps prompting laughter and high fives from his teammates. Abdullah wondered how such a kid could get caught up in *jihad*, but then he and Syukran had once taken the bait too.

Eventually the buzzer sounded and the players began to exit the field.

It was now or never.

"Amat!" Abdullah called loudly.

The sweeper immediately looked up, then lifted his chin and eyebrows. "What is it?"

"Some excellent game you got there. Hey, can I talk to you for a minute?"

"What, are you a scout or something?"

"Something like that," Abdullah smiled.

"Huuuuu," one of Amat's teammates teased, "too good for us, aren't you? Well, we don't need you. Don't come back." The others laughed.

Amat grabbed his sandals and water bottle and approached Abdullah. "We can't talk in front of these jokers. Let's talk outside."

They weaved through the flow of other teams leaving their fields. It was nearly sundown, but the oppressive heat in the tin-roofed building caused every player to be completely drenched in sweat. The smell was intense. Abdullah couldn't imagine how the girlfriend could stand it. He watched her stay at least a foot away from her probable boyfriend, who was taking off his soccer shoes with one hand and smoking a cigarette with the other.

Some of the team stopped at the snack bar tables, but Amat continued outside. The kid was fast; Abdullah was having a hard time keeping up with all the players going different directions.

Finally he made it out the door into the fresh air. The first players out were already on their motorbikes heading home. Amat wasn't in the parking lot. Where had he gone?

He spotted Amat walking toward the street and called out. Amat turned back and motioned for him to follow. By the time Abdullah crossed the parking lot to the street Amat was even further ahead of him, turning a corner. He started jogging to catch up.

When he turned the corner, Amat was nowhere in sight. He kept walking a ways, glancing to his right at the housing development—could he have slipped in between the homes?

As he passed a large tree on his left, he was so focused on the homes across the street he didn't hear the movement from behind him until it was too late.

A sharp pain jolted through the back of Abdullah's head and all went black.

Chapter 46

When Abdullah regained consciousness, the first thing he felt was a sharp pain in the back of his skull. He told his hand to feel for a bump, but his hand didn't respond. Neither did his other hand. His fingers felt around and discovered a thick rope bound his wrists behind his back. His legs also couldn't move—they were tied to something. He was seated on what felt like a hard wooden chair.

Abdullah opened his eyes and saw only blackness.

Had the knock on the head stricken him blind? Or was he locked in a dark room? He turned his neck to look around, and felt the scratch of burlap against his skin. There was a bag over his head. At least he wasn't blind.

He listened carefully for any sound that might give him a clue about his surroundings. There was a slapping sound behind him, near the floor. Could be the waves of the river splashing against a house on stilts over the water. In Banjarmasin, that meant he'd narrowed his location down to about half the buildings in the city.

The rickety tuk-tuk-tuk of a small boat engine passed by and the splashing increased. He was over the river. If there were any noises in the building they were being masked by the river.

He strained against the ropes on his hands, but that only chaffed his wrists. Wiggling his feet revealed only an inch or two of slack. His legs were longer than the chair's—perhaps he could try leaning forward and lifting the chair off the floor, but without sight, he might only succeed in stumbling forward out the doorway and into the river. He managed to lift the chair off the floor, then set it down again.

Something Sari had said invaded his darkness: *You're blessed when you're at the end of your rope. Well, here's the rope, so where's the blessing?*

The last thing he remembered was following Amat. Had Amat done this to him? If so, he had found one of the cell members. *Give yourself a pat on the back, Abdullah, you've got them right where you want them.*

In Afghanistan he'd been trained to handle interrogations. They'd taught him how to stall, distract, bluster, pretend to break and feed the interrogator false information, but most of all they'd taught him how to endure pain. He doubted anything these Indonesians would do to him could be as torturous as what the Pashtun instructors had done.

Stay focused and learn something. Provided they don't kill me.

He wasn't clear on what time of day it was, but judging by the stiffness in his joints, he'd been there for several hours when he finally heard a door open and feet shuffle in.

"Let's see if he's awake," a voice ordered.

Abdullah felt the bag jerk off his head and he blinked in the bright incandescent light. He was in a bare wooden room with a low plywood ceiling. The wooden window shutters to his right were locked shut. The door was directly in front of him, also shut. In front of the door were two men in black ski masks, and one of them was significantly bigger than Abdullah. The other one was probably the leader as he did the most talking.

"What's your name?" he asked.

"Abdullah. What's your name?"

"Why were you following Amat?"

"I just wanted to talk to him."

"Tell us what you want to tell him and we'll pass it on to him."

"Oh, so you guys are Amat's friends? Where do you know him from?"

The shorter man looked at the larger one, who backhanded Abdullah across the face. He could taste the blood on his lip.

"Tell us what we want to know and you might live to see tomorrow. What were you going to tell Amat?"

"I wanted to tell him that if he had any friends involved in the recent bombings, to tell them it's not too late to stop the attacks and save countless lives."

His answer seemed to surprise the speaker. The giant leaned over and whispered in the shorter man's ear.

"You were seen with a young man named Hafiz. What's your relationship with him?"

Ah, so the bigger man must be the one he saw approaching Hafiz at the bomb site. This is who Hafiz is afraid of.

"He's my former student. Was he working with you?"

The speaker pulled out a knife and touched it to Abdullah's cheek. "Tell me where Hafiz is."

Abdullah stared into the man's eyes. They looked cold as glass. "I don't know," he answered.

He felt the knife prick through his skin, the warm blood drip slowly down his cheek.

"A Muslim who opposes *jihad*. Perhaps I should carve a peace sign on your cheek." He outlined a circle on Abdullah's cheek but didn't cut through the surface. Then he put the knife to Abdullah's throat.

"Or perhaps I should kill you, pig. This is your last chance. Where is Hafiz?"

When Abdullah swallowed he felt the knife blade's pressure. "Please, he refused to let me take him to the hospital. He said he was afraid of something and had to get out of town. I put him on a bus to Batulicin. Maybe he has family down there, I don't know."

The knife-wielder hesitated, then put his knife away. He turned to speak to the giant. Abdullah strained to catch parts of it.

"Your turn. See if you..."

The shorter man left the room. He couldn't see through the big man's ski mask but when the man spoke, Abdullah imagined him smiling.

"Now you are mine."

The man's right fist plowed into Abdullah's left side and he heard his ribs crack. In over twenty years of martial arts he couldn't remember feeling a blow that powerful. The chair skidded across the room and tipped over an obstruction on the floor throwing Abdullah to the ground.

He saw the giant coming but could do nothing to defend himself. The man picked him up by the back of the chair with one hand and carried him across the room, then set the chair on a wooden crate with its back to the wall where they could be eye to eye. Abdullah searched those eyes for a hint of mercy, he'd even settle for a hint of humanity, but found none.

His jaw endured a crunching blow and he could feel a tooth rolling around in his mouth. Next a punch to his stomach that felt like it exited through his back. He couldn't breathe. Another shot to the opposite jaw. A stabbing pain went through his shoulder and he heard another cracking sound. He hoped it was the chair or the wall. His shoulder seemed to have more movement in spite of the throbbing pain; he guessed the chair had broken.

"Now you talk. Where's Hafiz?" The voice was low, guttural, without emotion.

Abdullah let the tooth fall out of his mouth, careful not to spit and further harm his chances of survival. He shook his hanging head and whispered, "Don't know."

Without warning he felt himself rising in the air, the ceiling fast approaching, then just as fast he flew crashing toward the floor. His back slammed into the floor, breaking the chair. Pain rushed up and down his arms and his spine and through the back of his head. He fought to stay conscious.

Cold steel glazed his ankles and he heard the sawing of rope. A large hand rolled him onto his side and his wrists were cut free. The bag came back down over his head. The man threw Abdullah's limp body over his shoulder and started walking.

There was no will left in Abdullah to fight. They'd let him live. That could only mean they hoped he'd lead them to Hafiz.

When he could walk again, he'd have to make sure this pain wasn't in vain.

Chapter 47

*K*haliq is at the door. Khaliq is climbing in the window. Khaliq is right behind you.

Whether in fitful sleep, or snapping awake at every sound, Hafiz was filled with terror. Khaliq was bound to find him.

So when the door creaked open softly just before dawn, he knew it was all over. Khaliq was here.

He lay perfectly still, holding his breath, straining to hear.

He heard the large man stumble and fall. He heard moaning. Hafiz lifted his eyes above the couch and though it was dark, he recognized Abdullah on his hands and knees.

"Pak Guru!" he called, leaving the couch to help Abdullah stand.

His former teacher waved him away. "Get Sari," he rasped.

Hafiz knocked on Sari's door, then opened it a crack. "Get up! Bapak needs you." He turned on the lights.

Between the two of them they got Abdullah on the couch. Sari scrambled for her first aid kit.

"Hafiz, bring the...motorcycle inside...through the side door," Abdullah instructed through gritted teeth.

"But my leg..."

"Just do it." Abdullah glared at him.

He limped out through the side door and found the keys still in the bike. *He thinks he's been followed.* Hafiz looked up and down the alley warily, but saw no one. Pushing the bike up the short ramp was difficult with only one leg to rely on, and it took him three tries. By the third he was sweating—not from the exertion but from knowing every second of delay someone might see him.

A few more days and maybe I'll be well enough to steal this bike and get out of town.

Back in the living room, he took a better look at Abdullah. Both eyes were red and puffy, his lip was cut and swollen, and he had dried blood on his cheek. Sari was doing her best to help with some ice, but Hafiz knew from his martial arts experience Abdullah's face would only get more colorful by evening.

Sari sent him to the kitchen for Panadol and a glass of water. He would've protested all this treating him like a slave, but he was too obsessed with one thought—*this had to be Khaliq.*

Hafiz sat on the floor and waited. The others weren't talking. He was afraid to ask, but had to know.

"Well, you gonna tell us what happened or what?"

Abdullah spoke softly, with frequent shallow breaths. "I found Amat…they caught me…tied me up…they wanted Hafiz…" He shifted his weight slightly and grimaced.

"Let me open your shirt," Sari said, and started working on the buttons.

"What did you tell them?" Hafiz demanded angrily.

"I said…you went to Batulicin."

"Did they believe you?"

"Your side is red," Sari interjected. "Does this hurt?" She poked Abdullah's ribs.

"Ahhhh…don't do that."

"Did they believe you?" Hafiz leaned forward.

"I doubt it…or they would have…killed me. They wanted to…follow me to you… I think I…lost them."

"You think? You think?" Hafiz pulled at his hair. "If they find us they'll kill all of us, you know that."

Abdullah looked at Sari. "I can't…do this anymore… I looked in his eyes… Non-violence is…it won't work… The only way…to stop him…is to kill him."

"Shhhh. Rest, Bapak. You want us to call a doctor?"

"No!" Hafiz protested. "No doctors. He'll be fine."

"How can you say that? Look at him!" Sari argued.

"No one can know. Khaliq knows Bapak's hurt. He'll be watching for doctors taking house calls in Kelayan. Then what are you gonna do? Call your little Christian gang, who learned how to fight from Playstation? They wouldn't last a minute against Khaliq. Nobody's gonna stop him. We need to run as far away from here as possible."

"Hafiz is right...no doctor."

"But Bapak," Sari pleaded, "you look terrible."

"And he's right...nobody's gonna stop him...if I don't... So as much as...I want to...no running."

"But—" Hafiiz began.

"I want to quit...so badly...but I can't leave...my city...in the hands of those men."

Abdullah dropped his chin to his chest and pointed behind his head. Sari's eyes widened. She grabbed some more cotton and peroxide to scrub the clotted blood away.

"You can't stop these guys," Hafiz continued. "They're killers. You're crazy to try talking to them. This—" he pointed at Abdullah's face, "—is how they listen."

"So Khaliq is the big one?" Abdullah mumbled.

"Yeah. He's the one who's going to kill me."

"And the one...he takes orders from? What's his name?"

Hafiz paused, mouth hanging open.

Abdullah continued, "You told the truth...about Amat... But you didn't...mention Khaliq."

"I guess I just forgot."

"No, you didn't... You're afraid of him... It's okay, I understand why." Abdullah moved the ice bag to his other eye. "But now you need to tell... me everything."

"I'm not telling you nothing."

Sari glared at him. "Hafiz, Bapak took this beating for you! He's given you a home, food and medicine, and now he's risked his life to keep you alive—look at him! If he would endure all that for you, surely you owe him something. Now tell him what he wants to know!"

I already screwed up and gave Khaliq's name. I'm probably dead anyway.

"Fine, you win," Hafiz groused. "The leader's name is Achmad. He was in Afghanistan. I already told you all the others."

"I need you to tell someone on the phone...everything you know about...every one of these guys, got it?"

"Whatever."

Sari reached for a pen and paper. "Let me write down all their names again. Maybe we can pray for them by name, right now, there may still be hope for some of them to change."

"That's the stupidest thing I ever heard," Hafiz grumbled, but he told her the names.

"Let the girl pray," Abdullah ordered, moving the ice pack to the back of his head.

Hafiz listened to Sari's idiotic prayer. *As long as you're asking, why not ask for cotton candy unicorns, or world peace, or other impossible stuff....*

Like my parents coming back from the dead.

Chapter 48

When the *Subuh* call to prayer reverberated through the window of Achmad's cheap hotel room, he was already wide awake. In fact, he hadn't slept all night. The digital clock by his twin bed read 5:10 a.m. Just past it he stared at Khaliq's empty bed. *What was taking so long?*

Most likely Khaliq had been overenthusiastic in beating his prisoner and the man couldn't walk, much less lead Khaliq to Hafiz. That was probably it.

I'll sleep when this is all over.

Achmad did his ceremonial washing, the *wudlu*, in the bathtub, then rolled out his *sejadah* on the floor and started his morning *sholat*. As he bowed and recited the prayers in Arabic, his mind wandered. Years ago the *sholat* had held a certain fervor of hope. *Jihad* was going to bring the world out of its darkness into the light. Recently, ISIS bringing to power a *caliph* to exercise Islamic government across the earth had reignited hope in many. But not in him. He was under no illusion that ISIS would succeed any more than Al Qaeda or a hundred efforts before them.

Yet he did his prayers faithfully, five times a day. It helped to center him, to keep him humble, and unattached to the world.

At the close of the *sholat* he whispered the "Peace be upon you," to his right and his left, though no one was there. He would need Allah's peace to face the test that was coming.

Jihad was a challenging occupation, but he had no regrets. Afghanistan had been his college education; Poso his apprenticeship. Now he was a leader in his field, and his pay was commensurate with the risks involved.

As he was rolling up his prayer rug, Khaliq entered.

"Is the boy dead?" Achmad asked.

"He got away," Khaliq answered.

"The boy got away?"

"No, the man. I was following him, but somehow he gave me the slip."

"Ya Allah! You giant moron! You useless son of a pig!" Achmad threw his prayer rug at Khaliq's head. "May Allah grant me the patience not to kill you instead! That man should be dead. Hafiz should be dead. Maybe you should be dead!"

"He said he's a teacher," Khaliq stammered. "But he's not just a teacher. I beat him unconscious. He could hardly walk, but he knew I was following him."

Achmad groaned in frustration, spun back to the bed and tossed his pillow to the floor, swinging around with a Beretta 92F in his hand. He pointed it at his partner. Khaliq stared silently at the gun.

"Great, just great. Until we're ready for the final act, you don't eat, you don't sleep, you find that man! Start with schools in *Kelayan*. I'll call you if I get any leads. They must be dead today, or you and I are done. You hear that, Khaliq? I kept you after Poso, but no…more…mistakes!" Achmad punctuated each of the final words with a tap of the Beretta against Khaliq's forehead.

The big man hadn't made eye contact the whole time. "Yes," he grunted.

Achmad stepped back, then flipped the pistol so he had it by the barrel and offered it to Khaliq.

"Take a gun this time."

"Khaliq doesn't need a gun."

Achmad shook his head. "Stubborn brute! Why do I bother? Go! Get out of here!" He waved toward the door with the Beretta.

Khaliq left.

Achmad threw the gun on the bed and grabbed his cell phone. He punched in Rio's number.

A sleepy voice answered, "What?"

"Are the packages ready?"

"Almost."

"Almost? Almost? And you're sleeping?" Achmad's voice echoed off the cracked cement walls. He grabbed the gun and mimed shooting the television. "I'm going to kill you all if there are any more delays! We will deliver them tomorrow on schedule or Allah help me I'll put a bullet through each of your sleepy eyeballs!" He hung up.

The adrenaline rush surged fresh energy through his body. He dropped to the floor and did fifty pushups, then grabbed his phone and called Baqri.

"*Assalamu alaikum,*" Baqri answered.

"The hack is tonight. Not next week, tonight. I expect no excuses. Do it or you're a dead man."

"Understood."

He texted the driver to be ready, did a hundred sit-ups, then texted Hidayat and Amat to keep looking for Hafiz until they heard from him.

The local cell members had only known his cold, calculating side. They were about to find out what he was truly capable of. Especially if they failed in their responsibilities.

He was not an unjust leader—he was equally hard on himself. It was his own fault, of course, for accepting Hafiz without a thorough vetting like he'd done with the others. A young idealist wanting to blow himself up just seemed too good to be true. This wasn't the Middle East—Indonesians weren't a suicidal culture. Achmad certainly wasn't planning to die that way. He knew he'd die a violent death, but he'd go down fighting.

And if his team didn't perform over the next seventy-two hours, he might have to give up his payday and slip away to fight another day.

After he killed all the other cell members, of course.

Chapter 49

The beeping cell phone aroused Abdullah from his sleep, but it took him a few moments to pull his mind out of the miry bog. When he touched the screen, he saw it was already past noon. The text message was from Joko.

His first attempt to sit up failed miserably. Tightening his abs sent his ribs into furious protests. Slowly he rolled onto his side and used his arm to push his body into a sitting position. After a few shallow breaths he opened Joko's text. It contained some valuable intel on the names Hafiz had given. *Finally we could make a plan, if I could just get out of bed.*

The bathroom mirror mocked him, telling him to go dig a grave and lie in it, but he kept moving, shuffling gingerly to the kitchen table. When Sari heard him come in she immediately started making coffee and brought him some pain pills and water while bubbling away.

"Bapak! How are you feeling? I'm glad you slept so long. Guess what? My friend Nina is here! She came into town last night to visit her mother who sent her over here to see me. Oh, how I missed her! She said she can stay a few days and help us. Maybe she can stay with me so you don't have to bother your neighbor anymore. Can I get you something to eat? There's still some yellow rice with a duck egg left over from breakfast."

Abdullah nodded, hoping that the caffeine and pills would take the edge off his headache. He took a few bites of the yellow rice, his swollen lip making chewing feel awkward. Then he pushed his plate away and asked Sari to call everyone.

Sari brought Nina into the kitchen on her arm. Right away he sensed something different about Nina. Maybe it was her more conservative clothes. Abdullah had watched Nina grow up from the little girl down the alley to the haunted young woman selling herself at clubs to provide for her family, and now she was married. He realized he hadn't seen Sari this happy in a long time, too. They sat on either side of him while Hafiz filed in last and sat across from him.

"Pak Joko texted me," Abdullah began. "Based on what Hafiz told him, he's dug up some intel on some of these cell members. Let me read it for you."

He read: Achmad, alias Pardo, alias Hussein, is a well-known terrorist from East Java, suspected of having been trained overseas. He appeared in Aceh fighting the Indonesian military, then in Sulawesi with the Laskar Jihad, then vanished a few years ago. He's on the 'twenty most wanted terrorists' list.

There is also a Rio, alias Maulana, on the top twenty list. He was trained by Abu Sayyaf guerillas in the Philippines to assemble bombs, and is rumored to have been involved in a church bombing in Sulawesi six years ago. If this Rio is in the cell, he's certainly capable of making the bomb that blew up the night club and the university auditorium.

Khaliq may be the large, unknown terrorist wanted in Sulawesi in connection with the beheading of three Christian girls.

For Amat we have no data. You said Pak Ardiansyah from IAIN identified him, so we can surmise he's a former student there.

Based on that, we checked out IAIN students of the same years named "Hidayat" and "Baqri." There are several, so again you'll have to do more legwork. But we did find an interesting possibility—one Hidayat is the son of Yusuf Anwar, former head of BULOG, now in Banjarmasin's Teluk Dalam Prison for corruption. The media reported that at the arrest of his father, Hidayat threatened revenge on multiple parties.

That's all I have to go on for now, but will keep digging and hopefully at some point be able to send you some personnel. Unfortunately,

RIGHT NOW ALL OUR STAFF ARE FULLY ENGAGED IN OTHER CITIES WHERE WE DON'T HAVE THE LUXURY OF SOMEONE LOCAL AS EFFECTIVE AND RESOURCEFUL AS YOU.

Abdullah wanted to laugh at that last line, but it wasn't worth the extra effort. He laid down the cell phone and addressed the others.

"Nina, can you take Sari out of town? It's not safe for you two here."

"No, Bapak! I'm not leaving." Sari was adamant. "Look at you! You look terrible, and Pak Joko said he doesn't have anyone to help you, so you're stuck with me."

"Don't be foolish, Sari. I'll work better knowing you're safe."

"Nina, he's right, you should go back to your husband. But Bapak, I'm not leaving you."

"I want to help, too," offered Nina. "Though I'm not sure what I can do."

"Then I guess the first thing you can do is drive Hafiz to the terminal and put him on a bus heading as far away from here as possible."

"Hey, wait a minute," Hafiz protested. "Are you trying to get rid of me?"

"Look Hafiz, you've done your part, you told us all you knew. I can't ask you to help us knowing Khaliq is looking for you. Get away from here, start a new life."

"But…but you're not sending me to jail? What about what I did to your son?"

"It doesn't matter. My two boys are gone. I don't want you to follow them."

Hafiz looked stunned. Slowly he rose and leaned on his chair.

"Fine…I'm out of here."

Nina and Sari stood. Sari grabbed the motorcycle keys from a nail by the door and handed them to Nina. Then she stepped toward Hafiz, and pulled him into a hug. At first his arms hung limp. But Sari didn't let go until he wrapped his arms around her too.

As Abdullah watched this exchange, he realized that his anger at Hafiz was gone. Once again Hafiz was his English student, his martial arts student, just an obnoxious, arrogant bully still trying to figure out who he really was. And now he was also a lost orphan boy trying to stay alive another day.

The door closed behind Nina and Hafiz. Abdullah and Sari stared at each other. Sari managed a sad smile. She took Abdullah's plate and coffee cup to the sink.

"I wish…" she started, but never finished the thought.

Suddenly the door opened, and Hafiz came back in.

"Where am I supposed to go? With Khaliq and the police looking for me, you might as well paint a bulls-eye on my head. I'm a dead man. Besides, you need me. A beat-up old man and a girl who's afraid of her shadow—you guys suck without me, you know that, right?"

Abdullah tried to smile but it hurt too much. "All right, son, sit down and let's make a plan." *Did I just call him "son"?*

Hafiz pulled out a chair next to Abdullah. "So what can I do that's the least likely to get me killed?"

Chapter 50

After a brutally hot and frustrating day, a bank of gray clouds finally rolled across the sun giving Khaliq temporary relief from the continuous streams of sweat that had drenched his black t-shirt and black jeans. He had visited several schools in Kelayan, but since it was Sunday, he knew he was wasting his time. Curse Achmad for his impossible demands. Abdullah and Hafiz would be dead soon enough.

The day hadn't been a total loss. Two purse snatchers had made a sudden u-turn in front of him. He had extended his arm knocking both of them off their motorcycle. Then he'd parked his bike and reclaimed the purse for the grateful woman to cheers from the crowd. Next he'd picked up both thieves and tossed them into the river. Finally, he'd raised their motorcycle over his head and tossed it into the river too. No one had cheered for him then; in fact, most of the onlookers had disappeared. He smiled remembering the fear on their faces as they scurried away like rats.

He was sitting at a *warung* on Kelayan B Street, drinking iced tea and watching the late afternoon traffic pick up, when the text message came in. Achmad had given him a school's name and address. No one would be there, but maybe he could break in and learn something.

Ten minutes later Khaliq pulled into the courtyard of the *Al-Mustaqiim Pesantren*. Two dilapidated buildings flanked the yard. Rusted corrugated aluminum roofs, plywood walls with chicken wire windows— a poor school for poor cowards like Hafiz who thought speaking Arabic would make them special. *When death comes, it doesn't care what language you speak as you beg for mercy.*

Khaliq heard a rustle behind the second building. An old man stepped around the corner, a bunch of weeds in his gloved hand.

"Assalamu alaikum. Can I help you? " the old man smiled.

"Wa alaikum assalam." Khaliq took off his motorcycle helmet and shook out his long, sweaty hair. "I'm looking for one of your teachers, Pak Abdullah. Can you tell me where to find him?"

"May I ask what this is about?"

Khaliq had prepared for this. "Pak Abdullah was given as a reference on a job application for his former student, Hafiz. But there was no phone number, just the school's address."

The old man continued smiling, but his eyes narrowed. "Pak Abdullah no longer works here. I'm sorry I can't help you."

"Perhaps you have a home address in one of your files?" Khaliq motioned vaguely toward one of the buildings.

The old man's eyes darted to the other building, then looked squarely at Khaliq. "I'm sorry, we're closed today. Come back tomorrow." His tone was final. This wasn't the gardener. Khaliq wondered if he was the school principal.

"What's wrong? Don't you trust me?" Khaliq approached the man, grinning as he came.

The old coot didn't back down. "Young man, unless you want to help me pull weeds, you need to leave."

"Might save you some time to use this." Khaliq pulled out a *keris*, a ceremonial knife about the length of a machete. He held it by the blade and offered it to the old man, who didn't respond.

"Go ahead, take it. My *ilmu kebal* protects me from knife wounds, so it won't help you against me, but at least you'll feel safer in the moments before I kill you." Khaliq anticipated the man's head in his hands, could hear the snap of his neck, and he grinned even wider. *Just like my first kill, when I took my uncle's life for what he took from me.*

"Those who live by the sword die by the sword."

Usually Khaliq could smell fear. This old man had every reason to fear, but chose not to. He respected that. This old man was not like his perverse swine of an uncle. This was an honorable man—he would receive an honorable death.

With a flick of his wrist he had the handle of the *keris*. He pointed it at the old man. "How about this saying, Teacher: 'Khaliq lives; you die.'"

With one smooth sweeping motion he severed the old man's head from his neck.

For a moment he closed his eyes and filled his chest with air. One breath, two breaths. He could feel his heart beating fast, pumping the life-blood through his veins. *No man can hurt me. I hold their puny lives in my powerful hand.*

Then he cleaned his sword on the man's pant leg and threw the head and body into the tall weeds behind the school.

The door the old man had revealed by his glance was locked. Khaliq tapped around the lock for a hollow place, then smashed his elbow through the outer layer of plywood, his fist through the inner plywood, and he could unlock the door.

This must be the school office. There were pictures of the current Indonesian president and vice-president on the wall, along with a calendar exhibiting an ornate mosque. There was a simple wooden desk and chair, a wooden bench facing it, and a dusty three-drawer metal filing cabinet behind it. The filing cabinet was unlocked.

It took just moments to find Abdullah's address and phone number. He wasn't sure how Achmad had known to send him here, but now he was back in business. Tonight after the 'Isya prayers he would kill Abdullah in his own bed. That would leave only Hafiz.

On a hunch, he searched through the student files and again found what he was looking for. The photo was younger, but unmistakable—Hafiz had been a student here too. Hafiz's home address was even closer to the school. Perhaps he'd see if the boy was home first. Yes, then he could boast to Abdullah that the beating he'd taken to protect Hafiz was all for nothing.

It turned out that visiting the school on a Sunday had actually been far better than waiting until Monday. Now he had everything he needed to finish the job tonight.

Chapter 51

"*Astaghfirallah al-adzim!*" Ibu Aaminah exclaimed when she saw Abdullah's discolored face. "*Ya Allah*, what happened to you?"

"Abdullah, what happened?" the RT, or neighborhood chief, echoed.

Aaminah had dragged the RT over to Abdullah's house after the evening 'Isya prayers because she was concerned about Sari, but there was more going on here than she had thought, and she wanted to get to the bottom of it.

Abdullah seemed less than forthcoming answering their question: "Someone didn't like something I said."

"Pak Abdullah, are you in some kind of trouble?" Aaminah asked.

"I'm fine," he answered. "What can I do for you?"

Ibu Aaminah nudged the RT with her elbow.

"You see, Pak Abdullah," the RT began, then paused to cough. "Well, Ibu Aaminah…" He glanced sideways and received an encouraging nod, "…and I are concerned about Sari. Specifically about what your intentions are." He took a quick breath and stepped backwards.

Sari had been busy preparing tea for the guests, but poked her head out of the kitchen. "Me? Why are you concerned about me?"

Aaminah took over. "Sari is the only Christian in our neighborhood, and as an orphan, we're all responsible for her well-being. As much as we feel for you, Pak Abdullah, in your family loss, and your recent misadventures, we will not stand by and watch this young girl being taken advantage of. It is our opinion that she is too young for you to marry, but if that is your intention, please make it clear; and whether it is or not, she shouldn't be living alone with you in this house."

Sari's eyes popped. Aaminah could tell Sari was young and naïve in the ways of men. Perhaps she hadn't noticed that at least two men in the neighborhood Abdullah's age had taken second wives not much older than Sari.

Abdullah shook his head. "Sari is like my own daughter. I would never hurt her. But if you want to take her to your house, please, go ahead. I'd certainly feel better about…keeping the neighborhood happy."

"That's very sensible of you," Aaminah smiled and nodded. She turned to Sari. "Get your things dear, my husband and I would be happy to have you live with us."

The tea kettle started whistling, but Sari was rooted to the floor. "Thank you, but—"

"The tea kettle?" Aaminah reminded her. "Now get the tea, dear."

Sari went to the kitchen and returned with two cups of hot jasmine tea. She knelt beside the coffee table and set the cups and saucers in front of the guests, now seated on the couch next to Abdullah. She returned the tea tray to the kitchen, then sat in the wicker chair opposite.

"Ibu Aaminah," Sari said.

"Yes, child."

"I understand that you believe it's improper for me to be here alone with Pak Abdullah. But what if someone else stayed here with us? Wouldn't that be okay?"

"That would certainly be different, dear, but who would you ask to move in here?"

Sari stood and headed down the hall. *What a curious girl! As unpredictable as her mother.*

She came back dragging a young man hanging desperately to a towel around his waist, protesting all the way. "What do you think you're doing, Monkey-face! If you wanted me naked, all you—whaaaa!"

"Pak RT, Ibu Aaminah, let me introduce you to Hafiz. He's living with us right now. Since both he and Pak Abdullah are recovering from some serious injuries, I think I need to stay here a little longer to nurse them back to health." Sari let go of Hafiz's arm, and he limped muttering back to the bathroom.

Pak RT stood. "You never told me you took in this boy. Who is he? I need to know these things."

Aaminah stood as well. "I really don't think this is a good environment for the girl, Pak Abdullah."

Everyone was talking at once when suddenly the door burst open and little Atoy ran into the room and wrapped his arms around Pak RT's leg.

"Grandpa, Grandpa! Grandma says you have to turn on the TV right now!"

Abdullah turned on his television to a breaking news report.

Ibu Aaminah gasped in horror at the images and fell back onto the couch, sputtering in English, "Oh my God! Oh my God!"

Chapter 52

Michael O'Malley showed his boarding pass for his Garuda Airlines flight to Jakarta, then walked down the stairs linking the waiting room to the tarmac, where a bus waited to deliver the passengers to the plane. He'd flown out of Banjarmasin's Syamsudin Noor Airport a few times before, but he'd never seen this many military toting machine guns in and around the airport.

They told me the cigarettes would kill me. I bet these business trips to unstable Third World countries will kill me first.

Why would God entrust some of the greatest natural resources of the world to some of the most idiotic people? He gave oil to the Saudis, diamonds to the central African nations, and Indonesia got liberal helpings of both, plus gold, timber, coal, rubber, palm oil, spices—enough to make them one of the richest nations on earth if they'd ever learn to manage it well. And if they could stop the endemic corruption long enough to invest their wealth back into their own economy.

He climbed on the bus and sat in the front. As usual in this part of Indonesia, he was the only *bule*, or white person, on board. The bus filled up quickly. A woman stood in front of him, nearly dropping her cabin luggage on his toes. She held the rail above with one hand, and the hand of her whimpering toddler with the other. How many times had he given up his seat for someone like her? But he was getting older, more easily tired. *Two more years to retirement, to living on a yacht in the Caribbean.*

But the yacht was pushed out of his head by the memory of the broken dragline excavator he had come to fix. It had taken longer than he'd expected. During his four days at the mining site, he'd realized their production delays were more complicated than a broken part. Two of their remote sites reported coal being stolen during the night, and they suspected the nearby military base was behind it. One mine was flooded. Rumors swirled of an impending strike. He couldn't wait to get back to Boston.

The bus was crammed full and smelled of body odor. He checked his watch—7:45 pm. They should have taken off by now. *Come on, driver, get off your frickin' cell phone.*

Craning his neck he could see the driver just outside the door. The thin old man's uniform was drenched right through with sweat, and he kept wiping his forehead with a handkerchief though a cool evening breeze wafted over the airstrip.

Michael blinked, and the old man had put his cell phone away and jumped into the driver's seat and closed the door all in one movement. He dimmed the interior lights and the bus lurched straight ahead.

Rowena…how I wish you'd be there waiting for me. I've no home to return to since you left.

He'd seen enough of the world. Everywhere he went he found broken parts to fix.

If only he could fix the broken parts he'd left behind.

The bus took a sudden turn to the right, and the toddler stumbled into Michael's lap. He helped the boy recover his balance.

"You okay little buddy?"

His mother replied, "Tank you, Mister."

Michael smiled at the boy, but could hardly make out the boy's face. He realized it had gotten darker. Swiveling back to the front, he noticed the driver had turned off the bus's headlights as well. They were driving into the dark, and picking up speed.

A murmur began on the other side of the bus, then turned to panic as passengers stared out the window. Michael couldn't see what they were seeing, but above the panicked cries he heard the roar of jet engines terrifyingly close.

He jumped up, but stumbled as the bus came to an abrupt stop. The roar was deafening now, drowning out the screams of the passengers.

Rowena, forgive me.

Chapter 53

Sari and Hafiz sat side by side on the couch, eyes glued to the news report. Abdullah had raced off, against Sari's protests, to see the destruction for himself. Pak RT and Ibu Aaminah had left right behind him. As they watched video of the carnage, they listened to the recounting of the event.

"I can confidently say that this was no accident. It was well-planned and required inside knowledge to make the timing perfect. Citilink Flight 872 from Jakarta was due to land at 7:30 p.m., but was running late. Meanwhile, Garuda Flight 537 was supposed to depart for Jakarta at 7:45 p.m., but was also running late. When driver Ali Fachruddin diverted his busload of Garuda passengers onto the airstrip and into the path of the Citilink plane, he had to know exactly when that plane would touch down. The police suspect that the driver received instructions from someone within the control tower, or someone who was listening in to the control tower.

"Right now I'm standing at the location of impact. This is where the front landing gear of the plane clipped the top of the bus, snapping off, driving the nose of the plane down into the runway and crushing the bus. You can see the marks where the plane and bus slid down the runway, shooting up sparks that I'm told were spectacular.

"As we walk down the runway, imagine that at this point the fuselage has split open just aft of the flight deck. Fuel leakage near the middle of the aircraft causes an explosion that tears off large portions of the wings. Those passengers who may have survived when the fuselage split are incinerated in the blast.

"Over there about five hundred meters from the original collision, you can see that only a heavily damaged nose cone and the tail section are intact. Both pilots avoided the explosion and are being treated for multiple injuries. All passengers and crew have been pronounced dead.

"So far no one has claimed responsibility for this tragedy. Once again, the police believe the driver had accomplices. Anyone with information, please come forward.

"And on behalf of this station, our heartfelt condolences to the families of all the victims, including the driver Ali Fachruddin's wife and his six-year-old daughter who we have just learned is in critical condition at the Ulin Hospital with tracheal cancer."

The news cut to a commercial break. Sari's stomach felt queasy, but she had to ask Hafiz her question.

"Did your group do that?"

Hafiz stood and stretched, shaking his head violently. "Man, I don't know. They never told me they were doing anything like that. That's insane." He rubbed his hand roughly over his head. "What was I thinking?"

The house phone rang, and Sari answered it. Nina wanted to know if she'd seen the news. They talked a few minutes about it. Nina told her that Hidayat hadn't showed at the prison today, but she'd go back and watch during visiting hours tomorrow.

When she hung up, Hafiz was still limping around the room, swinging his arms randomly, clearly agitated. *Maybe this was his moment of truth.*

"If they asked you to, would you have driven that bus?"

"I don't know, man, there were little kids on that bus. And on the plane. Maybe people we knew! That's twisted, man."

"What if Khaliq was standing right there and told you to do it?"

"That guy's freaky. You don't know if he's going to rip off one of your body parts, or maybe..." Hafiz stopped pacing and quietly looked out the window. "You're not talking about the plane, are you?"

Sari waited.

Hafiz nearly whispered his next words towards his reflection in the window. "I came to your house that night to scare you. It was my revenge for…well, for what your mom did to Syukran. They never mentioned raping you, till we were in your house and Khaliq changed the plan. I didn't want to do it. But I was scared. It was the first time in my life I was really scared. It was like I let someone else control me."

Sari waited again, but Hafiz didn't continue. She asked, "Why did you join them in the first place?"

"I wanted to be somebody. I wanted to do something great, strike a blow against the enemies of Islam." Hafiz's shoulders slumped. "I became a slave. I accidentally killed my best friend's brother, and I blew up my own parents…my own parents." He choked on the words.

She could see in his reflection in the window the saddest look she'd ever seen. She walked up behind him and put her hand on his shoulder.

"I'm sorry," she said.

"No, I'm sorry," he whispered. "I'm really, really, really sorry."

In the reflection she watched the tears pouring down his cheeks. She leaned her head on his shoulder and they watched each other in the window, as if in another world where life wasn't so painfully *real*.

After a time, Sari lifted her head. "I believe in redemption, do you?"

"You mean paying for all your sins?"

"No, I mean when God steps in and takes all our mess and still makes something good come out of it."

"I believe in fate. What happens must be Allah's will. And I'll get what I deserve."

"Then what's the point of mercy? If I'm willing to give you a second chance, surely God must be too."

Hafiz turned to face her with a pained expression. "I doubt there are second chances for kids who kill their parents."

Sari smiled sympathetically. "Why don't you sit down. I'll go make us some tea."

Hafiz turned off the television and sat in the wicker chair as Sari moved into the kitchen. She filled the tea kettle and turned on the stove. While she waited for it to boil she reviewed the words of Jesus she'd posted on the refrigerator. More and more she could see herself in the verses. Sometimes, like tonight, she could see Pak Abdullah or Hafiz in them too. Surely they were still in God's embrace; surely He would bring them through the darkness and into the light.

The kettle boiled, and she poured the water into two cups with teabags. The rich aroma of jasmine filled the air. As she inhaled, she smiled.

The front door creaked open, surprising her. Did Pak Abdullah forget something? She was about to call out to him when she heard Hafiz gasp from the living room.

"Khaliq!"

Chapter 54

Sheer terror coursed through every cell of Hafiz's body. Khaliq's silhouette filled the entire doorway. As Khaliq stepped into the light, Hafiz stared at the powerful muscles that would tear off his limbs, the merciless eyes, and the twisted grin. His brain screamed at his legs to run, but they refused to respond.

The memory of how he felt stepping into Sari's house to scare her flitted through his mind. *I deserve to die this way.*

He hadn't been ready to die when he planted the bomb, but he was ready now.

Khaliq's eyes scanned the room. He noticed the two-by-four near the front door and picked it up in his right hand.

"Where's the old man?" he growled.

Hafiz couldn't breathe, much less talk. He stood frozen across the room watching Khaliq slowly advance.

"Talk, boy," the giant grunted, then in a split second he raised the two-by-four and snapped it down over his knee. With a jagged weapon in each hand now, he took another step toward Hafiz.

Sari peeked around the corner from the kitchen and saw Khaliq. Hafiz watched her chest expand, drawing in a deep breath, then she screamed.

He had heard that scream before, and something inside him shattered like glass windows in an earthquake. He never wanted to hear that scream again.

Jim Baton

The scream diverted Khaliq's attention. He spun toward Sari with the quick pounce of a tiger.

She reacted by throwing both cups of boiling tea into his face.

Khaliq dropped his weapons, his hands flying up too late. He covered his burning eyes and howled. Then he flung one arm toward Sari but she had already retreated to the kitchen, and he only succeeded in knocking a lamp to the floor.

Suddenly Hafiz's feet felt a bolt of lightning propel him behind Khaliq toward the door. Khaliq heard him and lunged blindly, catching his knee on the corner of the couch. Still Khaliq reached one hand toward Hafiz, who stiff-armed it away, and he was out the open door.

"*Maling!* Thief!" Hafiz yelled running down the alley. He picked up a rock and banged it wildly against a metal telephone pole. Lights came on, doors opened, and the neighborhood men poured out of their homes. Hafiz knew they would defend one of their own. He pointed back to Abdullah's house but stayed behind the gathering pack, wondering if Khaliq would retreat or just kill them all.

Khaliq realized his overconfidence had put him in a disadvantageous position. His eyesight was returning, though his face still stung with the burns. But he had let the runt escape. There was a girl in the kitchen, maybe Hafiz's lover. That presented possibilities.

He found the girl trapped in the back of the kitchen holding a knife. She looked vaguely familiar. He blocked the doorway and glared at her.

"You burned my face. For this you will die."

The girl pointed the knife at him and stammered, "You...you won't win, you know."

Khaliq grinned. "Khaliq always wins."

She shook her head. "Love always wins."

"Shut up. Where's the man called Abdullah? This is his house, isn't it?"

"He's gone."

196

"So there's no one here to stop me from slitting your throat." He took two strides toward her. She feebly stabbed at him, but he caught her wrist, causing her to cry out in pain, then pried the knife from her fingers. He jerked her arm behind her and with the other hand brought the knife up to her throat.

But she wasn't the one he was after.

"Come with me."

Keeping the girl in front of him, Khaliq exited the house. A mob armed with long knives and various lengths of wood for clubs was gathering on the street in front of the neighbor's house, still offering him an escape route up the alley toward Kelayan B Street. When they saw him holding the knife to the girl's throat a blanket of silence fell over them. As always, Khaliq was in control. But the traitor Hafiz had run away like a cowardly dog.

He called out to them, "Come any closer and I'll drench your street with her blood." He pushed her quickly through the yard to the alley. No one moved.

When he had put about twenty yards between the mob and himself, he whispered in the girl's ear. "Today is your lucky day, whore. I want you to give Abdullah a message for me. Tell him that Khaliq is coming for him."

He touched the point of the knife to the side of the girl's neck just hard enough to draw blood and hear her squeal one more time. Then he threw her to the ground, saluted the crowd with the bloody knife, turned his back and walked away.

Chapter 55

Hafiz breathed a huge sigh of relief when he heard Abdullah calling to him to unlock the door. When he opened it, he saw there were still nearly a dozen of the neighborhood men on the porch and in the yard keeping watch. A few were playing dominoes and drinking the hot tea Sari had fixed for them.

Sari threw her arms around Abdullah, then she and Hafiz took turns telling him what happened, including Khaliq's ominous message.

Abdullah's brow furrowed in concern. "Are either of you hurt?"

They both shook their heads and showed him the small prick on Sari's neck. Hafiz noticed Abdullah shudder and mumble something in Arabic.

"I was a fool to expect they wouldn't discover my home eventually. I never should have let you two stay here. I can't believe you're both still alive." He touched Sari's shoulder affectionately. She was still trembling. Hafiz hoped he didn't look as terrified as he felt.

"Did you call the police?" Abdullah continued.

"Yeah," Hafiz answered, "one of the neighbors did."

"Pak Darsuni," Sari added.

"But thank God no cops came. They're useless anyway," Hafiz complained.

"Let me try Sergeant Eko." Abdullah called the sergeant on his cell phone, then put it on speaker phone for Hafiz to describe Khaliq. Sergeant Eko promised a manhunt would commence as soon as he had personnel available. They discussed the airline crash. When Abdullah asked for a plain clothes officer to assist Nina at the Teluk Dalam prison, Eko promised to send one.

"Where's the lamp?" Abdullah asked after he hung up.

"Bapak, I'm so sorry, it broke," Sari replied.

"It doesn't matter. The important thing is you two are alive."

"'You two?' Are you including me with your precious Sari now?" Hafiz smirked.

Abdullah didn't answer. "Pack your bags, for at least two or three days. It's past time for us to move to some place safer."

"No, Bapak! We're not leaving you here alone." Sari grabbed his arm.

"I mean all of us. Khaliq knows this house. We've got to lay low somewhere he doesn't know."

"We can't run from Khaliq," Hafiz protested. "He'll find us. Maybe not today or tomorrow, but he'll hunt us down. We'll never be free till he's dead."

"A lot can happen in 'today or tomorrow,' Hafiz," Abdullah countered. "Let's make sure we stay alive to do what we can to stop him."

An hour later there was a knock at the door and Abdullah welcomed David into the living room. Sari squealed with joy and gave her former youth pastor a hug. David smiled and held out his hand to Hafiz, who reluctantly took it.

"Hafiz! It's good to see you again," David said.

Hafiz nodded and turned to Abdullah. "Why couldn't you have called someone from the *pesantren*? I'm not staying in the home of a *kafir*."

Abdullah frowned. "I thought I'd call our school's headmaster first to see if we could stay with him. His wife said he went to clean the school yard and didn't come home for *Mahgrib* prayers. If Khaliq went there... I don't want to think what might have happened. Khaliq could have gained access to all the school's records. The safest place for us is with a Christian."

"But why do we have to stay with someone who's going to hell?"

Abdullah glared at Hafiz. "We're already in hell. Be grateful David is willing to risk his family to shelter us."

He turned to Sari. "It's time to leave this house. May God give you courage. Go grab your bags."

As Hafiz zipped up Syukran's old school backpack, he thought about asking to borrow Abdullah's motorcycle and head out of town. He'd have to avoid the police and Khaliq... But maybe if he started clean somewhere far away—a new name, a new look, maybe grow a long beard—maybe Khaliq would give up looking for him.

Then he remembered Sari's head on his shoulder. He thought of Abdullah carrying him away from the bomb site. Where would he find anyone who cared about him like these two did?

But staying in a Christian home? They were still his enemies...

I'll try it for twenty-four hours. If those Christians try anything suspicious, I'm out of here.

They said good-bye to the neighborhood men, who promised to keep a night watch for the rest of the week. Sari immediately jumped on Abdullah's motorbike and clung tightly to him, eyes closed, her backpack wedged between Abdullah's knees. He saw Abdullah grimace when she grabbed his side, but his former teacher pretended he was fine.

Hafiz was not fine. He kicked the ground, then clambered on behind David, his backpack resting between his stomach and David's back. David started jabbering away about how happy he was to have Hafiz come to his home, but Hafiz just tuned him out.

It's amazing what a guy will endure to stay alive...

Chapter 56

Chanting of the *Ayat Kursi* on his cell phone's alarm woke Achmad early on Monday morning. He stretched, flipped back the gray curtain, and saw a beautifully clear blue sky. He smiled. *Heaven must be smiling on me too. Today is a perfect day.*

The room service breakfast consisted of fried rice and a fried egg. He ate it watching the television coverage of the airplane crash. It had worked exactly as he had imagined it. He was an artist. Surely his backers would see that, and perhaps include a bonus with his paycheck.

After breakfast he added fifty extra sit-ups and twenty extra pushups to his routine. He felt so much power surging through him he thought about trying to bench press the creaky bed. He was high, and if the finale went as well as last night, they'd have to tie cement bags to his legs to keep him from floating off the ground.

Ah, the finale. Banjarmasin was already in chaos, gripped with a palpable terror, but they hadn't seen anything yet. Rio had checked in late last night, informing him that all five bombs were armed and would soon be hidden at the meeting location for tonight. Five bombs, five targets. Those who survived this wave of attacks would beg for a government that could negotiate with the jihadists and restore order.

His assignment would be fulfilled, and his bank account a million dollars richer.

Achmad didn't know who was paying him, only the go-between who had offered him the job. But he knew there was plenty of money out there from his previous assignments. It was probably some Saudi prince.

He didn't care. The go-between knew if Achmad didn't get his money, there would be hell to pay.

What will I do with a million dollars? Open a security agency? Buy real estate in Jakarta? He had let himself fantasize about this occasionally, but only for a moment or two. Success in this line of work demanded total focus, no distractions. He was the master of the details.

He whipped out his cell phone and confirmed with Hidayat, Amat and Baqri the meeting time and place for this evening. Only Khaliq didn't answer, and he understood why. He didn't leave a message. Khaliq knew the time and place already, and would surely be there, hopefully with the cheerful news of Hafiz and Abdullah's deaths. Now *that* would truly make it a perfect day.

He had chosen the five targets carefully. Each of them had heightened security, but he had spent months in this city surveying weaknesses in the system, and had found a way to smuggle a bomb into each of them.

Achmad reviewed the list in his mind: the Trisakti Harbor, Duta Mall, the downtown Bank Central Asia, the Regional Parliament building, and the City Hall. He had planned to blow them all at once, but Baqri convinced him to stagger the blasts by twenty-minute intervals to increase the panic. Since the airport was already closed, and the harbor was next, those fleeing the city would face jammed roads and police checkpoints, heightening the chaos.

Half a million people trying to find a way out of hell.

The harbor bomb was his. He'd trigger it from a speed boat a half-mile away, and by the time the City Hall exploded he'd be well on his way upriver to Palangkaraya, where he'd opened a new bank account six months ago under a different name.

He wasn't taking Khaliq this time. A sketch of Khaliq's face had appeared on the morning news. The idiot had not worn the mask last night. *Sorry, buddy, you play the fool, you end up playing alone.*

He checked his Beretta, then wrapped it in a *sarong* and packed his few possessions in his backpack. This would be his last night in a grungy hotel—from now on nothing less than four star hotels for him.

Achmad's memory returned to the day he had left for Afghanistan. His mother had cried, sure that he'd end up dead. His father had tried to shame him, asking who would take care of them in their old age. They had both been wrong; he was alive and about to be filthy rich. At seventeen he had figured out that *jihad* was where the money was.

He had played the game and won.

Chapter 57

Amat hung up the phone, Achmad's *"Al-jihad sabiluna"* reverberating in his head. This was it. The final act. Achmad hadn't said this was a suicide mission, but Amat couldn't fight the feeling that Achmad had been preparing them exactly for this. He would be expected to die for the cause.

So what should I do if this is my last day on earth?

Amat lit a cigarette and watched a *klotok* chug by on the river, probably taking tourists out to the floating market. One of the kids on the boat waved at him. He blew a puff of smoke out through his nostrils.

Smile now, kid. You may be waving at the guy who blows you up.

This life had seemed so glamorous when he was in college. He and Hidayat had stayed up many nights discussing how *jihad* gave true meaning to life, and about how dying as a martyr was the ultimate honor.

But now that his glorious moment had arrived, Amat wasn't sure he wanted to die.

He noticed a bird hopping on the grass nearby chomping a cricket in its beak.

We all have to die. I'm fortunate that I get to choose my own manner of death. Or is Achmad making the choice for me?

Maybe he should play futsal today. A final game, in which he'd score the winning goal. Give the boys something to remember.

His cell phone buzzed and he checked the caller ID—his uncle. He'd have to visit his parents later too, time to say goodbye.

"Hey Uncle Surya, what's up?"

"Today's the day. Are you ready?"

Amat jerked and nearly dropped the phone. *How could his uncle possibly know?* "What do you mean?" he stammered.

"Today's the day you and I deal with your apostate cousin, Lani. She's run away from home and is hiding at some Christian friend's house in Belitung. Meet me at the big mosque on Simpang Belitung Street in thirty minutes, and we'll deal with her once and for all. And if any Christians try to defend her, we'll kill them too."

The relief Amat felt that his uncle wasn't talking about the bombing quickly dissolved with hearing his uncle's plan. No matter how impossible it was to understand Lani's actions, he couldn't imagine plunging a knife into his own cousin.

"I don't know, Uncle, maybe we should talk to my dad first."

"Your dad is off to Jakarta. The time for talk is over. The time for action is now. Are you with me, or should I take little Adi along instead?"

"Uncle, please, Adi's too young to see death. Besides, he has to stay after school today for a boy scouts meeting," Amat lied.

"If you're not here in thirty minutes, I'm taking Adi. Come on, Amat. You're always talking about *jihad*. Let's see you prove you're more than just hot air. Thirty minutes."

His uncle hung up. Amat was torn between protecting Adi and protecting Lani. Watching either of them suffer was not how he wanted to spend his last day on earth.

He started his motorbike, then paused and pulled out his cell phone again. He tried calling his college mentor for advice, but the old man didn't pick up.

He could still hear his mentor's words: *Sacrifices must be made.*

He imagined shoving the bomb down the back of Uncle Surya's pants—let *him* make the sacrifice.

Amat dropped his cigarette on the ground and stepped on it. Then he spit. He wasn't sure if the spit was intended for his uncle, for Lani, for Achmad, or for fate that put him in this position.

He grit his teeth and roared off on the motorbike for home.

Chapter 58

When Amat pulled up in front of his house, a white van he'd never seen was parked out front.

I'm too late. Uncle Surya's got Adi.

Suddenly a bicycle shot out from behind the van, with Adi pumping the pedals for all he was worth. He nearly ran over Amat.

"Look, Amat! It's Peter's bike!"

Adi zipped past him chanting "Peter's bike, Peter's bike…" and narrowly missed getting tangled in the neighbor's low-hanging laundry. On the opposite side of the van he found his mother talking to a man probably in his thirties, with a nose like a sea gull and a big smile.

"Come here, Amat. This is Pastor Christianto." His mom was smiling too.

Pastor? Amat warily approached and shook the man's hand. "What's going on here?"

"Are you Adi's brother?" the pastor asked.

Amat nodded.

"It's nice to meet you. I was just telling your mother about how the recent fire at our church tragically resulted in some unfortunate casualties. Two boys were in the bathroom, afraid to come out. We didn't even know they had died until we found their bodies the next day. One was a second-grader named Peter who attended school with Adi. Peter's mother asked me to find one of Peter's Muslim friends to inherit his bicycle as a way of reminding us all to follow the children's example of seeing beyond race and religion and becoming true friends."

Amat was stunned. He had watched the church burn with glee. He'd never imagined one of his little brother's friends would be killed in the blaze.

"I don't understand," Amat responded. "But you, uh, you don't hate the Muslims for this?"

"We don't believe it was our Muslim neighbors who did this, but a mob incited by outsiders who don't even know us. But in any case, we're trying to follow the example of Jesus, who when faced with death, prayed that God would forgive those who wanted to kill him."

Adi screeched to a halt next to Amat and grabbed his brother's pants leg. "That guy said whenever I ride this bike, I can remember Peter. Isn't that cool, Amat? Why do you hate Christians so much? Why can't you be their friend?"

As Adi raced off, Amat could feel his face turning red and looked away.

"It's okay," the pastor said with a laugh. "It was great to meet you both. I should be going."

Amat and his mother thanked Pastor Christianto again and he drove away. Amat took his mother's arm and urgently warned her about Uncle Surya coming for Adi. She ordered Adi to take his new bike into the house with her, then she locked the door.

Back on his motorcycle, Amat headed toward Belitung. He thought he knew the home of the one Christian friend they'd both had back in high school.

He had to get there before his uncle and warn Lani.

Chapter 59

"Time is running out, Abdullah. Please give me some good news." The tic in Joko's eye seemed more pronounced today. Maybe it had something to do with his lunch order—a pot of coffee. Or maybe seeing Abdullah's discolored face and awkward movements revealed the unfortunate direction this mission was going. Abdullah lifted a spoonful of Banjar chicken soup to his swollen lips and swallowed hard.

"I'm just starting to figure out who the players are. I don't have enough information yet to turn them. The only truly hopeful lead I have is Hidayat's father in prison has agreed to help us. He knows his son is angry and hiding something, but we're not even sure yet if he's one of the cell members. And as for the others? Well, I need more time."

Joko leaned forward, tilting the rickety table and nearly spilling Abdullah's iced tea. "There is no more time! Our nation is descending into chaos. Angry mobs are forming. Civilians are getting killed. And because there were Americans on that plane, the CIA is on their way to Indonesia as we speak. When they arrive in Jakarta, the Detachment 88 will have a significant show of force to accompany them here to Banjar. Groups like Laskar Jihad have already threatened to mobilize a counterforce. This city will become a battlefield like nothing seen since our war for independence.

"The only way to avert this is to take out that terrorist cell now. If we hold a press conference announcing the cell is no more, Detachment 88 will deploy their troops elsewhere. Now tell me we can do this!"

Abdullah wiped the sweat from his forehead. "Let's hope that our stakeout at the prison will be successful today. If we can catch Hidayat and turn him, hopefully he'll lead us to the others. Right now, they've all gone underground, except Khaliq who is trying to kill Hafiz and me. I can't find the others. And I doubt I can turn Khaliq, or the leader, Achmad. What if violence is the only solution?"

"At this point, our primary goal should be to save the city; rehabilitating any cell members will have to be our secondary goal." Joko's teeth were clenched, eyes narrowed. "We need a breakthrough in the next twenty-four hours, Abdullah, you got it?"

Abdullah pushed his half-eaten meal away from him. "I got it," he replied. He felt bad for letting the old man down, but the guy was too much of an idealist. *There is only one way this will end—kill or be killed.*

His cell phone beeped. The text message was from Sergeant Eko, that Hidayat had just entered the prison. He texted back: YOU KNOW WHAT TO DO. BE THERE IN 30.

"Good news, we've got Hidayat at the prison." Abdullah stood. "Now what I need from you is your word that all the offers we discussed are a go. I'm not going to promise these guys something and have you back out of it."

"They've all been approved at the highest level, exactly as you proposed."

"Any chance you could stick around to talk to these guys with me?"

Joko looked at his watch, then drained the last of the coffee. "I'm on a plane to Banda Aceh in two hours. Things are even darker there than they are here. But if you succeed, I'll be back for the press conference."

Abdullah rolled his eyes. "Yeah, right. Much better chance you'll be back for my funeral.

"On second thought," he continued, the images of Bali's funeral stabbing through his mind, "don't bother."

Chapter 60

When Hidayat regained consciousness, he blinked at the bright light bulb above him. Suddenly the light was blotted out by a head. His father was looking down at him.

"Son, are you all right?" A drop of sweat fell from his father's forehead onto Hidayat's cheek.

He couldn't remember why he was lying on the prison floor. He tried to get up and discovered his hands were handcuffed behind his back. He didn't remember that either. Fear began to choke his breath.

"Dad, what happened?" he stammered.

"Some guards carried you in and dumped you in my cell. Son, what have you gotten yourself into?"

Hidayat wriggled to his knees and looked wild-eyed around the room. This wasn't the visitation lounge. This was a cell. There had to be twenty or thirty men crammed in here. And every last one was staring at him. He felt the bile rise in his throat and struggled to swallow it back down.

"Dad, I swear I don't know what's going on. There must be some mistake."

"They told me you're a terrorist, that you killed women and children." A tear slipped out of his father's eye. "Is it true?"

Panic began to take control. Hidayat felt his heart might explode. He was light-headed. He closed his eyes and collapsed to the floor.

"Dayat!" His father slapped his cheek gently. "Come back! We only have a few minutes and we need to talk."

Only a few minutes…were they going to execute him without a trial? Could they do that?

He stayed on the floor and kept his eyes shut.

His father leaned down to whisper in Hidayat's ear. "Son, can you hear me?"

He nodded slightly.

"Listen, you have to get out of here. There are evil men in here who will…who will hurt a handsome boy like you. And if you look to the other *jihad* maniacs to protect you, they'll make you promise to be a suicide bomber when you get out. Your path leads only to pain, humiliation and death. Believe me, I know."

Hidayat cracked open one eye to see his father's face. It had once been such a strong face, a powerful face. Now it just looked old and scared. "But…how?"

He felt his father's hand grip his shoulder. "If they offer you a deal, you take it. You hear me? You take it."

He heard a loud click and the groan of metal hinges. His head whipped around in time to see two large guards enter the cell, pushing through the bodies, coming for him. Each one grabbed one of his arms and roughly jerked him to his feet.

"No! Dad!" he cried as they pulled him away.

"Dayat! You take it! Hear me? Take it!" His father's yells echoed off the cement walls as he was propelled down the hallway, deeper into the stomach of the beast that swallowed men whole and spent years digesting them till there was nothing left.

He wanted to ask where they were taking him, but no words came.

Other prisoners banged on the bars and called to him. "Hey, Pretty Boy! Why you dressed for a party?" He tried to tune them out by focusing on his father's face. His foot caught on something and he stumbled. A roar of laughter arose from the prisoners. The guard on his right jerked his arm up so hard he felt a shooting pain in his shoulder and cried out, inviting more mocking jeers.

Is a living death still martyrdom? He doubted it.

At the end of the hall it was quieter. They turned a corner, then passed a series of metal doors, no more bars. At the last door on the left, the guard turned a key in the lock and opened the door into a small, barren room. The light from the open door allowed Hidayat to glimpse a metal cot bolted to the back wall and the floor, with a metal squat toilet in the corner. The other guard unlocked his handcuffs and pushed him into the room.

The door closed. He was plunged into total darkness.

The rough floor hurt his hand. He must have skinned his palm when he fell. He thought about feeling his way to the cot, but what did it matter? Should he beat the door with his fists and scream curses into the silence? Should he break down and cry? Should he think of a way to kill himself? His brain was going numb, he couldn't even think in this darkness. If it weren't for the sound of his breathing, he wouldn't even be sure this was real.

Maybe if I hold my breath I'll no longer exist.

He sucked in a long breath and held it, listening. Ever so faintly, he could still hear the rhythm of inhale and exhale, inhale and exhale—but that was impossible! His ears strained to isolate the sound.

Something near the door scraped the floor. He was not alone.

Chapter 61

Instinctively Hidayat scrambled on all fours away from the noise till he banged his head on the metal cot. His breath came in loud pants now, but he couldn't control it.

Surrounded by darkness and nowhere to hide.

He wanted to know, no, he *needed* to know who or what was in the cell with him, but he couldn't find the courage to speak. He clung to the cot as though it were a shield, knowing full well there was no one and nothing that could protect him from what would happen next.

Maybe that sound had been his imagination. He had to get control over his breathing so he could listen once again. He wrestled with his fears to slow down his breathing and calm himself. When his breathing was normal, he tried holding it again and listening.

He stifled a cry when suddenly a voice spoke: "You've been a bad boy, Hidayat."

The voice was strong, supremely confident. But it was human, and that fact strangely brought the tiniest sense of relief.

The voice continued, "We know you're part of the terrorist cell that has just killed hundreds of people and is tearing apart our city. Your life now belongs to us. We can leave you here to rot, make you disappear from the earth, or publically execute you. What we choose depends on how you answer this question: why did you do it?"

Hidayat wasn't sure what the voice wanted him to answer, but the man was waiting for something. It probably didn't matter anyway. He felt all his anger dissipate, leaving him empty inside. His life was over.

"For justice."

No response. He tried again. "Okay, for revenge. What do you want me to say? Someone hurt my family and I wanted to hurt them back." He waited.

There was an angry edge to the voice this time that sent chills down his spine. "And did you succeed? Did you kill the man that destroyed your father in the night club bomb? Or did you kill him with the university bomb? Did you kill him in the plane crash?" The voice was rising to a dangerous pitch now. "Hundreds of dead bodies, people with their limbs blown off, children left staring at their headless parents, and where is the man you wanted to hurt? He's not even here. He's in Singapore on a business trip.

"You know what I should do with you? I should invite the parents, the brothers, the sisters, the children of all the people you hurt into this cell, one after another, here in the darkness you created, to take their own 'justice' on you however they want, for hour after hour, day after day without a break, until all the pain you've left them with is satisfied. Maybe we should chain up your father in here with you to witness what his son has done.

"And if there is anything left of you when they are finished, who is going to hurt the most then, huh? The Chinese businessman? No. He'll be fine. Who you've hurt the most is your father. And yourself."

Hidayat tried to swallow, but his mouth was too dry. He realized he'd made a terrible mistake. But what was there to say?

After a few moments, the voice continued, "What I'm about to say, you don't deserve, but I'm going to offer you a way out—"

"I'll take it," Hidayat interrupted. He'd ignored his father's counsel enough, he wasn't going to miss this one. "I don't care what I have to do, just tell me. I'll take it."

A beam of light shot out towards him and he blinked repeatedly. It was a cell phone. Then the cell phone angled upward showing the features of a tall man with short hair, some bruises on his face, but with a strong jaw. The man used the light to walk across the room and sit on the metal cot. Hidayat stayed on the floor. Something about the light gave him a flicker of hope.

"My name is Abdullah. I know that the group you joined is planning to kill more innocent people. I need your help to stop them. If your information helps us succeed, you will be rewarded. If we fail, may Allah have mercy on our city, and on your soul."

"I'll do it. I'll tell you everything."

"Start by telling me the names of every member of the group."

"Yeah, sure. There's Achmad, Khaliq, Rio, Baqri, Hafiz..." he hesitated to give his college buddy's name, but was too afraid to take the chance, "...and Amat."

"Good start. I'll expect much more from you shortly." The cell phone illuminated Abdullah's right hand extended towards him. Hidayat took it weakly. "Don't you want to know how you'll be rewarded?"

"It doesn't matter."

"Let me tell you anyway. If we succeed, I have received approval from the authorities to put your prison sentence on hold. Instead, you will join a new Center for Ending Violence to learn how *jihad* can be a peaceful force for good. If you graduate, all charges against you will be dropped."

Hidayat could hardly believe this. He was sure it couldn't be that easy. But it didn't matter; he was going to do what his father told him and take it.

Abdullah helped him stand up, then walked over to the door and rapped on it. He turned back to Hidayat.

"What's more, once you graduate, I'll get your father transferred to the Center with a good staff position, how about that?" Abdullah shined the cell phone light on his own smiling face.

"You can do that?" Hidayat was stunned.

A key turned in the lock and the door opened, flooding the cell with light.

Hidayat turned his back on the darkness and followed Abdullah to freedom.

Chapter 62

Hidayat's information led Abdullah to an internet café on Hasan Basri Street frequented by university students. One of Sergeant Eko's uniformed officers walked through the room to cover the back exit. Abdullah stood in the front doorway. The second officer loudly announced, "Identity Card check!" and went customer by customer checking their cards. The third one looked about ten years old. The cop cuffed him behind his ear and told him to get to school.

Abdullah had already spotted which one was Baqri. He was seated in the corner pretending to rummage through his backpack for an ID card Abdullah was sure would not be produced. He had the puffy, slicked-back hair in front, shaved on the sides, and wore expensive-looking clothes, just as Hidayat and Hafiz had described. Abdullah observed with a wry smile as the kid feigned forgetting his ID card to the officer. He nodded to the second policeman, who joined the conversation, and suddenly each had a grip on Baqri's arms propelling him to the door.

Outside, they pushed Baqri into the back seat of a police cruiser, then stood watch while Abdullah climbed in the car alongside him.

"Hey, what's the big deal? Just let me go home and get my card, and I'll bring it to the police station."

"Forget it, Baqri, that's not why I'm here."

"Then what?" the boy protested.

"This is about the bombs destroying our city and you and your friends who are behind them."

In the blink of an eye the blustering teenager was gone. When Baqri next spoke, he had the icy calm of a poker player.

"You're here because you need my help. Make me an offer."

Abdullah was taken aback, but recovered quickly. "How about I offer to hand you over to the CIA for your part in the airplane crash? Be nice to have the Americans owe me a favor. I hear Guantanamo Bay's beautiful this time of year." He waited for that to sink in.

"I don't know what you're talking about."

"Don't give me that crap. You hacked the radar station, Baqri, and caused the deaths of over three hundred people, including four Americans—"

"You can't prove that."

"I don't need proof. The Americans will lock you up for years without a trial. Your family, your girlfriend, they'll only know what I choose to tell them. Face it, Baqri, you're screwed."

Baqri's fingers drummed nervously on his knee.

"So why isn't this car moving? You got another offer coming?"

"That depends on you," Abdullah leaned in. "Tell me why you did it."

"Did what?"

"This isn't a game. The slim chance you avoid Guantanamo depends on how you answer this question. Tell me why."

"Is this the part where I tell you I need a lawyer?"

"The CIA doesn't believe in lawyers. They put their trust in years of repetitive torture. You've got one hope, and it's me. Answer my question satisfactorily and you'll have options; refuse, and no one will ever see you again."

"So there is an offer coming?"

Abdullah tried to be patient. "If I like what I hear."

Baqri frowned. His fingers drummed faster. Then he took a deep breath and shrugged. "What was the question?"

"Why did you do it?"

He pursed his lips, like he didn't want the words to slip out. But they did. "I need the money."

"For what?"

Baqri's face turned away. "My parents. My mom is sick." He paused, still facing the car window. "I didn't want to hack the radar. Achmad threatened to kill me if I didn't. He'll kill me now for talking to you."

"Look at me." Baqri turned back toward Abdullah. He looked pale, even nauseous. Abdullah hoped he wouldn't vomit in the police cruiser.

"That wasn't so hard, was it? So here's the offer. You help me bring down Achmad and the rest, and I keep you out of Guantanamo, even out of Indonesian prison. Instead, you will be placed in a new Center for Ending Violence. When you graduate, you'll have a job interview waiting for you at BIN, national intelligence. That job will pay you far more than enough to take care of your parents.

"Two of your comrades are already on our side. Now help us stop these attacks before this city goes up in civil war."

Baqri's forehead creased in thought. He studied his loafers. When he spoke, the confidence was back.

"I'll do whatever you ask on one condition. I want to be on a plane out of here before sundown. Achmad's called a meeting for tonight, and if I'm not there, he'll find me and kill me. Get me out of town and I'm all yours."

Abdullah smiled gently and extended his hand. Baqri took it.

"Tell me everything you know."

Chapter 63

Face lifted to heaven, hands reaching up to grasp the unseen, Sari slowly twirled in her worship dance. While she mouthed the words, "Heavens open, healing rain, washing over me again," she wiggled her fingers as her hands descended slowly, like raindrops from above. Those drops may have been symbolic, but the tears falling from her cheeks were real.

At the end of her silent song Sari collapsed on the floor. She was alone in David's house. David and Angelina had taken their baby Josie and Hafiz out on the front porch. Sari had seized the opportunity to do what she always did when she was sad, or scared, or lonely, or a host of other things—she danced. When she was done, she didn't always feel better, but she always felt a deep assurance that *God sees.*

Abdullah was out there somewhere risking his life and here she was hiding indoors. Oh how she wished she had the courage to get out there and do something—*anything*—to help him!

She pulled out the scrap of paper with the words of Jesus she was meditating on that week: "*You're blessed when you get your inside world—your mind and heart—put right. Then you can see God in the outside world.*"

The outside world…were her mind and heart ready to try again?

Today is my day. God, help me, I'm going to walk out that door, down the street, until I find another human being to talk to.

She stood up slowly, took a deep breath, noticed her heart pounding even faster than when she'd been dancing, but put one foot in front of the other until she was standing in the front doorway.

"Hi Sari," Angelina called. "Want to join us?"

Sari flashed a smile, but didn't answer, keeping her focus on the gate up ahead. Step by step she crossed the small yard, then slid open the gate and stepped onto the asphalt. For a moment a wave of nausea threatened, but she prayed again and willed herself to start walking down the alley.

Up ahead two children were playing badminton with no net, watched by a young woman with a baby on her hip. Sari stood next to her.

"Hello, I'm Sari," she began. "What a cute baby!"

"You want to hold him?" the woman handed the baby to Sari without waiting for an answer. As Sari held out her hands to take him, she noticed there was no shaking. She smiled.

"What's his name?"

"Cecep. That's his older sister playing badminton, Citra. They live down there at number forty-four." She pointed out the girl and the house. "I'm their maid. Are you Pak David's family?"

"No, just a friend staying with him for a while. What's your name?"

"U'us. Is that your husband?" She pointed at Hafiz.

Sari laughed. "No, just a friend."

"He's handsome." U'us pulled her long hair back behind her ear.

Sari laughed again, and was delighted to see the baby responded by laughing too. "Come meet him." She started walking back to David's porch and U'us timidly followed.

"Cecep! Come play with Josie." Angelina motioned for them to join the group. She moved aside some glasses of iced tea, and Sari set Cecep down facing Josie. He flapped his chubby arms with pleasure and everyone laughed.

Sari was surprised to see how easily Hafiz was interacting with David, Angelina and Josie. It looked like their love was beginning to win him over.

U'us was staring at Hafiz from the bottom step. Sari pulled her hand to climb the steps and sit on the porch, then went inside to get her a glass of tea. When she came back, David and Angelina were trying hard to contain their laughter, while U'us was blushing and wouldn't look at Hafiz.

"Hafiz! What did you say to her?" Sari demanded.

"Nothing!" Hafiz shrugged innocently. "I just said the baby looks like her."

Now Sari had to stifle a laugh. She gently corrected him. "It's not her baby."

"Oh," was all the embarrassed boy could squeak out.

Somehow Cecep had gotten his face low enough to put Josie's foot in his mouth, causing a panicked expression on Josie's face. Angelina moved to break up this budding romance. Sari absorbed the scene—Muslims and Christians, rich and poor, old and young, enjoying life together. This was what would be lost if the jihadists succeeded in plunging the nation into sectarian violence. This was why Abdullah *had to win.*

Sari excused herself and went back inside. She needed to pray. Abdullah hadn't checked in all afternoon, and she felt keenly a struggle between life and death over the city, with Abdullah at the center of the storm.

She knelt by the couch and began to intercede with God. She prayed for each of the terrorists by name, that God would cause them to see things in a new way. She prayed for peace for her city. Most of all, she prayed for the man who had become her adopted father. Her city needed to experience the father-heart of God, and this was the man God had chosen for the hour.

Abdullah had to win.

Chapter 64

"Lani! It's me, Amat! I need to talk to you!" Though he spoke with urgency, Amat tried to keep his tone pleading, non-threatening. A face peeked through the curtains and Amat held up both hands to show he held no weapon.

The door swung open to Lani's warm smile. "Come on in."

"Uncle Surya is on his way here to kill you! You've got to get out of here now!"

Lani put her hand on his arm. "Relax, Mat. He's not coming."

"But—what do you mean?" he stammered.

"My mom texted me just five minutes ago. Uncle Surya called her from the police station to bail him out. He just got arrested for gambling. My mom told Uncle Surya it would take her some time to collect the money, but she told me she has no intention of bailing him out."

Amat breathed a sigh of relief and collapsed onto a brown batik-cloth sofa. "*Alhamdulillah!*" he exclaimed, eyes turned heavenward. Lani sat down next to him. She seemed so calm. If he knew someone was out to kill him, he'd be a wreck.

That reminded him of Khaliq and his appointment that evening.

Lani was talking. He pushed Khaliq out of his mind and brought his focus back to her.

"...how important religion is to you, but you haven't rejected me. That means a lot."

"Yeah, sure, Lani. I'm still worried about Uncle Surya though. He'll find a way to get out, and then he'll start hunting you down again. You need to leave town for a while. Do you have anywhere safe to go? Do you have any money?"

"I'm not afraid," Lani answered.

"Think about your mom. You want her crying at your funeral next week, never getting to see you get married and have her grandkids? This isn't just about you, Lani. Think about those who care about you."

Lani seemed to be mulling this over. Finally she reached a decision.

"I see your point. Before I go home and pack, I need to stop at an ATM machine and one other place. Will you take me?"

It was already 4:30, but he could probably squeeze it in before meeting Achmad and the others. He had wondered how he should spend his last day on earth. If he could ensure Lani escaped death, maybe Allah would count that as *amal*, credit to balance out his sins. Just in case his martyrdom didn't go as planned, he'd need as many good deeds tallied up as possible.

"Let's go."

After collecting a thick wad of cash from the ATM, Amat followed Lani's directions till he pulled up in front of the police station.

Confused, Amat protested, "Why are we here?"

"Come with me and see." Lani smiled.

"I don't know…" Amat nervously held back.

"What?" Lani queried. "Done something illegal this week?" She punched him playfully. He tried to smile.

If you only knew.

It took a few minutes for them to find the officer in charge. He was a large man, both tall and round, and every sentence he spoke sounded like he was interrogating them.

"What are you doing here?" he rasped, staring at them through suspicious eyes.

"I've come to bail out a man arrested for gambling this afternoon, Surya Salahudin."

"What?" Amat cried, grabbing Lani's shoulder and spinning her toward him. "Are you out of your mind?"

She smiled. "Trust me." Then she turned back to the officer. "How much is the bail?"

The officer looked her up and down, frowning. "You don't look like his family."

"I'm his niece."

The big man shuffled some papers till he found one with Surya's name. "This says bail is set at ten million rupiah." Amat wondered if that number was really written somewhere or if the officer had pulled it out of the air. His father had told him once that most problems with the law could be settled with an envelope of money at the police station before ever going to trial. But that was the old days. Indonesia was trying hard to clean up its reputation for corruption. Amat wasn't sure the police did that anymore.

While he was lost in thought, Lani had already begun negotiating. "I believe this is his first offense. He didn't hurt anyone. Look, I brought three million rupiah with me." She pulled some money out of her purse and started counting it.

"Gambling is a serious offense. Bail is never set lower than six million for gambling." The cop leaned over the counter trying to gauge how much money was in the purse.

Lani put her purse on the table and took all the cash out. "All I have is five million. If I have to go borrow another million from my cousins, I'm sure I could get it, but not until tomorrow morning. Will you be on duty then?" Lani turned her innocent brown eyes pleadingly toward him.

The cop's eyes were riveted to the money. "I guess for a first offense I could let him off with five million." He held out his hand. Lani pulled the money back a few inches.

"If you don't mind, sir, could I please see you sign the release first?" She smiled sweetly.

He looked away from the money with a grunt, then fiddled around on his desk till he found the right form, signed it, and called a junior officer. "Bring out this guy," he commanded, handing him the form. As soon as the junior had exited, he held out his hand for the money.

"Thank you, sir." Lani handed him the money. Amat watched it go straight into an envelope and into a drawer. No receipt was offered or requested.

All that was left was to wait for Uncle Surya. Amat figured his uncle couldn't kill Lani in the police station, but he never knew what the guy might do.

"Let me talk to Uncle Surya first," he told Lani. "Stay behind me."

A few moments later their uncle emerged, brash and cocky as usual. He saw Amat from across the room.

"You're like my own son! Let's get out of here."

Amat stepped toward him. "Uncle, I didn't bail you out. Lani did." He pointed behind him to where Lani was waiting. Uncle Surya stopped dead in his tracks, glaring at her. Amat stayed between them, and kept talking. "I told her to take her money and leave town. She brought all her savings here instead to get you out of jail. Nobody in your whole family showed up to help you but her. They would have all let you rot in jail. She's the kindest family you have." Amat got right up in his uncle's face and spoke quietly but firmly. "She lives, Uncle, she lives."

As he watched, the angry lines in his uncle's face softened. He blinked rapidly, looking from Amat to Lani. It felt like he even shrunk a couple inches there before Amat.

Then, with his eyes still over Amat's shoulder looking at Lani, Uncle Surya answered. "She lives."

Chapter 65

"**P**astor Chris!" David exclaimed. "So nice of you to drop by."
Hafiz looked up at the man approaching the porch, then ducked his head. He recognized the man immediately. It was the pastor whose church had been burned down. Would he recognize Hafiz as one of those in the crowd?

"Hi, David, Angelina," the pastor climbed the steps and hugged them both, then kissed the top of Josie's head. "And who is this?" He smiled and stretched his hand toward Hafiz.

"Just a friend," Hafiz answered, shaking his hand while looking at the ground.

"I came with some bad news." The pastor turned back to David. Relieved, Hafiz slipped behind Angelina and played with Josie.

"Please sit down." David motioned with his hand and they all sat again on the porch. "What is it?"

"Remember the church leaders you and Pak Abdullah spoke with? Two of them—the lawyer and the doctor—have decided to go ahead with a slew of lawsuits. Our chairman doesn't agree with them, but said he won't stop them. I know pastors shouldn't use this kind of language, but they're idiots. Here I am trying to rebuild trust with our neighbors and they're tearing it down faster than I can build it."

"I'm so sorry. I thought they really took what Pak Abdullah said to heart."

"I had hoped so too." The pastor took a deep breath and sighed. Hafiz had never imagined sitting on a porch together listening to a pastor share his troubles, much less hearing him share about all the trouble Hafiz had caused him. The last couple weeks had felt like he was in an action movie where he had thought he was the star, but it turned out he played only a minor character likely to die before the end.

"But I guess all is not lost," the pastor continued with a smile. "Today I took the bicycle of one of the little boys who died in the church fire to his best friend, a little Muslim boy named Adi who lives nearby. The kid was thrilled, shouting, 'Peter's bike!' as he rode circles around me." He chuckled. "Although his older brother, Amat, looked like he'd seen a ghost. Little Adi asked him, 'Why do you hate Christians so much?' right in front of me, can you imagine?" He laughed again, and David laughed too.

"You weren't offended, were you?" David asked.

"Of course not…." The pastor kept talking, but Hafiz wasn't listening. There were thousands of Amats in Banjarmasin. There's no way this could be… He had to know for sure.

"Excuse me," he interrupted. Everyone looked at him and his face turned red. "Did you say, 'Amat'?"

"Yes."

"Can I ask what he looked like?"

"He looked like a college kid, soccer jersey, modern haircut, nice-looking boy."

"Was it a Real Madrid jersey? Was he driving a brand new blue Shogun?"

The pastor looked taken aback, but replied, "Actually, I think it was a Madrid shirt, and there was a shiny blue motorcycle next to him. It might have been a Shogun."

Hafiz looked at David. "We have to call Pak Abdullah. I think we've found one of the…you know…" He raised his eyebrows and clamped his mouth shut.

David excused himself and stepped inside the house to make the call, but quickly returned with the news that Abdullah wasn't answering his cell phone.

"We got to do something!" Hafiz implored. "These guys are experts at disappearing. If we know where one is, we need to grab him fast!"

"What are you talking about?" the pastor asked. No one answered. Finally David asked him to wait on the porch for a moment while he and Hafiz consulted with Sari inside.

After a quick discussion, it was agreed that they needed Hafiz to confirm this was the correct Amat without being seen and spooking him. Chris would take David to the door and introduce him. Hafiz would be watching from down the street. He would call David's cell phone—one ring to confirm, two rings meant the wrong guy. It would be David's job to somehow talk Amat into meeting Abdullah.

Once they had a plan, Hafiz commented, "I'm surprised you're willing to get involved in this, Pak David. If things go badly, they could come after you too."

"Don't forget, if things go well, we could save a lot of people's lives," David countered.

Hafiz just shook his head. Sari said a quick prayer for them and sent them off.

Fortunately Pastor Chris was willing to help, no questions asked. Hafiz rode in the pastor's van, David on his motorcycle.

As they drove off, disturbing thoughts raced through Hafiz's mind. *What if Khaliq is watching Amat's place? What if it's a trap? Or what if he's watching us right now, leaving the girls helpless behind us?*

Is there any way this movie gets a happy ending—one with me still alive to see it?

Chapter 66

"*Allaaahu Akbar, Allaaaaaaahu Akbar.*" The *adzhan* had just started blaring from the mosque speakers calling the faithful to their sundown prayers when Amat heard the knock at his door.

"Adi, go see who's at the door," he instructed. Amat needed to pray. He needed Allah's help to tell his parents good-bye and walk out that door in a few minutes for possibly the last time. He slipped into his bedroom and took his *sejadah* off a shelf, unrolling the small carpet next to his bed. He had just assumed his standing position facing Mecca when Adi burst into the bedroom.

"It's the bicycle guy. He wants to talk to you."

"Tell him I'm praying."

Adi took his hand and pulled him off the prayer rug. "Come on, older brother."

Amat gave in. He followed Adi through the empty living room toward the door. His mother was already doing her *sholat* in her own bedroom. Amat was never sure where his father was, maybe off to Jakarta again?

He was surprised to see two men at the door. "Can I help you?"

"It's Amat, right?" the older one began. He nodded. "I'm Chris, I met you earlier today. My friend David here really wants to meet you." Amat shook David's hand. "I need to be going. Bye, Adi!" The older man waved at Adi, then walked away.

Amat couldn't help but be suspicious. "What's this about?"

David smiled. "Please, this will only take a few minutes. But perhaps it's best the two of us speak on the porch." David glanced at Adi.

"Go inside, Adi," Amat said. He closed the front door and they sat on dirty white plastic chairs on the porch.

David leaned forward, elbows on knees, fingers intertwined, and spoke softly. "I'm here to tell you that if you want a way out, there's a way out." Then he sat back and waited.

Amat tried to keep from jumping out of his skin. *How does this guy know exactly what I'm thinking? A way out…if only. Achmad had made it clear time and time again, the only way out was death.* His eyes began to blur. He turned his head and blinked rapidly, bombarded by panicky thoughts. *Who is this guy? What if it's a trap? What can I say that won't give myself away?*

Almost unconsciously his hand drifted toward his cell phone. *I could call Achmad. Or maybe that's exactly what he wants.*

No, he had to face this man alone.

The man looked unarmed. He scanned the neighborhood for signs that he was surrounded and saw no one. He gave David a searching gaze. This was one smiley, cool-headed pro, or a naïve fool about to die.

He had to say something.

"Uh, I'm not sure what you're talking about. Who are you again?"

"My name's David. I'm a friend. I'm not with the police or anything like that. But I have a friend who helps people facing impossible situations like you're facing, and helps them get out before it's too late."

"What are you talking about?" Amat needed to stall until he could figure out what was going on.

"Look," David leaned in again and spoke in hushed tones. "I know you have a meeting tonight. If you go, hundreds of people will die, maybe even you or someone you love. You don't have to go. Come with me. My friend will arrange protection for you and explain a way out of this mess."

Amat wiped the sweat from his forehead. *This guy knows everything! We're screwed.*

Or could it be possible that there is a way out?

He looked through the front window at Adi, playing with a toy car on the coffee table. Did he really want to leave Adi and his parents? Was *jihad* going to make a better life for them as he'd been taught?

He sprang out of the chair and started pacing on the porch, confused. This was decision time, the point of no return. He would go to the meeting tonight ready to become a martyr and tomorrow enjoy the pleasures of heaven. Or he could follow this stranger down an unknown path with a vague promise that tomorrow he'd still be alive.

Lani's face popped into his mind. She wasn't afraid to die for what she believed in. So why was he?

Or is the problem that I no longer believe?

Achmad's face came next, then Khaliq's. They'd kill him if he tried to walk away.

Uncle Surya's face appeared, murderous, calling for executions. Then it changed to the shocked face he'd seen at the police station when Lani paid his debt and set him free.

Too many faces…he was losing his own. *Who is Amat, anyway?*

And what path should I choose?

Chapter 67

"**M**ake the call."

Abdullah sat in the back of an unmarked sedan with Baqri, the two cops now wearing street clothes seated up front. They were parked on Kolonel Sugiono Street, just outside Losmen Tokyo, a seedy little motel where Baqri was supposed to pick up Rio for tonight's meeting. Abdullah seemed to recall this motel being a center of drugs and prostitution fifteen years ago. Now they were serving terrorists planning to blow up the city.

Baqri opted to text that he was waiting outside.

Soon a middle-aged man emerged. He squinted through his glasses left and right searching for Baqri. Abdullah understood why it was so hard to track a terrorist in Indonesia—250 million people, and nearly all the men looked like someone who was your doctor, your child's teacher, or the guy who picked up your trash. No one would ever suspect the hands that now held a newspaper had just assembled a bomb.

Baqri nodded and the two cops headed toward Rio. A few paces away Rio realized something was wrong and started walking quickly away. One of the cops yelled at him to stop. For a moment Abdullah thought Rio was going to run. But he slowed, then stopped, turning slowly to face them, hands in clear view.

Abdullah started to climb out of the car, but Baqri objected, "Wait! Don't leave me here alone!"

"Don't worry, I'll send one of the cops back to guard you."

Clearly Baqri was terrified of Khaliq. Abdullah's eyes quickly swept the scene for anything out of place as he approached Rio.

Rio stood silently, shoulders sagging, a cop at each elbow.

"My name is Abdullah. I've been looking forward to meeting you, Rio."

No answer.

Abdullah didn't want to talk to Rio in the car with Baqri. He spied an empty police post across the street. The patrolmen were probably at the nearby mosque for the *Mahgrib* prayers. He told one of Eko's men to stay with Baqri in the car, then crossed the street with Rio between the other cop and him.

They sat on hard wooden benches facing each other while the cop stood at the front of the post.

"Rio, we know you were on your way to a meeting tonight with Achmad and the others. You're not going to make that meeting. I'm here to offer you a choice.

"There is a long list of bombings all across Indonesia for which you'll have to stand trial. You will be convicted to life in prison or death." He paused. Rio showed absolutely no reaction. "Or you can help us stop the attacks tonight, and give us information on other *jihad* cells around the country, and we will treat you well. You may even be able to avoid a trial altogether."

Abdullah paused again.

"Come on, Rio, aren't you tired of the endless cycle of death? I'm offering you a chance to put it all behind you."

Finally, Rio spoke. "Sorry, you've got the wrong guy. May I smoke?" He took a pack of cigarettes out of his shirt pocket. Abdullah nodded, and Rio calmly lit up, blowing the smoke out slowly through his nostrils. After three such puffs, he asked, "Are you arresting me, or can I go now?"

Abdullah pulled out his cell phone and scrolled to a phone number Joko had provided him, then dialed the number. A woman's voice answered.

"Hi, this is Abdullah. Remember I told you I'd try to get him on the phone for you? Here he is." He handed the phone to Rio, who took it nonchalantly. "Yeah?"

"Is it really you, honey?" the woman said. Abdullah could also hear precisely what he'd asked to hear—two children's voices calling loudly, "Hi, Daddy! Are you coming home?"

Rio's whole body stiffened, then began to shake. The voices continued through the phone.

"Answer them," Abdullah gently nudged.

Then he stood and walked out of the police post to wait with the policeman.

Traffic was light, as usual during the prayers. A teenage boy came flying around the corner on his motorbike with no helmet. He glanced up, startled to see anyone at the police post, but the cop just gave him a glare and let him go on his way.

The prayers were coming to an end at the Agung Mosque. He could hear the final words, "*Assalamu alaikum warahmatullah, Assalamu alaikum warahmatullah,*" the pronouncement of peace upon those on your right and on your left. *If only that practice could make it out of the mosque and into the world.*

He waited a couple more minutes, then reentered the police post. He could hear the quiver in Rio's voice as he said, "I gotta go...Yes, I miss you too. Good-bye."

Abdullah sat down and took back the phone. Rio looked down at the floor. "Why did you do that?" he asked Abdullah.

"When I was young I left my wife—she was pregnant with my oldest son but I didn't find out until almost a month after he was born—and joined the *mujahidin* in Afghanistan. Now nearly twenty years later, I look at what that decision cost me. My youngest son died in *jihad.* My wife left me because of it. My oldest son was killed by someone in your cell. I brought this plague of death to my family, and now I'm sentenced to a life without them.

"I just don't want that for you."

Rio poked at some trash on the floor with his sandal. "Believe me, I know how this ends. Stay or leave, I'll die. Better to die as a *syahidin* than as a coward."

"Help me save this country from destruction, and I'll make sure you see your wife and children's faces again."

Rio picked up the smoldering cigarette again and took a long drag. "I'm not saying I'll help you. But know this—as long as my leaders are alive, I'm probably a dead man for even talking to you. You'd best lock me up in your most secure cell to keep them away from me. After they're dead, I'll consider your offer."

"I could really use your help to capture them."

Rio snorted. "Capture them? Not going to happen. Killing them is the only way to stop them."

He stood, dropping his cigarette and smashing it under his sandal. Then he stretched out his wrists. "Let's go."

Chapter 68

The peaceful scene below him did nothing to soothe Achmad's highly agitated demeanor. As he gazed down from the upper window of an abandoned logging warehouse, he could see the Banjaraya night fish market just beginning to stir. The first of the food vendors was setting up his stall, anticipating a crowd of customers that would peak closer to midnight as the catches of fresh fish would arrive at the dock below.

He looked at his watch again. It was ten past eight, and none of the group had arrived on time but Khaliq, who he'd put on watch on the opposite side of the warehouse. Achmad turned from the window and called out quietly to his partner.

"See anything?"

"They're not coming," Khaliq answered.

"They're coming," Achmad retorted. "Or I'll kill every last one of them myself. We're so close…"

He glanced down at the four Styrofoam ice chests favored by fish merchants, now stored under a table in the corner. Four suicide bomb vests. Four bombs that needed to go off tomorrow morning right after his.

"Why are you here, anyway? I told you not to come unless Hafiz and Abdullah were dead. Why aren't you out there finishing your assignment?"

"I told you, they're on the run. I thought you might need me here."

Achmad glared at Khaliq. "On the run is not DEAD!" He struggled to keep his voice down. "They should be dead! And if you can't take care of that, we're finished. Now get out of here! I'll wait for the others alone."

"But I got a bad feeling…"

"Shut up! They'll come. Go do your job."

Both men turned back to the windows. Everything looked as before. Khaliq climbed down the scaffolding and headed for the door under Achmad's window where he paused and looked up.

"It's clear. Go!"

Khaliq turned the doorknob and swung the door outward. At that moment Achmad noticed the man who was setting up a food stall let go of the tie-down rope and lunged for something under a tarp. Out of the corner of his eye he caught a slight movement in the trees to his left as well.

"Get back!" he yelled. Khaliq jerked his body back from the doorway just as a spray of bullets peppered where he'd been standing. The explosions from the shots echoed around the empty building.

Achmad cursed. They'd been sold out.

He whipped out his Beretta, broke the glass, and put a bullet through the fake food vendor's head, then fired a few shots into the trees, and before anyone could fire back, he leaped from the scaffolding to the floor and scrambled up the scaffolding on the other side. Shadows in the darkness were moving towards the building. He broke that window and fired a round randomly, chasing the shadows into cover. Then he leaped to the floor where Khaliq was waiting.

"We're surrounded. We're going to lose the bombs." Achmad cursed vehemently.

"Khaliq can take them," the giant offered.

"You fool. That's the Detachment 88 out there. The best we can hope for is to blow a few of them up."

He ripped the lid off one of the ice chests and pulled out a suicide bomb vest.

"Take the lids off those ice chests." Khaliq obeyed.

They could hear sporadic fire toward the windows above them and the front door. Achmad piled the vests one on top of the other. Then he led Khaliq to a trapdoor. The warehouse was built over the edge of the river so that logging boats could pull up alongside and deliver their goods. The trapdoor allowed wood scraps to be swept back into the river.

"Can you swim?" Achmad asked Khaliq.

The big man nodded. Achmad secured his pistol in his belt, gave a desperately longing look in the direction of the bombs, then motioned for Khaliq to drop quietly into the water. Achmad held the trapdoor open until he, too, was in the water.

"On the count of three, we go under and swim with the current to the south," he whispered. He lowered the trapdoor and began dialing one of the throwaway cell phones Baqri had provided, while he counted: "One...two..."

On "three" he pushed CALL and ducked under the water.

Chapter 69

Back at David's house, Abdullah sat on the living room floor drinking a glass of warm tea, with the bullet-proof vest Detachment 88 had loaned him propped up behind him to lean back on, and pondered what to do next. Angelina had left them to put Josie to bed a few minutes before ten o'clock. David, Hafiz, Sari and Amat had been spellbound by Abdullah's story of the botched capture and ensuing bomb blast.

"But did they find the bodies?" Hafiz asked.

"So far they've found no body parts, but there is a lot of rubble to dig through," Abdullah answered.

Hafiz looked knowingly at Amat. "They're still alive." Amat nodded. Abdullah thought they both looked a little pale at the thought.

"Yes, we should assume for now that they're still alive." Abdullah was frustrated. "Those Special Forces guys spooked them. I told them to let me go in first and try to talk to Achmad, but they wouldn't listen."

"Achmad probably would have killed you," Amat said.

"Or have Khaliq do it," added Hafiz.

"But look where the violence has gotten us now—another bombing, and our one chance where we knew Achmad's location wasted. How are we going to find him now?"

"Maybe since Detachment 88 is here he'll run away," Sari interjected hopefully.

"You know him best, Amat," Abdullah prodded. "What will he do next?"

"He'll follow orders."

"Whose orders?"

"I don't know. But I've seen him checking with someone on his cell phone. If he's still got assignments to do, he'll do them. But I don't know what—we were supposed to find out the next assignment at tonight's meeting."

"Where would he go to hide out?" Abdullah asked.

"I don't know where he stays. We always met in a different place—could be an abandoned place like tonight, or in a public place in broad daylight."

Abdullah took a drink of the warm tea. He was exhausted, and sore from the tumble he took when the warehouse blew up. But there seemed only one option left.

"I'll have to draw him out. He wants me dead. I just need a way to let him know where I am… Amat, dial his number and let me talk to him."

"Bapak, no!" Sari protested.

"I'll arrange to meet him, and take Eko's men as backup."

"Ha!" Hafiz slapped his thigh. "Detachment 88 gets their butts whipped, and you want to try again with regular cops? You're delusional!"

"He's right, Abdullah," David said gently.

"Dial the phone, Amat."

Everyone sat in stunned silence as Amat dialed. After two rings, a strange look crossed Amat's face and he hung up.

"It said, 'the number you have dialed is no longer in service.'"

Abdullah would have loved to punch something, but didn't have the energy. He stared at the ceiling. *A little help here, God?*

His phone rang. It was Joko. "I heard what happened."

"Then you heard we lost them. They're still out there, Pak Joko. What am I supposed to do?"

"Look, in a few minutes a military plane will touch down at Syamsuddin Noor Airport with more Detachment 88 personnel and two CIA experts. You've done well, Abdullah. I heard you were able to turn Hidayat, that's something." He sighed. "Our experiment was worth a try."

"Actually, Baqri and Amat have seen the light as well."

"Wonderful! Well done, my friend, well done. Make sure they're at the airport before the military plane takes off at midnight. I'll have the three of them kept in a secure location until your boss Pak Ramadani gets his rehab center set up, and they'll be part of his first class.

"For now, just stay out of harm's way and pray Detachment 88 can find these two without tearing apart the city."

David kindly offered to take Amat to the airport, and Abdullah reluctantly accepted.

As Amat said his good-byes, Abdullah held out his hand. "Amat, I still can't believe David found you and brought you here! I was afraid we'd lost you. And I'm so glad you accepted my offer. You had a part in creating this nightmare. Now is your chance to have a part in saving lives, in saving our nation, through understanding rather than violence."

Amat shook Abdullah's hand. "Yes, sir. But I still have one question—why would you risk your life to save all those people you don't even know?"

Sari answered for him. "He risked his life to save you, Amat, to save you."

Chapter 70

The *ding-ding-ding* of the *bubur* cart passing by the window woke Hafiz the next morning. His back was sore from sleeping on the floor, and the dreams of Khaliq coming for him had made it a restless night. He lumbered to the bathroom and splashed some water on his face. The cut above his eye was leaving an intimidating scar, perfect if he wanted to pursue a life of violence, but he wasn't so sure that's what he wanted any more.

What do you want, Hafiz?

The image in the mirror looked lost and confused. He dragged himself to the breakfast table where everyone else was waiting.

Angelina had bought *bubur* for everyone. Hafiz examined the bowl of steaming hot rice porridge, with its shredded chicken, duck egg and cilantro sprinkled on top, wary of any pork the Christians might try to sneak into it. It looked pretty normal, so he grabbed a spoon and dug in.

"Ohhh, hot!" He'd burned his tongue. Sari laughed at his contorted face. Abdullah barely noticed. He looked like he'd slept even less than Hafiz, with bloodshot eyes and sagging shoulders. Hafiz wondered if Abdullah would take Joko's advice or not. He would bet a pack of Marlboros Abdullah would not.

David called them all to attention. "Usually in our house we pray before we eat. Would that be okay with you?" Abdullah nodded. Hafiz shrugged. Then David took Angelina's hand on his left and Sari's hand on his right. Sari reached out and grabbed Hafiz's hand. At first he jerked away, but he saw Abdullah accepting Angelina's hand and reaching for Hafiz too. Pak Abdullah gave him *the look* he'd seen so many times in the classroom. Hafiz rolled his eyes and accepted holding Abdullah's and Sari's hands.

These Christians are so weird.

Then David closed his eyes and prayed. "Dear Lord, we're grateful to be alive and safe. We thank you for bringing Amat and two others back to the light. Today we pray your help and protection on Pak Abdullah to find these other two lost souls. Have mercy on them, and on our city. Bless this food we're about to eat. Amen."

Abdullah and Sari echoed the "Amen," but Hafiz didn't. Even back in his school days he'd known Pak Abdullah was a different kind of Muslim, but this, this was going too far. He let go of Sari's hand and wiped his hand on his jeans, then dug into the *bubur* once again.

"So Abdullah," David began, "do you have a plan?"

"I need to find Achmad and Khaliq before Detachment 88 does," Abdullah answered. "I spent much of the night trying to imagine how, but I just don't know where to look."

"Why can't you let Detachment 88 handle it?" Angelina prodded.

"I'm just afraid of a shootout where innocent civilians get caught in the crossfire." Abdullah glanced around the group. "Do any of you have an idea how to flush them out?"

"We'd have to be able to communicate with them," Hafiz said. "Without a cell phone connection, I don't know how. Do they watch TV? Listen to radio? With Detachment 88 everywhere, if I were them, I'd be holed up where no one would find me."

"God will make a way," Sari interjected.

Abdullah took a deep breath, then started eating his *bubur*. A part of Hafiz wished he could help the old man finish his quest. He was a pretty amazing guy, in spite of his questionable friendships. But another part of him…

"It will be hard for those two guys to get around town," David added between bites. "Last night I had to go through several check points to get to the airport and back. The police are everywhere."

"I hope none of the local fundamentalists react by attacking the police, like I heard is happening in Makassar and Banda Aceh," Angelina said.

Hafiz imagined that he'd never joined the *jihad* cell. Would he be in the streets protesting police brutality against Muslims? Maybe. He still wasn't sure who were the true good guys and bad guys in this world—and which side he was on.

As people finished their breakfast, Angelina began clearing away the dishes helped by Sari. Abdullah stayed at the table, drumming his fingers. David looked at him sympathetically.

"Be patient, my friend. God will tell you what to do."

Hafiz rolled his eyes again and was about to leave the table when Abdullah's phone rang. Hafiz sat back down and scooted close enough to eavesdrop.

"Hello?" Abdullah answered.

"Pak Guru, this is Fani." Hafiz could hear the high-pitched voice of his former classmate, but it sounded higher than usual. "Pak Ardiansyah and I are in trouble. Can you help us?"

"What kind of trouble, Fani? Where are you?"

A different voice spoke through the phone, much lower in pitch, and ice cold in tone. "We have the professor and the boy. We want to make a trade. Bring the traitor Hafiz to the professor's home in one hour and these two will live. If you're late, or if you bring any police, they'll both die."

Click. The line was disconnected. Abdullah turned to Hafiz, who was shaking. "You heard?" he asked.

Eyes wide, Hafiz nodded slightly. He stood slowly, the room starting to spin around him. He needed to get out of there before Abdullah tied him up like one of the cows sacrificed at *Idul Adha.*

His eyes searched the room wildly until he spotted his salvation—Abdullah's motorbike keys. He grabbed them and pushed his way out the door. Hands trembling, he started the bike, nearly clipping the open gate on his way to the alley. Then he was on the main street heading north. He'd leave town, go to Palangkaraya, where there was no unrest. Detachment 88 could deal with Khaliq. He never wanted to see Khaliq, Achmad, the pork-eater David, or that lunatic idealist Abdullah ever again.

Chapter 71

PAK JOKO, ACHMAD AND KHALIQ HAVE TWO HOSTAGES THEY WANT TO TRADE FOR HAFIZ AND ME—WHAT SHOULD I DO?

Abdullah looked down at his text message and hit SEND. He was in over his head and he knew it.

After twenty minutes he got his answer: TELL DETACHMENT 88, LET THEM HANDLE IT. STAY SOMEWHERE SAFE. IT'LL BE OVER SOON. He read it twice, shook his head, and told the others, "It's time to go." David handed over his motorcycle keys with a knowing sadness in his eyes. Angelina gave him a hug. Sari's tears as she held him tightly began to weaken his resolve, and he had to gently pry her hands off of him. When he closed the door he saw the three of them holding hands again in prayer.

As Abdullah sped across town to the university, his thoughts were racing too.

Once again, I'm on my own. What resources do I have? So far threats and persuasion have been enough. But with these two? He remembered his own words to Hafiz: "The only way to stop Khaliq is to kill him."

Joko's ideals of non-violence might work on some, but will I be ready to kill again if that's what I have to do to save this city?

How did they find his connection to Ardiansyah? How would they respond when he showed up without Hafiz? He couldn't blame Hafiz for running.

He heard Sari's prayers in his mind, and thought he'd add his own: *Ya Allah, nothing I can do will atone for all my sins. But answer the prayers of that pure-hearted girl. Have mercy on me.*

As he passed through the gate into the IAIN campus, there were no students anywhere. Probably with all the bombs, they'd closed the school.

He thought he glimpsed a large figure—Khaliq?—hidden in some trees on his left. *Watching for police, most likely.* If he stayed put, that meant there was only Achmad to deal with at Ardi's.

Abdullah imagined every scenario he could think of to sneak up on Achmad and disarm him, but the slightest flaw in his plan could get Ardi or Fani killed. His terrorist days were too far behind him. He wasn't a killer any more. He'd have to talk his way through this and hope for a miracle.

Abdullah knocked on the door, then called out loudly, "It's Abdullah. I'm unarmed. I'm coming in." He pushed the door open, and with hands raised, slowly made his way through Ardi's house until he found them in the study.

Ardi and Fani were sitting in the two wooden chairs facing Ardi's large desk. They were not tied up, but might as well have been they were so frozen with fear. Achmad leaned against the desk facing them. As Abdullah entered, he saw the pistol move from Ardi to him.

Achmad smiled. "The teacher comes to save the pupil. Now where is the traitor, Hafiz?" Achmad leaned to look behind Abdullah into the hallway. Abdullah stepped to his right away from the hostages and nearer Achmad, revealing that he was alone.

Immediately Achmad's demeanor changed. "What? You didn't bring Hafiz? I told you to bring Hafiz!" He jumped forward and pointed the gun at Abdullah's pelvis. "If I don't like your answers, you'll leave here only half a man."

"Hafiz left town. He—"

"Liar!" Achmad shouted. "Khaliq saw him at your house! Now where is he?" He took a step closer, the gun now just three feet away from Abdullah's waist. He tried to ignore it and keep eye contact with Achmad.

"You have me. Why don't you let these two go? They're good Muslims who don't belong in this struggle between us."

"If you had brought Hafiz, maybe I would have made a trade for both of them," Achmad sneered. "But since you only offer yourself, I guess I don't need one of them."

He pointed his gun at Fani, who whimpered. Then he pointed it at Ardiansyah. The professor murmured indignantly, "You'll regret this."

"Got a coin, Teacher? Flip it for me. Heads, the boy dies; tails, the old man dies." Achmad jerked his gun quickly from one to the other while keeping his eyes mostly on Abdullah.

Abdullah could smell their fear, but he kept his focus on Achmad. The man was highly agitated. His trigger-finger seemed ready to contract any moment.

"A coin! Now!"

"Wait!" He inched closer as he said it, right hand slowly moving toward his front pocket. "I have something better—I know where your missing *jihad* members are. They've decided to stop this madness. You can too." Abdullah reached slowly with thumb and forefinger into his pocket for his phone.

"Impossible! I spent months indoctrinating those guys. And you could turn them in a day? Ha!" Achmad spit on the floor.

"Here's my cell phone. Call one of them and see I'm telling the truth." As he finished speaking, the phone slid slowly up out of his pocket, then slipped from his hand. He bent down casually to pick it up, his foot accidentally bumping it a few inches away to his right behind a short rolling bookcase.

As Abdullah pretended to reach for the phone with his right hand, he launched his lowered left shoulder into the rolling bookcase, sending it crashing into Achmad. Achmad swung back around and fired but the impact caused him to shoot over Abdullah's head. Abdullah flung himself at his unbalanced foe. His shoulder hit Achmad in the chest propelling him into Ardi's heavy desk.

He felt the butt of the gun pounding against his back. Another shot echoed around the room. He heard Ardi gasp and curse, and Fani scream. Abdullah knew he had to get that gun. He smashed his right fist into Achmad's jaw, then turned to grab Achmad's right arm with both hands, getting Achmad on his back. He brought the arm down so violently against the desk he heard Achmad's forearm crack and Achmad roar in pain. The gun fell to the ground. He kicked it away just as Achmad's left arm circled his neck cutting off his breath.

Abdullah lunged backwards toward one of the tall bookcases, slamming Achmad's back against it, but the jihadist wouldn't let go. He tried again, then a third time. He desperately needed air. The room was beginning to swirl around him. He lost his balance and stumbled forward. The rocking bookcase behind them fell on top of them.

In a fog he heard someone shouting, "Shoot him! Shoot him!" He glanced across the room in time to see Ardi wrest the gun from Fani's hand, point it straight at Abdullah's head and fire.

Chapter 72

There were at least a dozen police blocking the road north to the jungle, checking every motorist fleeing town in a line nearly a kilometer long. Hafiz panicked and quickly pulled off the road. In his haste he had forgotten to grab a helmet. He was driving someone else's motorbike. He didn't even know if the registration papers were under the seat or in Abdullah's wallet. There's no way they would let him through. And what if they were looking for him?

He gazed past the roadblock at the green fields of rice and mangrove trees. Out there was the tropical rain forest. Out there was the peaceful town of Palangkaraya, with none of this madness. Out there was freedom.

He cursed out loud. He cursed the police. He cursed Achmad and Khaliq. He cursed himself. A toddler sucking on a lollipop stared at him from a nearby kiosk. "What are you looking at, kid? Get lost!" He shooed the boy away with his hand, and the boy started crying.

He wanted to curse Abdullah and his noble quest. But then he remembered waking up from bombing the university, and there was Abdullah's face, concerned, caring, Abdullah's strong arms carrying him home.

He should have died that day. But then he would have gone straight to hell for killing his parents.

Maybe there was still a way out of hell for him. And that way didn't lead north to freedom.

He released one more expletive, yelling it this time, then turned the bike around and headed for IAIN, talking urgently on his cell phone as he went.

When Hafiz passed through the campus gate, he slowed down and came to a stop in front of the library. The others weren't there yet. He knew Abdullah would have still come alone, but realized he had no idea where to find Abdullah and Fani. He swiveled around looking to see who he could ask for help and noticed a motorbike coming up fast behind him. It was Khaliq.

He spun Abdullah's bike out of Khaliq's path just in time, Khaliq's grasping hand just missing his head. He gunned the bike and raced back out the gate to Banjarmasin's busiest roadway, A. Yani Street. He turned right into the oncoming traffic, knowing that if Khaliq caught him this time, his death would be far worse than a traffic accident.

He knew Khaliq would be right behind him. Horns blared, angry drivers yelled at him, but Hafiz kept weaving in and out of the oncoming rush of cars, trucks and motorcycles desperate to get away from the ghost of his nightmares.

The police station was only a half mile away. If he could make it there perhaps Khaliq would give up the chase. Even if he got arrested for all his traffic infractions, he'd stay alive one more day.

At a slight break in traffic he glanced over his right shoulder and couldn't locate Khaliq. Had he lost him?

Suddenly he felt a thump against his bike from the left. He corrected, just barely missing a motorbike carrying a family of four, the smaller child standing up between her parents. He shot a quick look left just as Khaliq's foot kicked his bike again, harder this time. Hafiz fought to maintain control. As he righted the bike, a truck bore down on him, and the only thing he could do was jerk the motorcycle to the right and off the road.

Fortunately, he missed the ditch by mere inches and swung dangerously into a narrow alley, clipping a pedicab driver as he did. The man yelled and waved a long, curved knife at him. But Hafiz ignored him and kept speeding down the alley into a crowded neighborhood.

Around the first corner he hit his brakes to avoid a mother hen and family of chicks in the road, then slowly weaved through a group of kids playing soccer. He turned another tight corner and nearly ran into a satay cart coming toward him. He could smell the skewered chicken roasting on the portable grill. Gingerly he circumnavigated the cart and found himself blocked in by two motorbikes parked side by side in the alley.

He dismounted and started to move the first bike to the side when he heard a roaring motor behind him. He looked up just in time to see Khaliq accelerate around the corner and collide head-on with the satay cart. Hafiz heard a hiss that must have been the gas tank, then watched in horror as the satay cart exploded.

The satay seller had been knocked onto someone's porch by the collision, but Khaliq was directly over the cart when it exploded, and when he climbed out of the wreckage he was on fire. It reminded Hafiz of that movie with the Human Torch. A few more steps and Khaliq would set him on fire too.

For a moment they stood there staring at each other. Then Khaliq spun right and left looking for any sign of water. The alley was so narrow, there was nowhere to go except through one of the houses, all of which would have been built on stilts over the swamp. Khaliq rushed into a doorway setting the curtains on fire as he passed. Hafiz could hear people screaming as the fire attacked the wooden structure. A woman carrying a baby emerged from the front door, then two more girls, all of them crying. The woman called for help and suddenly the alley was alive with neighbors bringing buckets of water or trying to rescue items from the house. Hafiz joined in, carrying out the television and a small mattress before the house got too hot. In only a few minutes the walls were blazing, showering the air with sparks and thick black smoke. Those neighbors who could take the intense heat turned to throwing buckets of water on their own houses to keep them from catching on fire.

He heard the wail of the fire brigade coming from the main street and decided he'd better get out of there. He moved the other motorcycle aside and slipped through the alley.

Khaliq hadn't emerged from the fire. Burned alive—what a horrible way to die. Hafiz was still trembling with fear, but he headed back to IAIN. He had to know what had happened with Abdullah.

Chapter 73

At the sound of the gunshot, Fani cried out, "No!" and rushed over to Abdullah. He strained to push the bookcase aside and get to his teacher under all the books. "Help me!" he called back to Ardiansyah.

"Step aside, Fani." Ardiansyah raised the gun again.

Fani looked back, alarmed. "No! No more shooting!" He blocked his adopted father's view of the two men. "Put down that gun and help me!" Fani's pleading eyes eventually won the moment. Ardiansyah put the gun somewhere behind the desk and stooped to brush books off the two men.

Fani heard someone moan, and hoped against hope it was Abdullah. But it was Achmad trying to free himself from the mess. He let go of his grip around Abdullah's neck and tried to roll off him.

Fani ignored him. With Achmad gone, he could see Abdullah's head matted with blood. He glared up at Ardiansyah. "You killed him!" He pushed some more books aside and tried to get Abdullah's motionless body free.

Through teary eyes Fani watched Achmad struggle to his feet, his shattered right arm dangling across his chest. He reached with his left hand towards Ardiansyah, who stepped back, nearly causing Achmad to fall. But on the second try he grabbed Ardiansyah's shirt and pulled his face close.

Achmad slurred, "What would you do for a million dollars?"

The professor raised one eyebrow and frowned. "Your time here is done." He put his hand on Achmad's broken arm and pushed.

Achmad roared and let go, stumbling backwards. "You haven't seen the last of me yet." He took a good look at Abdullah's lifeless body and lurched down the hallway.

Finally Fani got Abdullah extracted and dragged him to a sitting position. Fani couldn't see any sign of breathing.

"How could you do this!" he wailed at the professor. "He was one of the only people who was ever kind to me." He slapped Abdullah's cheek and called his name, but to no avail.

"I was trying to shoot the other guy," Ardiansyah defended himself. "I didn't mean to."

Fani tried to remember what they'd learned in the martial arts club about helping people who couldn't breathe. He laid Abdullah flat and breathed into his mouth, then pushed down on his teacher's sternum.

"Come on, Pak Guru, please don't be dead." He tried again. The tears were pouring down his face now.

After several tries he pounded his fists in frustration on Abdullah's chest. He could feel Ardiansyah's hand on his shoulder trying to pry him away, but he didn't care. He kept beating his teacher's body and crying out, "Why? Why? Why?"

A small cough. A desperate gasp for air. Abdullah's arms shot up to protect himself and easily threw Fani aside.

Surprised, Fani picked himself up and giddily crawled back to Abdullah. "Pak Guru! You're not dead!"

Abdullah's eyes scanned the room. "Where's Achmad?"

"He left. We thought you were dead."

Abdullah tried to sit up, but immediately grabbed his head. "Whoa." His eyelids fluttered. "You let him go? We've got to stop him!" He tried again to stand but only made it as far as kneeling before swaying and holding on to a chair to keep from falling.

"Just stay still, Pak Guru, you're hurt. Pak Ardi got his gun. We'll go after him." Fani stood and looked at Ardiansyah, who nodded and retrieved the gun.

"No, bad idea," Abdullah muttered through closed eyes. "Let him go. The important thing is that you two are alive."

"And you, too, Pak Guru!" Fani wiped the tears from his cheeks and beamed at his teacher. "You saved us! Can I get you something? Maybe a drink?"

Abdullah removed his hand from his head and looked at the blood on his hand. "Maybe you better get me a doctor."

"Sure, Pak Guru, whatever you say." Fani looked at Abdullah's calm face and knew everything would turn out all right.

He was so focused on Abdullah he barely noticed Ardiansyah leave the room.

Chapter 74

By the time Hafiz made it back to IAIN, Udin and Juki were waiting for him at the front gate.

"Where's Kiki?" Hafiz asked.

"Said he'd be late," Juki answered.

"Kiki never makes it to New Year's until February," quipped Udin. "Now what's this all about?"

"There's no time to wait for him," Hafiz said. "Some dude has got Fani and another guy held hostage in one of these buildings." He waved at the campus around them. "Pak Abdullah went to stop him, but the guy is planning to kill our teacher."

"Whoa." Udin looked wide-eyed at Juki. "Are you serious?"

"Dead serious," Hafiz retorted. "Let's spread out and search the campus. You find them, call the others first before you walk in and get killed, okay?"

"Okay," Udin answered.

Juki nodded. "This place looks like a ghost town."

As their motorbikes cruised slowly past the library, a gunshot rang out.

"I think it came from behind there!" Hafiz pointed to the ornately structured building in front of them with a flagpole out front. The sign read, "Office of the President." They zoomed past it onto the muddy back street searching for the source of the shots.

After they'd past a few places and wondered if they'd missed it, a second gunshot broke through the still morning air.

"Over there!" shouted Juki.

Hafiz followed Juki's lead, but couldn't help thinking, *What if Abdullah's dead? I'll be next. If it's too late to save anyone, why walk into this deathtrap?*

But he had to know.

They pulled up outside a building that looked like a private residence. There were two motorbikes in front.

"Is this where the shot came from?" Hafiz asked Juki.

"I don't know, man, I think so."

Udin looked worried. "You didn't tell us the dude had a gun. How are we supposed to stop a dude with a gun?"

"I don't know. I didn't have time to plan anything," Hafiz responded irritably.

"We're sitting ducks out here. Maybe we should hide."

Juki interjected, "Let's try to get a look in the window."

"Good idea," Hafiz agreed. They snuck around to the side of the house, but the curtains were closed. Hafiz put his ear as close as he could and thought he heard Fani's high-pitched voice shouting, "No!"

"It's Fani!" he told the others. "This is the place."

"So what are we going to do?"

They all stared at each other. Hafiz broke the silence.

"There's only one thing to do. We're going in."

They three boys returned to the front of the house and paused at the bottom of the steps to the front door.

"Well," said Udin, "you're the one who invited us to this party, Hafiz. Lead the way." He motioned with his hand for Hafiz to go first.

"Yeah, right." Hafiz looked both his friends in the eye. "Stay close to me, okay?"

"Let's do this already," Udin prodded. "I've still got a bank holdup and a mad bomber to stop before lunch."

Hafiz turned to face the front steps. He remembered the rush of sneaking into Sari's house, and shame flooded over him. This feeling was nothing like that. This feeling was like having his neck magnetically drawn into the guillotine. *It's too late to turn back now.*

As he put his foot on the first of the three steps, the front door flew open.

Hafiz stood face to face with the man who had recruited him to ISIS.

Chapter 75

"If you need anything, just use that intercom on the wall to buzz me. I'll be in the next office, okay?" The gray-uniformed Intelligence staff nodded at them, then exited and locked the door.

Amat looked around at their "holding cell." Hidayat and Baqri were relaxing on the L-shaped fake leather couch, white with black trim, opposite him. He was seated on a love seat from the same sofa set. Between them was an ornate glass coffee table on curved, silver-plated legs. Under their feet was a plush dark blue carpet. A ficus plant stood watch over them from the corner. The freshly painted white walls held the customary photos of the president of Indonesia and the head of BIN. A small television in the corner opposite the ficus was tuned to a news channel. Their driver from the airport last night had mentioned they'd be kept temporarily at the BIN headquarters in South Jakarta.

"Sure beats Guantanamo Bay," Amat remarked.

Baqri crossed his arms and stared sullenly at the television. Amat's ears perked up hearing the word, "terrorist."

"...in spite of the terrorist attacks around the nation. The first presidential debate between Ali Bin Husaini and Muhammad Rizky Ramadani proceeded as planned last night in Bogor. The main topic was how to deal with ISIS in our nation. Pak Husaini argued that the military needed better weapons, greater breadth of authority, and more consistency in supporting the Islamic values of the majority in our nation. Pak Ramadani countered that violence empowers violence and the road to peace requires all parties to engage with and understand each other so that* *we can seek solutions together. When asked what message each would like to give to the victims of the—*"

Hidayat rose and turned the television off. No one protested. He crossed the room to look out the second-story window. "Hey, check this out," he summoned the others.

Amat joined him. Hidayat pointed out various places of interest around the BIN campus: "Those look like houses, that's a kindergarten playground, there's a tennis court—"

"They have a soccer field!" Amat interrupted. "You think they'd let us out for a couple hours of exercise each day?"

"This isn't vacation, doofus," Hidayat scorned. "More likely they let us out to stand down the end of that shooting range for target practice." He pointed past the soccer field.

A turtledove flew down and landed on the windowsill. Amat wished he had some food to offer the bird. They looked at each other through the glass, Amat mirroring the bird's head cocked to one side. Hidayat laughed.

"Look at the human, caught in a cage," Hidayat quipped in bird-voice.

Amat turned the latch and the window opened, frightening the bird away.

"Check it out, the window's not even locked. Want to plan our escape?"

"Yeah, right," Hidayat objected. "Like I'm that stupid. Right now if they want me to jump, I'm asking, 'How high?'"

He returned to the couch, and Amat followed.

Hidayat was puzzled. "Why are they treating us like this? Why don't they throw us in a dungeon and feed us bread and water?" He pointed out the cups of hot tea and the pastries on the coffee table. "Remember Amrozi, and Imam Samudra, the Bali Bombers? They were executed."

"I know, man," Amat replied. "This whole experience has been surreal. I can't believe that not that long ago we were all excited about Islam finally having a *caliph* in the Middle East to lead us, about ISIS, then meeting Achmad and imagining a whole new world.

"Then it was 'kaboom' here and 'kaboom' there, the whole city is going crazy, and then we're caught..."

Amat paused. "Do you think our *jihad* accomplished anything? I mean, *anything*?" He sat back on the love seat and waited for his friend's response.

Hidayat only shrugged.

Amat looked to Baqri. "What do you think, buddy?"

Baqri spoke without looking at him. "The important thing is, it's over, gotta move on, gotta be survivors. Don't talk too much. Keep your heads down. This could all go sour on us in a heartbeat."

It was a sobering reality, reminding them they were prisoners, after all. Amat stared at the other two for a minute, glad he wasn't in the Intelligence headquarters all alone.

Hidayat picked at a pastry and took a drink of tea. "You know what that guy told me, Mat? He said if I do well in this program, whatever it is, he might get my dad out of jail. Could he really do that? *Would* he?"

"If he works with Intelligence I guess anything's possible," Amat replied. "This Abdullah guy, he's...I don't know, I can't figure him out. But I think he's the real deal. If he said it, he'll probably do it."

Amat wanted to tell his friend about his visit to David's home, about the pastor and the bicycle, about Lani. But there were too many other thoughts on Hidayat's mind right now, most likely about his father. He decided to save those stories for another day.

"All I know is..." Amat concluded, "...somehow we got lucky, 'cuz this is not what we deserve."

Chapter 76

Hafiz forcibly swallowed the bile rising in his throat and tried to act brave. Achmad looked way too happy to see him. But *Alhamdulillah* he saw no sign of a gun. And Achmad was holding his arm funny, like it was hurt. The bravado Hafiz had lost since his parents died surged back into him.

"Where's Pak Abdullah, jerk-face?"

"Where you're going to be, traitor, he's dead."

"So are my parents! You made me kill my own parents!" Hafiz screamed the words, finally given a new focal point for all the anger and hatred he felt for himself.

With a cry of rage Hafiz exploded up the steps diving for Achmad's legs, but the older man nimbly skipped aside and kicked Hafiz in the ribs, spinning him sideways into some potted plants.

When he picked himself up, brushing the dirt off his head, he saw Achmad was already down the stairs. There Juki and Udin were waiting in martial arts stance.

Achmad feinted left, then aimed a kick at Juki's chest on the right. Juki sidestepped and blocked with his right arm, stepping forward to jab at Achmad's face with his left. But he found only air—Achmad had spun out of his T-kick into a backwards roundhouse kick, his right foot catching Juki in the face and sending him sprawling.

Just in time Achmad turned to catch Udin coming at him fast with a combination of kicks targeting Achmad's knee and shoulder. He nearly caught Achmad off balance, but not quite. Achmad dodged and with his left hand managed to grab Udin's foot off the high kick and flip him onto his back.

Hafiz launched himself off the porch wrapping both arms around Achmad's neck. When Achmad tried to flip him over his shoulder onto the ground, Hafiz refused to let go, and Achmad was catapulted forward. Achmad extended his broken right arm to steady himself and collapsed howling on top of it. Hafiz took the advantage to land some strong blows to Achmad's body and head before he was finally thrown off.

Achmad rose slowly to his feet, blood on his face, fury in his eyes. Hafiz, Juki and Udin stood in defensive positions all around him.

"Come on, guys, all at once now!" Hafiz urged.

All three rushed Achmad, but the more experienced fighter managed to spin away from Juki pushing him into Udin while landing a straight jab to Hafiz's face followed by a kick to his thigh that nearly knocked him off his feet. He reset his stance in time to see Juki go down with a cobra kick and Udin take a sharp jab to the face and retreat. All three boys were breathing hard, unsure how to take Achmad down.

Achmad's face relaxed, and he straightened up. "Impressive! You have been trained well. You are worthy candidates for the *mujahidin*. Join the cause of Allah and you will be rewarded more greatly than you can imagine."

"We were trained by Pak Abdullah, dirtbag," Udin responded, "and our reward will be taking selfies next to your ugly mug behind bars."

"I will never go to prison," Achmad snorted. "You'll have to kill me first."

"That's not the way Pak Abdullah taught us," Juki objected. "He taught us to never use violence to hurt others, only to protect others." Hafiz was taken aback. *That's true. I had forgotten he said that.*

Suddenly Achmad made a break for the motorbikes, pushing Udin aside with his left arm. He was nearly there when Hafiz tackled his legs from behind and Juki dove onto his back forcing Achmad's face and broken arm into the dirt. Udin joined them and twisted Achmad's left arm behind his back. Achmad writhed in obvious pain.

Hafiz came to squat beside Achmad's face. "Why did you fail? Number one, because you lost your team. Alone you are nothing. Number two, because you risked coming out of hiding to kill Abdullah, not realizing that Abdullah is more than just one man. Abdullah lives in me, in these guys, in thousands of others who will rise up to stop this senseless killing."

"Well said, little brother." Achmad spoke out of the side of his mouth with his face still on the ground. "I need a new team, and you require a new teacher. Come learn from me, and my employers will reward you with a car, a house, whatever you want."

"What employer?" Hafiz asked suspiciously. "Who do you work for?"

"The Devil," answered a deep voice from above them. Hafiz and his friends craned their necks to look behind them into the barrel of a gun and dove for cover. A shot rang out. When they looked up, Achmad lay still on the ground with a bullet hole in the back of his head, blood pooling on the grass around him. Standing above him was a large, balding man with glasses holding a pistol. None of the boys moved.

"It's okay, I won't shoot you," the man called, lowering the gun. "That terrorist nearly killed me, and no doubt has killed many others. He deserved to die."

"Did he kill Pak Abdullah?" Hafiz asked while rising to his feet.

"Very nearly, but he's alive. Go see for yourselves."

Hafiz, Juki and Udin rushed past the shooter into the house. They found Abdullah sitting in a chair holding his head. Next to him was Fani shouting into a cell phone.

"Bapak!" Hafiz cried, kneeling beside him. "You're alive!" Juki and Udin knelt beside Hafiz.

"Juki, Udin," Abdullah greeted his former students. "Hafiz, you came back." He smiled briefly, then a sad expression crossed his face. "But I'm afraid Achmad got away."

"No, Pak, Achmad's dead. So is Khaliq. We did it." Hafiz put his hand on Abdullah's knee. "*You* did it. The cell is no more."

Fani interrupted them. "The ambulance is coming."

Udin turned to Hafiz. "You said you killed your own—"

"Later," Hafiz cut him off, pointing with his lips toward his injured teacher.

Abdullah put his hand on Hafiz's hand. "Well go on, son, tell me everything."

Chapter 77

Sari was overjoyed to see Abdullah walk through the door, head bandage and all. She ran over and hugged him tightly.

"Oh, Bapak! Oh, thank you, God!"

He winced, but returned her hug.

"What happened to your head?"

"A bullet just grazed me. I'm lucky to be alive."

Sari couldn't stop the tears of joy. She called David and Angelina, who welcomed Abdullah back with hugs as well.

The door opened again and Sari saw Hafiz smiling at her. She squealed in delight and ran to hug him. He embraced her whole-heartedly. Behind him she saw Udin and another guy that must have been Hafiz's friend.

"What's up, lizard-hand?" joked Udin. Sari smiled warmly and welcomed both the boys in. They seemed to already know David, who began introducing them to his wife and daughter. She returned to Abdullah who was now sitting on the couch.

"So what happened?" she asked, curling her legs under her on the couch next to him.

"Patience, my daughter," he answered. "Let me make a phone call."

"And let me make you some iced tea."

Sari went to the kitchen to make tea for everyone. While waiting for the water to boil, she thanked God for answering her prayers. Abdullah was alive. Hafiz was back, and looked different. *It looks like his fear is gone, or his anger, or both.* She could hardly wait to hear the story.

When she brought the tea to the coffee table, everyone sat down and gave Abdullah their attention.

"That was Pak Joko on the phone. He's flying here this afternoon for a press conference at eight o'clock tonight. Once I've made my appearance there, I expect to go home and sleep for a month."

Everyone laughed. David asked, "Why the press conference?"

"To tell the world that Banjarmasin is now a *jihad*-free city."

Everyone cheered. Josie clapped her hands too.

"So, tell us, Bapak, what happened?" Sari prodded.

"My apologies to Juki and Udin, there's much to this story you don't know. Let's just say Hafiz was helping me to stop the guys who have been bombing our city. The last two were waiting for us at IAIN today holding Fani and the professor hostage…"

Abdullah proceeded to tell his part of the story, then Hafiz his part. When they finished, Sari could hardly believe God's goodness to them.

"It's a miracle!" she exclaimed.

"It sure is," David agreed. "And a miracle worth celebrating! Let's order some barbecued chicken and barbecued fish and have a *syukran* feast." The boys enthusiastically agreed. They went outside discussing with David which place was best to order from. Angelina took Josie into the kitchen to cook more rice. Sari and Abdullah were left alone.

"I want to thank you for your prayers. So many times I wanted to quit. I should have been killed more than once. But somehow…here I am."

"I wish I could have been out there helping you more."

"You were right where you needed to be."

Sari held Abdullah's upper arm with both her hands and leaned her face against his shoulder. She remembered her dream of dancing with her Christian friends, leading them to join the Muslim girls in a choreography that beautifully displayed their distinctiveness, but weaved them together in something greater than their dances alone. *Was all that had happened connected to her dream?* Meeting Amat…the *syukran* planned for tonight…she was right where she needed to be.

"I think I'll go lie down," Abdullah sighed.

Sari told Angelina, who offered Abdullah their comfortable bed. He made Sari promise to wake him for the barbecue.

She slipped into Josie's room and took out her journal. There was so much to catch up on. She started writing:

> *Dear God,*
> *…and Mom,*
> *…and Bali,*
> *…and Dad,*
> *Every sacrifice you made, everything you wanted for me, I want you know that it wasn't in vain…*

Chapter 78

After a noisy morning of fire trucks seemingly encircling the police station, things finally quieted down in the afternoon enough for Rio to take a nap. The cot in his police cell was about as soft as sleeping on cardboard and the enclosed space felt like a sauna, but that didn't stop Rio from sleeping. He was tired. *So very tired...*

An obnoxious clanging on the bars of his cell awakened him in what felt like only minutes later, but most likely had been hours. He reached for his glasses and looked up to find a young officer rapping with his large metal key ring against the bars.

"Wake up, towel-head. Word is you're one of the jerk-hadists behind those bombs. Is that true? Better answer me if you know what's good for you."

Rio had nothing to say. His life was probably over anyway. At least he got to talk to his wife and kids. They occupied most of his thoughts since he'd been captured. *I don't even know what my kids look like now. I wonder if they—*

The officer interrupted his thoughts. "Arrogant dog! You think Bin Laden will swoop in to rescue you? Bin Laden's dead. You belong to us now. And when we—"

"When we what?" a commanding voice echoed through the prison hallway.

The officer snapped to attention. "Here are the keys you requested, sir!"

"You want to finish that sentence now, Private?"

"No, sir." The officer remained at attention.

"Give me the keys." The taller man held out his hand. "This prisoner will remain untouched. Jakarta has asked to have him transferred there safely tomorrow. If he's not in perfect health, we'll all be in trouble, understood?"

"Yes, sir!"

"Dismissed." The doors to the cell opened, and Rio sat up to see what the tall, lean policeman wanted.

"I'm Sergeant Eko. I have a text message for you from a man named Abdullah." He scrolled through his cell phone, then read: ACHMAD AND KHALIQ ARE DEAD. BANJARMASIN IS AT PEACE ONCE AGAIN. WILL YOU HELP US SAVE THE REST OF THE NATION? WILL YOU AND YOUR FAMILY FIND PEACE FOR YOUR SOULS?

Rio was stunned. "They're dead? But how?" He took off his glasses and rubbed his sleepy eyes. "How do I know this is true?"

"Oh, it's true. The media is buzzing about it. There will be a press conference tonight, I'm told. Detachment 88 is packing their bags and moving on to one of the other hot spots as we speak."

It had never entered his imagination that Achmad and Khaliq would die. He knew he would die, and probably the young bucks, but not those two. They had died and he had lived. And now he had a choice to make.

"If I agree to help you, can Pak Abdullah keep me out of prison?"

"I'm not authorized to make any promises. It may depend on the quality of help you have to offer."

Rio thought some more. He did know several individual *mujahidin* scattered around the country, perhaps forming cells like this one. If he gave information about those who were about to be annihilated by the Special Forces anyway, no great loss. But if they escaped, there was no place he could hide—they would come for him.

And what about my ideals? What would Allah think if I betrayed my brothers?

Meanwhile the lure of his family was strong. *Curse Abdullah for that phone call!* The longing in his children's voices begging him to come home haunted him constantly.

"Well?" Eko asked.

He needed time to think. Better to play along for now. In time he'd see more clearly what they wanted and what he was willing to give.

"Sure, I'm in."

The tall officer arched an eyebrow skeptically. "Prove it. Tell me something we don't already know."

Rio wracked his brain for something he could say that would convince the sergeant of his cooperation without endangering any of his brother *mujahidin*. His fingers drummed on the prison cot. *How to help the enemy without betraying his brothers, the cause, or Allah...*

Finally he came up with something innocuous. "Okay, how about this? Not all the bombs were in that warehouse that blew up. When they arrested me, I left the last bomb in my small green suitcase at the Losmen Tokyo. Achmad said he would pick it up today. When they killed him, did they find the bomb?"

Now both of Eko's eyebrows shot up. "I'll pass on this information. We'll check into it."

He hustled off down the corridor leaving Rio alone with his children's pleadings once again.

Chapter 79

The IAIN campus was abuzz with police, Special Forces, television and newspaper reporters, and of course the entire student body returning to their campus to find out what was going on. This was all easily seen by the imposing figure wearing a helmet that hid his face, seated astride a stolen motorcycle just outside the campus gate.

The clothes he wore were too small. The tiny patches of hair that had survived the blaze still smelled like smoke, and his body reeked of the swamp. His skin felt like it was still burning underneath the clothing. But it was nothing compared to the volcano inside of him.

It had taken too long to break through the bathroom floorboards and submerge his body in the swamp, then duck under the adjacent houses until he was far enough from the fire to re-emerge and steal what he needed to get back here. Now he wouldn't be able to get anywhere near the house.

Khaliq smiled to himself. *They're probably all here to see Abdullah's decapitated head on a fence post.*

He engaged one of the students walking out of the gate. "What's happening down there?"

"Oh, man, it's crazy! One of our professors shot a terrorist! They say he was the one behind all the bombings. Our professor is a hero!"

Khaliq's world suddenly reeled. Someone killed *Achmad?* That wasn't possible!

"Just one body? What did he look like?"

"Dude, I don't know. You'd have to ask Professor Ardiansyah. See down there the big bald guy talking on the microphone with the SCTV reporter? That's him. He's the one who saved our city."

Khaliq had to be sure. He gunned the bike and pulled up behind the white SCTV van where he could listen in without being seen.

Ardiansyah was speaking: "...really it was a partnership between myself and BIN that stopped the terrorist and/or terrorists. I can't say any more at this time, you understand, but I've been told that Pak Abdullah and BIN will be holding a press conference at eight this evening at the Swiss-Bell Hotel. You'll get all the details that we're allowed to give there. Thank you. Now if you'll excuse me, I'm exhausted. I need to rest."

Khaliq spun the motorbike around and made his way back out of the gate, joining the flow of traffic on A. Yani Street.

No Achmad. No one to tell him what to do. What was he supposed to do now? Think, Khaliq, think!

It had been over ten years since Achmad had found him in a rice storehouse in a village in Sulawesi, an orphan chained to metal rings in a cement wall by his uncle. He'd been a violent child. The local witch-doctor couldn't cast the demons out of him. He laughed at the memory. Adding dark powers had always been better than trying to get rid of them.

Achmad understood that. Achmad was the only one who ever understood him. Now Achmad was gone.

What would Achmad do?

He was almost to the edge of town when it hit him—the bomb. The bomb Achmad was supposed to detonate at the harbor as he and Khaliq left town by speedboat. He needed the bomb.

He made a u-turn and sped back toward downtown. Along the way he considered, should he bomb the same target, or choose a new one?

Achmad picked that target. But that was when we had five bombs. Achmad was good at changing the plan to fit the situation.

But Achmad was a genius. How can I possibly do what he did?

Khaliq heard a voice whisper in his mind—*We'll do it together.*

Was it Achmad's voice, guiding him from beyond the grave? He answered aloud, "Yes, together."

Rio was not supposed to have checked out of his room, so Khaliq expected it to be undisturbed, but was surprised to find the door unlocked. He entered warily. The room was empty. The green suitcase was gone. He checked the bathroom, the closet, under the desk and bed.

The bomb was gone.

He marched straight to the front desk. A young woman with a tight red shirt unbuttoned so low he could see her black bra peeking out smiled coyly.

"Can I help you?"

"Number 11. My friend sent me for his suitcase. Where is it?"

"Dunno, honey. You want a special order for tonight?"

Khaliq reached over the counter and grabbed her long, curly hair. "Where's the green suitcase? Who took it?" he demanded.

She clawed at his arm with her long fingernails, ripping into his already burned flesh. He slammed her face down into the counter and stomped out.

Where is the bomb? What do I do now? Spirit of Achmad, help me.

The voice whispered to him a second time.

Khaliq smiled. Now he knew exactly what to do.

Chapter 80

The Swiss-Bell Hotel in downtown Banjarmasin boasted a beautiful view of the Martapura River. The evening lights of Pasar Baru across the river performed a lively dance on the waves. Sari watched for a moment, enchanted. So much she had missed by hiding herself away for the last few weeks. But though the pain remained, it was much smaller without the fear standing on its shoulders.

She breathed in the cool night air. Everything was perfect. Pak Abdullah looked distinguished in his red *batik* shirt. She'd encouraged him to cover his head bandage with a hat, but he'd refused. Hafiz even looked nice with a green *sasirangan* shirt borrowed from David. She wore a long, flowing dark green dress with a short black sweater, both borrowed from Angelina, to cover her wrists and ankles. *Better to be conservative in this crowd.*

In the lobby, an old, thin, silver-haired man approached them and pumped Abdullah's hand enthusiastically.

"You must be Sari," he smiled widely, and shook her hand too. "I'm Joko. Quite a man, your Abdullah, quite a man."

"Yes, er, thank you," she managed.

Pak Joko already knew Hafiz's name as well, then moved on to greet other guests. *Does he know everybody here?*

"Freaky guy," Hafiz whispered. Sari giggled.

Next Abdullah introduced them to Professor Ardiansyah, then Sergeant Eko and various members of the police. Sari had heard Abdullah's stories about these people, and now she could finally see them for herself. Hafiz left her to hang out with someone named Fani. Since Abdullah seemed busy with Sergeant Eko, she decided to wander over to the hotel restaurant.

The restaurant was on the ground floor just off the lobby. It was dimly lit, with red velvety chair covers and dark wooden tables. She glanced through a menu. New Zealand steak for Rp.200,000—that was like a month's tuition payment in college! So expensive! Then she remembered her inheritance money from her birth father. Technically, she could afford it now. But she knew she'd never spend that money on steak. She had bigger plans for it.

The crowd was moving up the wide staircase to the ballroom on the second floor. She followed at the back of the crowd, trying to locate Hafiz. At the top of the stairs two large doors opened into an ornate room with a plush red and gold carpet below, a glorious chandelier above, and enough space for several hundred people. *I should have my wedding here, and my reception out in the parking area overlooking the river.*

She saw Abdullah step onto the stage behind Pak Joko. The lectern had been pushed back to accommodate a long table on the platform. Even from the back of the room she could read the placards resting on the red tablecloth at each seat. In the center was the governor of South Kalimantan; next to him was the mayor of Banjarmasin on his right, and the chief of police on his left. Next to the chief was a Lieutenant Colonel with Detachment 88. Beside the mayor sat Pak Joko of BIN, and on the end was her adopted father. Sari felt so proud.

The front two rows of the audience were filled with journalists flashing photos. Sari looked again for Hafiz. *He better have saved me a seat!*

Someone tapped her on the shoulder. She turned expecting to see Hafiz, and was surprised at the large man peering at her through his spectacles.

"Excuse me, Sari is it? Remember me? I'm Ardiansyah, the professor, a friend of Pak Abdullah."

"Oh, yes, of course. You took in his student, Fani. That was very nice of you."

"Just a small kindness, really. He's a sweet boy. Abdullah speaks very highly of you, by the way."

"Thank you." Sari felt herself blush.

"He's an extraordinary man." The professor adjusted his glasses. "You know, I'm glad I ran into you. The students from my university sent a giant flower arrangement to honor Abdullah at this event. I could really use some help bringing it from my room here to this ballroom, and I can't find Fani anywhere. Would you be so kind?"

"Sure, no problem." Sari returned the older man's warm smile and thought of how delighted Abdullah would be to see such an extravagant gift from the students. Ardiansyah motioned for her to precede him through the double doors and guided her down the hallway toward his hotel room. She wondered why he needed a room just for an event that should be over in an hour. *Well, maybe he needed it to store the flowers.*

I hope Hafiz saved me a good seat. I don't want to miss all the excitement!

Chapter 81

I *should have taken more aspirin.*

Abdullah's head was throbbing. He was having a hard time paying attention as one by one the other civic leaders at the table took their turns presenting different aspects of what ISIS had done to the city, how they had attempted to thwart the terrorists' plans, and what this successful resolution meant to them. Abdullah's turn was last. He looked at his watch. At the rate everyone was talking, he'd get to speak about ten o'clock.

His eyes wandered through the crowd looking for Sari. Hafiz was easily distinguishable, and had an empty chair next to him. *Who else would Sari even know to sit with?*

The news from Rio was disturbing. The police still hadn't found the final bomb. Hopefully it would turn up without some child accidentally setting it off. But with no more terrorists to hunt down, someone else could deal with that detail. Abdullah was craving a good night's sleep in his own bed.

His mind drifted back to Sari. Did this mean she would move back into her own home? He'd gotten so used to having her near—the daughter he'd never had. Of course she had her own life to live. *But honestly, I'm not ready to let her go. She's all the family I've got.*

The mayor mentioned his name. He nodded to the applauding crowd. This was one of his least favorite parts of the job. He'd always been a man of action. Now he was learning to war with words. But face-to-face suited him more than the spotlight.

Along the side of the room he watched Fani walking quickly toward the front, all the way to the stage, where he knelt by Abdullah's side facing away from the crowd. As he had approached, Abdullah thought he looked upset, but up close he could see Fani was crying.

He put his hand on the boy's shoulder. "What is it, son?"

With a trembling hand Fani held out an envelope, unmarked on the front except with the Swiss-Bell Hotel return address. Abdullah took it. Before he could open it, Fani held out a cell phone in his other hand. On the phone was a photo. What Abdullah saw sucked the breath right out of him.

It was a photo of Sari, eyes closed, with a gun to her head.

"I'm so sorry, Bapak," Fani blubbered in a whisper, then he turned and ran out the door. Abdullah watched Hafiz get up and go after him.

No one else paid any attention to this. They were clapping for another of the mayor's statements. In a daze, Abdullah opened the envelope.

There were two sheets of paper, both handwritten. One seemed to be a speech of some sort. He decided to start with the other one.

DO EXACTLY AS I SAY OR I WILL KILL YOUR BELOVED SARI. REMEMBER, I'M WATCHING YOUR EVERY MOVE ON BANJAR TV.

Abdullah glanced up at the large television camera filming the whole event. Everyone on the stage would be visible. He continued reading.

THERE IS A BOMB IN THE BUILDING. I HOLD THE DETONATOR IN MY HAND. YOU ARE GOING TO DIE TODAY. BUT IF YOU FOLLOW MY INSTRUCTIONS, SARI WILL LIVE.

Sweat broke out on Abdullah's forehead. His heart thudded so loudly in his chest he glanced over at Pak Joko wondering if he could hear it. Then he remembered the bomber was watching him and he looked down at the letter again.

STAND UP AND GO TO THE LECTERN. ASK THEM TO TURN ON THE MICROPHONE THERE. READ THE SPEECH THAT I HAVE WRITTEN FOR YOU, WORD FOR WORD. IF YOU DON'T, I SHOOT SARI AND BLOW THE BOMB.

He pretended to be reading the papers slowly, wracking his brain for a way out. If he tried to warn everyone, they'd probably be blown up anyway, and he'd lose Sari.

Why should Sari have to pay? He, Pak Joko, the police—they all knew the risks of fighting terrorists.

Why Sari?

Abdullah knew he couldn't stall forever, he was on TV. He slowly rose to his feet. His knees felt weak. He felt light-headed, and steadied himself by grabbing the back of Joko's chair. As he moved in slow motion toward the lectern, the mayor began to notice something was amiss and paused his speech to turn and watch Abdullah. There was a brief buzz among the journalists, then a hush fell over the crowd.

Abdullah reached the large, ornate lectern and stood behind it, placing the page of handwriting before him. He gripped the sturdy teak wood to keep himself upright. His foot brushed up against something and he glanced down.

Hidden in the lectern was a green suitcase.

Chapter 82

Khaliq needed to find a way into the hotel. That's where the man had taken the suitcase.

He had spotted the man pulling the small green suitcase through the parking lot nearly an hour ago. But when he tried to follow the man through the front door, he found cops everywhere. So he had retreated and watched.

But now it was after eight o'clock. The press conference was already starting, and still there were two policemen guarding the door.

He drove the motorbike around back to the service entrance. It was bustling with activity—too many people to just slip through.

Achmad, I need a plan.

He waited, and when it came to him, he grinned. He parked the bike and approached one of the hotel staff.

"My brother's friend said he works here. Big guy, likes to lift weights. You know him?"

"Oh, you mean Andri, the maintenance guy?"

"Yeah, Andri. Can I talk to him for a minute?"

"I guess so. I'll see if I can find him for you. Wait here."

Khaliq watched caterers unloading a van. A couple housekeepers exited the door going home for the night. Finally the woman returned with a beefed up young guy with a crew cut. He wasn't as big as Khaliq, but he would have to do. He winced as he gingerly slipped the helmet from his scorched scalp.

"Hey, Andri. My brother said you guys have a good fitness center here. Can I see it?"

Andri stared at him. "Sure, dude. Who's your brother? And what happened to your face?"

"An accident. You know my brother, Udin, right?" Khaliq picked the most common man's name in Banjarmasin.

"Yeah, right." Andri looked away from Khaliq's burnt face and down at his chiseled body. "Dude, you're massive! Where do you usually work out?"

"Here and there."

Andri shook his head in awe. "Massive, dude. This way."

He led Khaliq through the service door and down several hallways to the hotel's Borneo Fitness Center. He pointed out the treadmills, the stationary bikes, the rowing machine, the Life Fitness set and the free weights. Khaliq nodded approvingly.

"Can you show me where the changing room is?"

"It's through here."

At the far end of the fitness center they entered the men's changing room. It was equipped with benches, lockers and showers. Khaliq looked through it thoroughly and saw no other customers. He pointed under one of the sinks.

"Looks like you have a leak down there."

When Andri bent over to take a look, Khaliq karate-chopped him on the back of the head, dragged his body into one of the showers and pulled the curtain. A few seconds later he emerged wearing Andri's maintenance uniform.

He made his way back down the main hallway toward the lobby. Carefully avoiding the front desk, he climbed the stairs to the ballroom. He slipped through the doors quietly and made his way along the back wall pausing at an air conditioning control unit. He pretended to make some adjustments while searching the crowd for the man who brought the suitcase.

His target wasn't on the stage. But the teacher was. *A more formidable foe than I anticipated. Your time is coming.*

But after two surveys of the crowd, he couldn't spot the man with the suitcase.

Panic began to swell up inside him. *I lost him again. Spirit of Achmad, guide me to him.*

A boy was speaking to the teacher. He looked familiar. Khaliq watched him run out of the room, clearly troubled. Another boy rose and followed him.

The traitor Hafiz!

This was his sign. He followed the two boys out of the ballroom and down the hall. He heard them arguing.

"Fani, wait up! What's going on?"

"Stay away from me!"

"I just want to help."

"Don't follow me. You'll just make it worse."

The younger boy picked up speed and Hafiz hesitated. Khaliq turned his face away and pretended to knock on a door. When Hafiz took up the chase again, he was around the corner before Khaliq could react.

He sprinted to the corner just in time to watch Hafiz fighting with someone to let him into a hotel room. Khaliq arrived just as Hafiz won the fight and threw open the door.

There before him were Hafiz and the younger boy, the girl he had nearly killed in Abdullah's home, and a man holding a gun.

The man with the green suitcase.

Chapter 83

Abdullah tapped the microphone at the lectern until he heard it echo-ing around the room. He closed his eyes for a second.

Ya Allah, ya Robbi.

The speech was handwritten neatly enough that he could read it. It was only one page long. Only one page stood between him and the detonation at his feet.

At least this close to the bomb, I won't feel a thing.

Actually, that sounded kind of nice, not feeling a thing. He'd lived a full life—mostly full of regrets. He'd lost both his sons. Maybe it was his time to join them.

But not Sari. He couldn't let her down, couldn't let Bali down. Whatever happened to him, Sari had to live.

Which meant he had to read the speech prepared for him.

"Ladies and gentlemen, honored guests…" he stammered. Then he paused and looked up. "I apologize for this interruption, Mr. Mayor, this is urgent and it won't take long."

He held his breath. The bomb didn't explode. He looked back down at the script.

This time he noticed something that had been there all along. Below the front edge of the lectern, unseen by the audience, was a laptop. On the laptop screen was a PowerPoint with the headline, "ISIS No Longer a Threat in Banjarmasin, Press Conference, Swiss-Bell Hotel" and the date. He followed the laptop's cable with his eyes to the left corner of the stage where an LCD projector was transmitting onto a large white screen. Perhaps one of the presenters at the table was planning to show some graphs or statistics.

He coughed, then picked up the speech and placed it just above the laptop on the lectern.

"Pardon me. Let me begin again. The statement I have to make today is of vital importance to all of you." He looked at the TV cameraman. "If you could please zoom in on me so as not to miss a word.

"Ladies and gentlemen, honored guests…" As he read the words of the speech slowly and carefully, he deleted the headline of the PowerPoint and began to type in a replacement.

"M. Rizky Ramadani is a fraud. He speaks of peace, but he is a supporter of terrorist activities," he announced. The crowd gasped in horror.

Meanwhile, he typed: *Emergency! Everyone please SILENTLY leave the room.*

"I have assisted Pak Ramadani in provoking unrest, mob violence, and recruiting the very terrorists that destroyed out city."

He kept typing: *I am being watched. On the stage is a bomb.*

Another gasp from the crowd. Feet could be heard shuffling, chairs scraping. Abdullah began walking across the stage drawing the television camera away from the LCD screen, yelling as he read.

"Ramadani is a liar! He doesn't want peace. He will ruin our nation!" He spoke slowly but loudly. The cameraman was glued to him, allowing the men at the table to slip away to the left. Once they were safely gone, Abdullah motioned for the cameraman to leave as well.

"Dark days trouble our nation. We need strong leadership if we are to survive. We need a leader who understands the challenges ahead and is not afraid to act." He paused, giving time for the last few people to make it to the exit.

"For all of you watching on television, the time to choose your president is now! For this is what happens to those who follow M. Rizky Ramadani."

It was the last line of the speech. He was alone in the ballroom. Abdullah's eyes drifted to the lectern, waiting for the blast.

Instead he heard something muffled in the distance, yet very distinctly the sound he was desperate not to hear.

A gunshot.

Sari!

His heart went out to her, dying alone. He hadn't protected her as he'd promised. His knees buckled and he found himself kneeling on the stage, holding his bandaged head in his hands, wishing the bomb would go off quickly and put an end to this cursed cycle of death.

Chapter 84

Panic was fighting for control of Sari's mind. Sitting on the floor between the television and a gun, simple things like breathing became a struggle. Her eyes began to blur. The familiar waves of helpless terror welled up to tsunami size to smash her.

Not today. Abdullah needs me to be strong today.

She took courage from the television. There was Abdullah's face—his strong, courageous, beautiful face—filling the screen, proclaiming loudly, "M. Rizky Ramadani is a fraud. He speaks of peace, but he is a supporter of terrorist activities." She turned to look past the pistol pointed at her to her captor's face. It was radiant with triumph.

And just beyond Ardiansyah, on a small desk, she saw a cheap cell phone. Hadn't the professor just snapped a photo of her on a nice smart phone, handed it to Fani and sent him away? Something told her this cheap phone was important, but why? She wracked her brain.

Then it hit her—she remembered Abdullah explaining how terrorists used cell phones to set off bombs.

She needed to get that cell phone.

But before she had a chance to make her move, the door burst open and Fani rushed in, trying to close it behind him unsuccessfully.

"Close the door, Fani!" Ardi yelled at him.

"I'm trying!"

Suddenly the door flew open and Hafiz fell into the room. "Sari?" he exclaimed. Then he stopped short at the sight of the gun.

Sari looked over his head and gasped. There was Khaliq filling the doorway. His long hair was gone, his face and bald head raw and oozing, but his merciless eyes were just as she remembered them.

From the TV she heard Abdullah's voice: "…the very terrorists that destroyed our city."

"Fani, you fool!" Ardi shouted and stood up, pointing the gun alternately at Sari, Hafiz and Khaliq. Everybody froze but Khaliq, who stepped inside the room and swung the door closed behind him.

"Give me Achmad's bomb," the giant demanded.

Sari watched Hafiz's eyes widen and face grow pale. Fani was trembling. She was surprised that she hadn't screamed yet. It was like a supernatural calm had come over her.

I have to save Abdullah. She glanced at the television. There was Abdullah's face yelling to her: "…We need strong leadership if we are to survive."

"Shut up, you dumb animal!" Ardiansyah barked at Khaliq. "If you worked for Achmad, then you really work for me. Who do you think was paying Achmad?"

"Khaliq works for no one."

"Make yourself useful. Kill him." Ardi pointed with the gun toward Hafiz. But Khaliq wrapped an arm around Fani's neck instead. With his other hand he gripped Fani's skull. "Give me Achmad's bomb or I'll kill your boy."

"Go ahead, kill both boys. Just leave the girl alive until we set off the bomb."

"No 'we.' *My* bomb." Khaliq threw Fani to the floor, pushed Hafiz aside and took a step forward.

"I'm warning you." Ardi's voice grew higher in pitch. Sari could see his gun hand above her start to tremble. As he took a step back, Khaliq took another step forward, his eyes narrowed like a tiger about to pounce.

Ardi's hand was shaking violently now. On Khaliq's next step he pulled the trigger.

The gunshot echoed around the hotel room. Sari instinctively ducked and covered her ears. When she looked up, Khaliq had taken a step back, and blood was seeping from his left shoulder. He looked at Ardi with simmering rage and started to come again. Sari watched Ardi raise the gun once more.

"No!" she shouted, and reached to push the gun away.

Ardi fired again, but her push redirected the bullet to crash into the wall just over Khaliq's right shoulder. She saw a tear in his shirt where the bullet had grazed his collarbone.

Khaliq kept coming. Sari grabbed the gun barrel and tried to wrestle it away from the much larger man. Another gunshot went off. Sari looked to Khaliq, where blood began seeping from his belly.

Khaliq's giant hand enveloped hers, grabbing for the gun. She let go and fell to the floor. When she looked up, Khaliq was throwing the pistol through the glass window.

Ardi was on the floor now, scrambling backwards away from his predator, hand reaching behind him for the cell phone on the desk as he spoke. "Wait! I promised Achmad a million dollars—it's all yours! Don't hurt me…"

With Khaliq's right hand he lifted Ardi up by the neck, Ardi's feet dangling beneath him. Sari saw her chance and darted for the cell phone, throwing it across the room to Hafiz and Fani. Fani caught it.

"Fani, push CALL—blow the bomb," Ardi choked out.

Sari looked in Fani's eyes. "No more death," she said quietly but firmly.

"But I'm…your father."

Sari shook her head.

Fani hesitated, looking wide-eyed from one to the other, then thrust the cell phone into Hafiz's hands and collapsed on the floor crying.

Ardi's lips were turning blue.

Khaliq snarled, "You killed Achmad. Khaliq kills you."

Sari edged between them, gently placed her hand on Khaliq's chest and looked up at his eyes. "No more death," she repeated.

Khaliq growled and tightened his squeeze. Ardi gurgled, eyes bulging, arms swinging wildly but to no avail. Sari listened for Abdullah's voice to strengthen her, but the television had cut to a commercial jingle for children's vitamins: "*I'm an Indonesian child, healthy and strong…*"

"You're not an animal. You're not a killer." Sari tried to get Khaliq to turn his gaze to her. "You need a doctor. Now let that man go."

Finally Khaliq's eyes left Ardi for her. She stroked his chest and smiled. "Just let go."

Khaliq released Ardi's limp body to the floor, already unconscious. He almost collapsed, but Sari guided him to the bed where she helped him lie down on his back.

"Hafiz, take that to Abdullah and bring him here."

"I can't leave you alone with—"

"I'm fine. Fani, get a doctor. Now hurry!"

Hafiz and Fani ran out of the room. Sari looked at the growing blood stains on Khaliq's shoulder and stomach and wished she knew what to do. She stroked his forehead.

"Don't worry, we'll get you a doctor. You'll be all right."

Khaliq's eyes were open, but no longer seeing her. "They're coming for me," he muttered.

"Yes, the doctor's coming for you."

"Dark shadows. I hear them talking. They want to take me." A shudder of fear passed over Khaliq's face.

Sari grabbed Khaliq's hand and squeezed as hard as she could. "Tell them, 'No!' Tell them, 'I'm done with darkness, I choose the light!'"

She couldn't make out what Khaliq mumbled next. "…too strong."

She was pleading with all her heart now. "God's love for you is stronger! Call out to Him. God's love—"

Khaliq sighed, and Sari watched horrified as a black mist arose from his mouth and nostrils, causing goose bumps on her skin. It floated around the room, then out the broken window.

"—always wins."

She couldn't bear to look at the fear etched for eternity on Khaliq's face, so she closed his eyelids and tried to smooth the wrinkled skin with her tiny hands. His singed hair and eyebrows and the burned skin of his face brought forth in her mind a vision of torment that she couldn't bear to imagine.

It seemed only yesterday she had closed Bali's eyelids in much the same way.

At least Bali died in the arms of someone who loved him. This poor soul looks like he never knew love at all.

Abdullah and Hafiz found her hugging Khaliq's hand to her heart and crying softly.

Chapter 85

The birds chirped gaily outside Abdullah's window as though the events of the past two weeks hadn't bothered them in the least. He yawned and stretched. His head and his ribs still hurt, but they'd heal fast enough, as long as he didn't get beat up or blown up again today.

What would I give for a day of perfect peace…

He thought he heard movements in the kitchen and decided to see who was up first, Sari or one of the boys. He grabbed some khaki slacks and a white tank top. Was that coffee he smelled? He smiled to himself. It was almost like his wife and kids were starting a normal school day.

If I could do it over again… No point dwelling on the past, Abdullah. The future is hurtling at your face and there's no time to dodge it.

He passed Bali's bedroom. The door was cracked open, and he could see Sari curled up under her own white comforter. In the living room he had to step around Hafiz on the floor. Fani had spent the night too, on the couch, and both were still snoozing.

At his dining table sat Pak Joko sipping a cup of coffee.

"I see you finally dragged yourself out of bed. Coffee?"

Abdullah nodded and sat. The guest poured his host a cup, then waved at the cream and sugar. Abdullah shook his head slightly and took a sip. The two men eyed each other.

"I hope you're not here with another assignment."

"No, no, nothing like that. Just thought I'd have breakfast with you before I fly off to Makassar this morning."

"Good. Whatever work I do today needs to be of the un-intelligence sort."

Joko smiled. "I thought you'd like to hear what our esteemed professor had to say when he woke up."

Abdullah's eyebrows rose. "Go on."

"After we laid out the charges against him, we offered him a plea bargain if he would name his donor and how they got connected. He claims it was the campaign manager of our presidential candidate Ali Bin Husaini. He was told that he was one of five people in five major cities offered both a million dollars and a seat in the cabinet if he could create enough unrest to swing the election Husaini's way."

"The 'Five Five' you told me about."

"We've tracked deposits to his bank accounts through various shell companies back to Husaini. And now we have the search warrant necessary to track Husaini's disbursements through the same companies to discover who the ringleader is in each of the other four cities. By this time tomorrow, we hope to cut off four heads and see if we can kill this hydra for good."

"You suspected Ardiansyah from the beginning, didn't you? Why didn't you tell me?"

Joko shrugged. "We needed evidence, and that meant getting close to him without spooking him. How better to do that than to ask him for help?"

"You sly old fox. You nearly got me killed. Ardiansyah pointed me to Amat, and his friends were ready to ambush me."

Joko smiled. "I would call that a fast track to the cell leaders."

"I prefer the term 'a right bloody beating.' And did you know about Husaini?"

"We had our suspicions. Again, we needed evidence."

"What's going to happen to him?"

"Once we have the other four in custody, we'll start leaking information about Husaini to the press. We need the general populace to turn against him before we arrest him, or we could end up with the very civil war we're trying to avoid."

Joko gave him a thumbs up. "Which means your man Ramadani will most likely be the next president! Are you interested if he offers you a cabinet post?"

"I'm no politician."

"Ah, yes, the quiet man of action." Joko smiled and leaned forward, his eye starting to tic again. "Remember when we first met I told you that we had our eye on you? Judging by what you've achieved here, I think you're well-suited for a role in Intelligence."

Abdullah smiled wryly. "I'm honored, but no thanks. I think I'll be plenty busy with Ramadani's peacemaking team. Besides, I've got to get Sari back in school. And I've got to do something with those two slackers." He waved toward the sleeping boys.

"You're starting an orphanage?" Joko quipped.

"Not an orphanage—a family."

The older man leaned back and took another long swig from his cup. He cocked his head to one side and said, "With kids both Christian and Muslim? You know, you remind me of a story about one of my heroes growing up.

"Civil war in India between Muslim and Hindu radicals once prompted Gandhi to go on a fast. He vowed he would not eat again, even if it killed him, until both sides agreed to lay down their arms and reconcile. Well, a group of Hindu radicals entered the Muslim home where Gandhi had chosen to fast and pray, offering to lay down their weapons. One of the wildest of the group begged Gandhi to break his fast, saying, 'Here! Eat! I'm going to hell; but I do not wish to have your death on my soul!'

"Gandhi responded, 'Only God decides who goes to hell. Tell me, why do you say you are going to hell?'

"The man answered, 'I killed a small Muslim child! I dashed his head against the wall because they killed my little one.'

"'I will tell you a way out of hell,' Gandhi said. 'You find a Muslim child whose parents have been killed. Then you and your wife bring him up as your own.'

"I'm very curious how this little experiment of yours will play out, Abdullah. And when you're ready for a new challenge, you know how to find me."

Joko stood and offered his hand. Abdullah took it. "Thank you."

"It is I who should be thanking you for saving a city," Joko protested.

"No, I mean thank you for saving those three boys from a life of *jihad* and believing in Ramadani's Center for Ending Violence."

"That Center is a dream come true for me as well. After so very many years of hunting, capturing, and killing extremists, only to see them multiply, perhaps we're finally starting to see the light."

Abdullah waved good-bye to Joko while making a mental note to himself to find time every so often to visit those three young men from Banjarmasin at the Center just to see how they were doing.

Chapter 86

"Let's go for a walk."

At the sound of Abdullah's invitation, Sari was pleased to discover that she felt no hesitation in saying "yes."

They exited Abdullah's gate and turned left down the alley toward Sari's house, but Abdullah led her right on past it. At Nina's mom's house, little Rini waved to her from the window, and Sari waved back. The dilapidated shack had a brand new corrugated aluminum roof—perhaps Nina's husband had put it on for them? She'd been cooped up so long she had no idea what was happening in the neighborhood.

Where the alley became so narrow cars could no longer squeeze through, they turned around and headed back toward the main street of Kelayan B. By the time they passed Abdullah's house she could feel beads of sweat on her forehead and neck from the high humidity.

She waved to Ibu Aaminah, sitting on her front porch instructing her husband which flowers to water. Ibu Aaminah waved back with a quizzical expression. Sari laughed to herself.

The whole alley belonged to her again.

They turned left on Kelayan B and walked north toward the outdoor market. All this time Abdullah said nothing, and Sari was content to enjoy his presence. More than content, she marveled at the world around her. An old man wearing an equally old fedora sat by the road selling thin cardboard wallet-sized pictures of Barbie to a little girl in a pink Disney princess dress. Sari smiled at them both. The old man smiled back, only one lower tooth left in his mouth. The princess waved her sparkly magic wand at Sari probably wanting to turn her into either a frog or a prince.

They came upon the spot where Sari had crashed her motorbike and felt her panic attack. She paused there on the street and looked all around her. The rich colors of the vegetables and fruits in the market sang out to her. The *toot-toot* of the *bakso* cart's horn joined in, as did the sounds of traffic and bargaining and laughter, and the waves of the river across the street lapping against the homes built on stilts above them.

This used to be her mother's market. Now it was hers. Her people, her street, her river. Her source of never-ending wonder.

She led her adopted father across the street to sit by the river and watch the small canoes bearing their produce home from the market pass by.

"Thank you," she said simply. His nod was nearly imperceptible. For a few minutes they kept their silence, watching the river life. She reached back and pulled her long hair up over her head, letting the breeze off the river cool her neck. Across from them some small boys did cannon-balls into the water.

Eventually Abdullah broke the stillness. "I used to see this city as my place to hide who I was. Now I'm beginning to love it as the place I can be who I truly am."

He turned his face slightly toward her. "How about you? Would you be better off somewhere else, a fresh start after all the traumas you've been through?"

"I told Hafiz I believed in redemption. I still do."

"So are you ready to move back into your home? I mean, it's okay if you're not, you can always stay with me." Sari thought she heard the faintest wisp of *longing* in the request. *Did she mean as much to Abdullah as he meant to her?*

"You're so kind to me, Bapak. I never could have made it through this last year without you. I would love to be your daughter. And as for where to stay, well, I have another idea for my home." And she shared her dream with him, prompting an exuberant smile.

"That's a beautiful idea. Let's make it happen."

They watched a man downriver from them catch a small fish on his line and throw it back.

"You pray a lot," Abdullah commented.

Sari was surprised. "I guess so. There wasn't much else I could do to help."

"Well, your prayers helped a lot. Honestly, I doubted I would ever see even one jihadist turn, much less four, if you count Hafiz. It seemed so impossible."

"Not to God," Sari shrugged.

"I think I had pretty much given up on prayer. Maybe it's time for me to start my *sholat* again."

Sari smiled. "And you can pray with me anytime you want."

They watched the fisherman pull in a larger fish this time and drop it into a bucket next to him on the dock.

"If you feel up to it, there's something else I could use your help with…" Abdullah seemed to be fishing as well.

"Of course, Bapak, anything!" Sari answered.

"David told me that Pastor Chris called him last night. After all that's happened in our city, and the disappointing response of his senior church leaders, Chris feels a burden to appeal to the young generation of Christian students to do something to break the walls of prejudice between our faiths. He wants to gather all the Christian campus organizations for me to speak to them."

"That's wonderful!"

"But you're their age. I was wondering if you'd like to speak to them with me."

"What could I possibly say?"

"Just tell them your story."

Sari's eyes opened wide at the thought of standing on a stage. Images flooded her mind of Abdullah on television behind a lectern, speaking as if his very life depended on it, which in a way it did. He had such courage. Could she find the courage to tell her story too?

"Huh...maybe could I bring my Peace Generation friends to help me?"

"Absolutely! It's going to take a whole lot of your generation to turn the tide—the more the better."

"Hafiz and Fani too?"

"Them too."

Sari wasn't sure she was ready to say out loud what she'd experienced...her mother...Bali...Khaliq's knife to her throat. But by telling Pak Abdullah "yes," she would be putting God on the spot to give her the grace when the time came.

As they started their walk back home she began imagining what she wanted to say.

Chapter 87

That evening Sari and Nina cooked up a feast. They made fried chicken, fried eggs on top of fried rice, fried noodles—all Banjar people seemed to love fried food—with watermelon and Sari's favorite fruit, the tiny but sweet *muli* bananas for dessert. They made enough to feed twenty, though Abdullah's house wasn't that full. Besides Abdullah, Hafiz and Fani, Udin and Juki were there, as was David's family of three. Hafiz and Fani had moved all the furniture out of the living room and borrowed a couple large Persian carpets from Ibu Aaminah to create more space by having everyone sit on the floor.

Abdullah prayed in Arabic the *Do'a Selamat*, thanking Allah for keeping them all safe through the terrible events of late. Everyone said a hearty "Amen," dipped their fingers in their washing bowls, and dug into the food with their hands.

Sari did her best to be a good hostess, making sure everyone had enough to eat and drink, though she hated running back and forth to the kitchen because she didn't want to miss anything. All of the tragedy behind her somehow made her appreciate *this* moment so much more.

Hafiz retold for the guests the scene in the hotel room. "...Sari had a chance to run, but instead she got right up in Khaliq's face and talked to him. I couldn't believe it! And he listened! That girl is certifiably cuckoo!" The others laughed appreciatively. Sari blushed.

Hafiz continued, "And she grabbed the cell phone that was supposed to set off the bomb and tossed it to Fani. And that professor dude's like,

'Blow up the bomb. Luke, I'm your father.'" He tried to imitate Darth Vader's voice. Sari noticed that Fani didn't join the others' laughter.

"Fani, you did the right thing," Sari said encouragingly.

"Then why do I feel so bad?" the boy asked. "Why do I feel like I killed my own father?"

Out of the corner of her eye, Sari noticed Hafiz close his mouth abruptly. She looked back at Fani. "No true father would ever ask his son to kill for him, right, Bapak?"

"She's right, son," Abdullah smiled. "He may have opened his home to you, but at the end we discovered that he never truly had a father's heart for you."

"But he was going to put me through college." Fani looked despondent. "Now where am I going to live? What am I going to do?"

"You're always welcome to live here with me," Abdullah offered with a grin.

"Really? With you and Sari and Hafiz too?" Fani's eyes lit up.

"Hold on there, buddy," Hafiz jumped in. "Now that I'm well, I should be moving on."

"Awww," Fani whined.

"Hafiz, I'd like you to stay with me too, if you want to. Sari said she's staying." Abdullah looked from one to the other. Hafiz looked away.

"I'd like it if you stayed with us too, Hafiz," Sari added.

Hafiz looked up at her and frowned. "With you losers? Forget it, I'm out of here."

He stood abruptly and headed toward the washing area where the motorbikes were parked at night. Everyone looked at each other, shocked. His plate was still half full of food.

In a few seconds he was back. "Ha! Got you!" he crowed, holding something behind his back. "Well, maybe I could stay here for a little while, till I figure out what I want to do, something that would make my parents proud... Or maybe till I get me one of these." From behind his back he pulled out a wooden plaque. He turned it to face them, the words "Peace Champion" freshly polished and gleaming.

"Bapak's plaque! Hafiz, you found it!" Sari exclaimed, hands on her cheeks.

"I saw it out the window and wondered how it got there. Once I got a closer look, I realized it would make a great, you know, like a memento if we ever succeeded." He handed it to Abdullah, who hung it back on the wall where it used to be.

Abdullah was touched. "You waded through the swamp?"

"Hey, a hero's got to do what a hero's got to do."

This elicited hooting from Udin and Juki and a high five for Hafiz from David. Little Josie clapped her hands, not wanting to miss out on the excitement.

"I hereby declare," Abdullah announced, raising his glass, "that this plaque shall no longer be mine, but shall belong to all the heroes assembled here today, for we are all Peace Champions."

Everyone raised their glasses and clinked them together. "Hear, hear," David said.

Sari stood up next. "Hey, I have something I want to share with everyone too." She went to the kitchen and returned with a small white paper from the front of the refrigerator. "Listen to this:

You're blessed when you can show people how to cooperate instead of compete or fight.

That's when you discover who you really are, and your place in God's family."

"The words of Jesus," said Angelina.

"Isn't that verse just perfect for *us*?" Sari gestured around the circle with her hand. "Through all that's happened I discovered that I'm much weaker than I thought, but I'm also much stronger than I thought. I'm discovering who I really am, and who you really are."

She pulled her long black hair back behind her ear and looked slowly around the room, letting her gaze linger on each one. "And you are all amazingly beautiful."

The origin story of Sari and Abdullah's path to peacemaking

In the midst of a global clash between international terrorism and an American congress-man's peacemaking effort, a poor Muslim-majority neigh-borhood in Indonesia holds the keys to victory. While some in the neighborhood are making efforts to understand the truth behind the Muslim-Christian divide and build new bridges across it, others are determined to perpetuate and intensify the hatred that has plagued the re-gion for years.

When a tragedy reveals an unexpected villain, it will be up to two unlikely heroes to set aside their differences and save the day. What will it take to keep hope alive? And who will be willing to make the ultimate sacrifice for the sake of peace?

This intense thriller will encourage you to reexamine your understanding of love and forgiveness, and reconsider what it means to be a true peacemaker.

Available online at **Amazon** or at **www.jimbaton.com**

"Where has Jim Baton been all our lives?! This is one of those rare 'first novels' that demands another. There are many academic books outlining the tensions and differences between Christians and Muslims, but beyond a riveting story, this book enables us to enter into the existing deep emotions, convictions, and inherited prejudices which otherwise elude us. The Batons know it because they've lived in the center of it for decades. I couldn't put it down. ...and I don't even read novels!"

Greg Livingstone, Founder, Frontiers
Senior Associate, World Outreach, Evangelical Presbyterian Church

"Hatred, persecution, fear, terrorism–just daily life for millions around the world. This book takes us through it all to the other side, to the hope for peace. I highly recommend it for peace-lovers everywhere."

U.S. Congressman Mark Siljander (ret) President,
Bridges to Common Ground
Author of *A Deadly Misunderstanding*

"SOMEONE HAS TO DIE will make you squirm, cry and smile. You will squirm as you realize that we are all fraught with stereotypes about Christians and Muslims. You will be confronted with the hypocrisy of your own faith, regardless of what side of the chasm you find yourself. You will cry as you are confronted with the ugliness of hate and the gentle power of self-sacrifice. You will smile because love is stronger than hate, and evil doesn't have to win."

Erik Lincoln, Peace Activist
Author of the bestselling series, *Peace Generation*

"It's easy to demonize those different from us. It's a bit harder to research facts in order to understand them. It's even more of a stretch to step into their world and to

walk in their shoes. But Jim Baton has gone one step further: he's told their story. The story is about conflicts between Christians and Muslims in Indonesia, a country where Baton has lived for many years, but it is more than that. It's also a story about us, whether Christian or Muslim. It challenges us to look at the truths about ourselves, about the prejudices, ignorance and anger that are in each of us, and that, if left untouched by God's love, can spill out to ravage nations, communities and families. Yet there is hope. God can and does change hearts, as Baton so beautifully testifies to in this warm and uplifting story."

Dr. Rick Love, President of Peace Catalyst International
 Consultant for Christian-Muslim Relations

"An incredibly realistic portrayal of relationships between our Muslim and Christian friends with fascinating lessons for peacemakers."

Rob Rice, Executive Director, Community Based
 Rehabilitation International

"I believe there is a grace that God sends with this book that goes beyond the words on the page; a grace for reconciliation, healing, and bridge-building. I have many beautiful, peaceful Muslim friends on the one hand, and on the other hand, Christians I know have experienced profound loss and violence because of terrorist Muslims. After reading this book, I HAD to go and pray about it. I had to connect with God and see what he felt and thought about what happened to my friends and about my own experiences with violence in an Islamic country. And what I came to was the COMPASSION Jesus has for the most misunderstood people; a compassion so beautifully displayed through the characters in this book, both Christian and Muslim. I had to go beyond the understanding of my experiences and think about what God feels about the conflict that happens between Christians and Muslims.

And then, not only that, I was up till past 4AM reading it and couldn't put it down. You cannot fall asleep reading this book."

Jim Baton

"Lola," American Christian woman living many years in the Middle East

"SOMEONE HAS TO DIE ably weaves narratives of individual lives of Muslims and Christians within the context of events that could be the leading story of tomorrow's news or echoes of yesterdays. Love and light transcends religion in this novel, as do unforgiving hearts, regardless of religious - who use religion as a cover for their self-centered deeds. SOMEONE HAS TO DIE reminded me of something C.S. Lewis wrote 'All day long we are, in some degree, helping each other to one or other destinations... There are no ordinary people. You have never talked to a mere mortal. Nations, cultures, art, civilizations—these are mortal...'

I read this book during travel flights this week - the hours went fast. I wanted to dance in the most gracious Creator's pleasure after I had read this novel."

"John," American military personnel involved in the Middle East

"Thanks, Jim Baton, for this gift of a book. It's better than a text book in how Christians and Muslims can live together and honor and love one another...or not, as sadly, some of the characters in your book choose to do, causing much pain and heart ache. The very real characters along with their personal dramas, global issues, and the suspense of a terrorism attack make SOMEONE HAS TO DIE a thrilling read. Set in a city village of Banjarmasin, Indonesia, using local language interspersed with details of life and culture in a Muslim majority country not only makes the story really interesting, but also thought provoking, poignant and sweet at times. I laughed at some of the characters' antics, I cried, I held my breath but I couldn't put it down. I've also bought a number of hard copies to give to friends and family as I know it will help many on their journey in 'loving our neighbors as we love ourselves'."

"Chrissy Van," Christian expatriate living in Southeast Asia

"In SOMEONE HAS TO DIE Jim Baton eloquently writes a beautiful story clearly depicting a paradigm-changing message on how relational healing is what will bring Muslims back into the Father's House. I highly recommend this book."

Ché Ahn, Founding Pastor, HROCK Church, Pasadena, CA
            President, Harvest International Ministry
            International Chancellor, Wagner Leadership Institute

"SOMEONE HAS TO DIE reads like a classic novel like Uncle Tom's Cabin, Ramona or Ivanhoe as it has the effect of changing public opinion. I feel that this is a very important book for our times."

Jill Davis, Frontier Ventures Resource Center

Sari's story continues in Jim Baton's third book of the Peace Trilogy

A Violent Light

The Youth for Peace Fresh Start Initiative gathers ten Muslim and ten Christian youth from ten nations around the world to learn new paths to peace. But the camp staff have some highly unorthodox teaching techniques. And when one by one the youth start disappearing, some of them wonder if the staff might not have an entirely different agenda. Those left behind must work together to solve the mystery before they also disappear. Meanwhile, unbeknownst to them, the entire world is watching…

Jim's third thriller follows Sari's adventures facing terrorists in her home country of Indonesia in *Someone Has to Die* and *A Way Out of Hell* to America, where prejudice is just as strong and just as ugly. She learns that pursuing world peace today will require a generation committed to a deeper level of trust and cooperation than ever before.

Coming in 2017—watch for it at **Amazon** or at **www.jimbaton.com**

About the Author

Jim Baton lives in the world's largest Muslim nation, building bridges between Muslims and Christians who both desire peace.

Find out more at **www.jimbaton.com**.

Made in the USA
San Bernardino, CA
14 December 2016